"I've got it," said Dickie suddenly, "I've thought of a name for us and for this camp. This is Lone Pine Camp, and we'll be the Lone Pine Club ... Now let's have something to eat…"

Both suggestions were approved.

"This must be a real secret," said Peter, "particularly from grown-ups who generally spoil everything, however nice they are."

The twins were indignant.

" 'Course we wouldn't say a word."

"We'd better all swear after," said Dickie.

"We'll sign in blood!" said Mary.

Malcolm Saville's
LONE PINE CLUB

Mystery at Witchend

For two Rs and two Js

Scholastic Children's Books
7–9 Pratt Street, London NW1 0AE, UK
a division of Scholastic Publications Ltd
London ~ New York ~ Toronto ~ Sydney ~ Auckland

First published by George Newnes Ltd, 1943
This edition published by Scholastic Publications Ltd, 1995

Copyright © Malcolm Saville, 1943

ISBN 0 590 55918 4

Typeset by TW Typesetting, Midsomer Norton, Avon
Printed by Cox & Wyman Ltd, Reading, Berks.

10 9 8 7 6 5 4 3 2 1

Contents

MAP of the
Witchend Country
drawn by David Morton
after the
Great Adventure

ROAD ROUND THE MOUNTA

VILLAGE

TRACK ALONG TOP OF MOUNT

LONE PINE

WITCHEND VALLEY

WITCHEND
WOOD

WITC

TR.

TRACK

INGLES

TO
WARDS
FARM

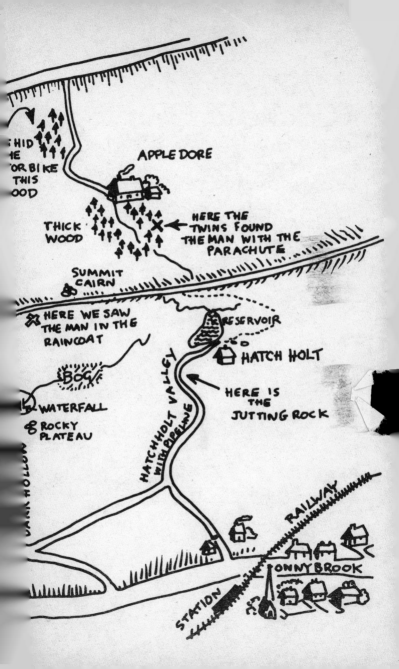

Foreword

Much of what Bill Ward told the children is true. There is actually a mountain called the Long Mynd in the highlands of Shropshire – a wild, rolling hill, with steep and lonely valleys or "gutters" as they are called locally, on the eastern side.

Caer Caradoc, like a crouching lion, does guard the vale between the Stretton hills, and over towards the borders of Wales another lonely range called the Stiperstones is crowned with black rocks which are hidden by the mists as "he" takes his seat on his throne.

The country in which this story is set is real, but if you are ever lucky enough to explore it for yourself you will not find Witchend or Appledore or Hatchholt and its reservoir. There is no village called Onnybrook and all the people you will read about in these pages are imaginary and have no reference to any living person.

M. S.

Chapter 1

Witchend

They changed trains at Shrewsbury.

"Promise me, twins," said Mrs Morton, when they had managed, with the help of a friendly but overworked guard, to get their trunks out of the van, "promise that you'll stay here with the luggage and look after Macbeth. Don't move till we come back. David is going to find a porter, and I'll see if I can get something to eat."

"All right, Mummy," said Richard. "Trust us."

"We swear," said Mary solemnly as she sat herself firmly on a trunk and hoisted an agitated little black dog up beside her. Macbeth was grateful for this attention and licked her face. He hated trains and crowds. People trod on him.

David didn't feel particularly grown up as he went up the long platform. He knew he ought to be. He remembered what Daddy had said. "Take care of Mummy for me, old chap, and look after those awful twins as well. I know you'll all love Witchend, and I want you to have a good time while I'm away... But be sensible and remember that I trust you not to do silly things."

He still felt a bit chokey when he thought of Daddy going off in his new uniform. "Do all you can to help your mother," he had said.

The crowds were thinning out now. The guard waved his flag, and the long chocolate and cream train slid out on its way to Chester and Birkenhead. David watched the last coach disappear round the bend, and when he turned an old porter was standing just behind him.

"And where be you going, young man?"

"Onnybrook," said David. "Will you come and help us with the luggage, please?"

He was a nice old man, and it was a pity that Macbeth proved so troublesome about guarding the luggage. He made so much noise that Mrs Morton came running out of the refreshment room with four buns in her hand and spoke to him sternly.

On the other side of the station their new train was waiting. The guard got up leisurely off the step of the van as they came up.

"Push 'er in, Albert," he said with a wink to David. "Doan't stand loiterin' about, man, and keep us all waiting."

He looked at the labels.

"Onnybrook, eh? Where are you staying, lad?"

And here the twins chimed in.

"We're going on a great adventure," said Mary.

"Our Daddy is in the RAF," said Richard, "and we're going to Witchend to live. We had bombs in London."

"Witchend?" smiled the guard. "Maybe you'll have your adventures up there all right by that old rascal mountain."

The compartment chosen by Mary had a sailor in it – a brown-faced, blue-eyed sailor with very white teeth. With apprehension David saw the twins exchange a meaning

4

glance. Strangers were apt to be fascinated by their strange likeness, and it was an old game for them to select a victim and proceed to play with him. More often than not they had the same idea at the same time, and had no need to put their thoughts into words, and this habit could be very disconcerting.

But this sailor proved a willing victim. He helped Mrs Morton in with the bags, laughed at Richard and Mary, patted Macbeth, slapped David on the back and accepted a bun. Long before the train started they were all friends, and the children had told him who they were and where they were going.

"If you like adventures you'll find plenty at Witchend," he told them. "I've lived in Shropshire all my life and it's the grandest county in England. We've got everything – mountains, moors, streams and rivers and waterfalls, and on the Long Mynd where you are going there are hidden valleys with wild ponies in the bracken and heather and little dark brooks which you can follow up to their source."

"Tell us some more about the Long Mynd," said David.

"You'll have to find out its secrets for yourself," he winked, "but take care when you're up there and watch the weather. Many a man has been lost in the snow and fog up on the Mynd. You'll see it soon looking bare and innocent in the sunshine, but there are bogs and pools at the top, so remember what I tell you."

He looked over to Mrs Morton.

"See they take care," he went on, "for the Mynd is a mountain of moods – not black and cruel like the Stiperstones…"

5

"Tell us about them. Say about the Stiperstones."

"Well, they're different. The Long Mynd is smooth and rolling. It's wild and lonesome, as I say, but the Stiperstones, way over the other side, are rugged and cruel, and those who live near 'em know they're evil, too."

"Gosh!" said Richard. "Go on. Tell us."

"At the top of the Stiperstones is the Devil's Chair – a big outcrop of shining black rock. My father told me once that these rocks are the oldest in England and that long ago, when all this part of the country under sixteen hundred feet was buried under a sheet of ice, the Devil's Chair stood up like a black island. But that's as may be. What we do know is that one day Satan came with giant strides out of the west, and you can still see the imprint of his foot on a stone in the brook which he crossed in the valley below. He was on his way to the Long Mynd to fill one of the valleys – we call 'em Gutters – with stones which he was carrying in his apron. We reckon the old devil was a bad walker, for they say he picked up a stone in his shoe and sat down in his chair to rest. He undid his shoe and flicked out the pebble which lies nine miles away in a field near Bishop's Castle. Some say this great stone turns round when the church clock there strikes thirteen."

"Go on," said Mary. "Tell us."

"Well, he rested on his chair a bit, but when at last he got up to step across the Mynd his apron string broke and all the stones dropped out, and you can see 'em there today."

Mrs Morton was smiling at him.

"Sometimes we smile, too," he said, "but there are

many as still hold that he comes back to his throne. Only when his chair is vacant can it be seen by mortal eyes. When it's clear and can be seen a long way off we know the weather will be fine, but sometimes while we watch a mist comes up from the west and hides it, and he comes back to his throne and the cottagers below go indoors and put up the shutters ... And that's why I tell you, young man," he went on, turning to David, "not to trust too much to the weather on these mountains. Always watch the west, where the bad weather comes racing over from Wales, and if you're doubtful turn back and be careful to keep to the tracks."

"Are there any other ghosts?" asked Richard. "Real ghosts, I mean. Not just old devils."

"Bless you, yes," said the sailor. "The Mynd and the Stiperstones are crowded with ghosts. Dad used to tell me about a Shropshire leader of the English when we were fighting the Norman invader. I forget his name, but he was a coward and betrayed his soldiers and his country-men by making peace with the enemy. They say he still haunts these mountains in the shape of a great black dog. And then of the Stiperstones there's the Black Huntsman on a great white horse, but I don't rightly know what he did. Others, I've heard, tell of gates which fly open at night without being touched, and there's stories, too, of birds of ill-omen called the Seven Whistlers."

Their new friend was still yarning when the train started. He told them of the other mountains they would see – Caer Caradoc, where, it is said, the British Chief Caractacus made his last stand – and of those other hills called Lawley and Ragleth.

He told them that his name was Bill Ward, and of his father's big farm away down in the plain some seven miles from Witchend, and invited them all to come down and see him.

"Do you like castles, Mary?" he went on. "You do? Real castles with a moat and battlements and turrets with narrow windows at which fair ladies sat and worked their tapestry as they waited and watched for their knights to come riding back to them?"

"Gosh!" said Mary. "I love castles like that."

"There's one at Ludlow," said Bill. "You can go and see it for yourself and climb a twisting turret stair and from the watch-tower look across a broad river to the Marches of Wales."

Mary clasped a protesting Macbeth to her.

"I just can't wait to begin," she said.

The train stopped at a funny little station. Their friend the guard had a word for everyone, but nobody hurried and London seemed a thousand miles away.

"Come this side," said Bill after a little, "and you'll see Caradoc. He looks like a crouching lion. Look! There he is."

They crowded over. Alight in the westering sun, grim and crowned with rocks, he seemed to guard the way into a new country. But the children's first view of the Long Mynd – the mountain which was to mean so much to them – was not so exciting. It was, as Bill had said, a long, smooth, rolling mountain without a peak like Caradoc. The slopes were bare of trees, and so suddenly did the mountain grow out of the plain that it seemed as if they might lean from the windows and touch it. As they watched, the sun slipped down behind it, and a great shadow was flung across the country to the train. The slopes that had looked so smooth and inviting were now dark and mysterious as black clouds came rolling up from the south-west.

"Better get your things ready," said Bill. "Onnybrook is the next stop, and you'll be running into a storm, I'm thinking … Look at the mountain now, David, and you can see the valleys I told you about. You'll want to explore them all."

The train stopped and the guard opened the door.

"Come and count your baggage, young man, and then get under cover quick, else you'll be wet through before you start."

Bill helped them out and shook hands with them all except Mary, who hugged him.

"I'll knit you a scarf," she promised.

"We're not very good at it," said her twin, "but we'll do it somehow."

Then an aged porter came along with a barrow just as the first heavy drops fell, and Mrs Morton ran for the shelter of the booking office.

"See the luggage out, David," she called, "then come in here with us. We'll see if the car has come. Come on, twins! Goodbye, Mr Ward, and good luck and thank you…"

The last bundle was on the barrow and David was checking everything methodically when there was a commotion down by the level-crossing gates.

"Stop! Stop!" a man was shouting excitedly. "Wait for me," and as he ran up the platform he banged David and sent him falling back against the loaded truck. Then he began to turn their luggage over and look at the labels.

"My parcel," he shouted. "My parcel! What have you done with it? Addressed to Thurston. Where is it?"

The porter told him there was no parcel for Thurston and the guard searched his van again. But still the stranger wasn't satisfied. They must telephone to Shrewsbury, he said, and find out whether the parcel was there, and while he was shouting he started again to turn over the Mortons' luggage.

Although David was really more angry than hurt, he had banged his elbow, and, to his shame, felt the tears in his eyes.

"Please leave our luggage alone," he said stoutly. "We haven't got your parcel."

The guard waved his flag and Bill leaned from the window and saluted as the train pulled out. The rain thrashed down fiercely and the old porter trundled his barrow over to the shelter of the booking office. At David's denial the man seemed to notice him for the first time, and was now staring at him with bright, piercing eyes. He was short, thick-set, with remarkably long arms.

Suddenly David shivered. He felt angry and oddly afraid and wanted to be with the others. He turned his back and ran through the rain alone.

"The car's here, David," said Mrs Morton, "but we can't get the luggage on for a minute. It's too wet. What did the funny old man want?"

"D'you know what he is?" said Mary.

"I'll tell you what he does," said Richard at the same time.

"He's a wizard of the mountain," said Mary.

"He changes into a black dog at night," went on her twin.

"He practically looked like a black dog as he came lolloping up the platform."

Then Macbeth, from under the barrow, began to growl, and they looked up to see the stranger in the doorway. Mary grabbed the dog's lead and held on with all her strength as the man called out to the porter:

"Hi, you! Have you telephoned about my parcel? I must have it. When is the next train?"

"No more trains tonight, mister," said the old porter with a grin. "Better ask station-master if you want to telephone."

Scowling and muttering to himself, the man rudely looked the Mortons up and down before striding out into the rain. A few minutes later they heard the noise of a motor-cycle.

"That's what he is…" began Mary.

"A wopping great, wizard black dog!" finished Richard.

"Reckon we should 'pologize for bad manners at Onnybrook, ma'am," said the old porter. "Folks aren't like him round here … somewhere other side of Mynd he comes from … Now, you must be Mortons, I reckon, coming to live at Witchend. Old Agnes was telling us all you was coming. She'll be expecting you, and as rain is laying off a bit we'll get busy … Come on, John, and help get this luggage on. That's if your old barrow'll stand it!"

And old John, the driver of the decrepit car, soon proved himself to be another friend. As Mrs Morton said,

"You're all so kind and friendly it seems as if we're coming home instead of arriving as strangers."

Somehow they got the luggage stowed away – some on the roof, some on the back and some on the front seat with John. Then the twins squabbled as to who was to sit in the front, and David settled the problem by pushing them both in the back with his mother and Macbeth, and somehow wedging himself in beside John.

At last they were ready to start, but got no farther than the level-crossing gates. A brown-faced signalman leaning from his window smiled at them through the rain, and Richard called out: "May I come and pull one of those levers one day?" but he couldn't hear the answer as a goods train clanked by. Some of the long, low trucks carried tanks, and as they passed old John said, "I've got a lad in one of them things in Africa."

At last the gates opened and they started on the last stage of their journey. The road crossed a brown, rushing stream and then turned up a long hill between woods. The rain was still pouring down, and it was dark and gloomy under the trees. Even the twins stopped chattering, and suddenly David felt oddly homesick for the sights and sounds he knew.

The climbing road twisted and turned for another mile before the trees thinned out, and they rushed out to the crest of a long hill. Ahead was rolling country with their road threading its way like a ribbon into the distance, but before David had time to exclaim old John braked and turned sharp right into a lane flanked again by trees.

"Are we nearly there?" he asked.

"Just through the wood, son, and you'll see Witchend."

The rain had stopped now and the clouds were breaking in the west above the rolling grandeur of the Long Mynd. To their left the mountain sloped abruptly away to its southern extremity. To their right it stretched hard across a skyline aflame with the scarlet and gold of the setting sun.

"Please stop for a minute," said Mrs Morton.

For a moment there was silence and then Richard said, "That's where the devil got a stone in his shoe, I s'pose ... Sittin' up there on the top."

"You silly ass," said his sister tersely. "You don't listen, Dickie. That's your trouble."

"Be quiet, twins," said their mother. "But where's Witchend? Show us..."

Old John pointed ahead.

"There's her smoke. See the larch wood down the side of the hill like a black wedge? Look again at the corner of the wood and you'll see a patch of grey – that's the side of the house, and I see her smoke against the trees. But we'll be moving, and I'll have you home in five minutes."

"What do you think of it, children?"

Only Mary answered. "If it wasn't for Daddy not being here it's like a good fairy story, Mummy."

They rushed down the hill and pulled up as some cows straggled across the lane into a farmyard. A man in khaki raised his hand in a cheery salute to them as they crawled past.

"That's your near neighbour – Alf Ingles. He's a great one for this Home Guard ... always crawling about the country on his stomach. I tells him he'd be better lookin' after his cows, for that old Hitler's not goin' to bother

13

about us up here … not that we wouldn't give him something to remember if he did!"

They were now almost at the foot of the Mynd, and in its shadow. Above them a dense wood of swaying larches clung to the side of a steep valley. Their lane came to an end and the car stopped on a level of close, springy turf against a white gate between a wall of loose stones.

Beyond the gate they could see the gleam of water and the shadow of a long barn and, on the right, the house. In the dusk Witchend looked bigger than they had imagined. Under the roof in front two gabled windows jutted, while at the back the hill was so close that it looked as if the house was leaning against it.

A stream came tumbling under the wall and ran chattering round the edge of the turf on which they were standing until it disappeared under the hedge at the bend of the lane.

Old John opened the car door for Mrs Morton. "Witchend, mum – and welcome to your new home."

The twins scrambled out and for once stood still.

"Gosh!" said Richard.

"Maybe that gate'll open by itself," whispered Mary.

"It won't," laughed their mother. "Open it yourself, so that we can get the car in. Then knock at the door and see if Mrs Braid has heard us. We must be quick because it's dark early this evening and we'll have to black-out soon. Come on, David! No time for dreaming now, but lots of fun tomorrow."

By the time the car was through the gate the front door had opened, and a tall, thin, forbidding-looking woman came out on to the step.

"You'll be Mrs Morton, I'm thinking. Ye're late. I've been expecting you this half-hour gone."

David didn't hear what his mother replied, but he did hear Dickie muttering, "She's a witch. She must be, Mary. Just look at her."

The next hour was a desperate muddle. Old John carried the trunks up the narrow stairs, but they all helped to bring in the other bundles, and Macbeth got trodden on and yelped.

Mrs Braid did not seem a friendly sort of person, and once snapped at Richard for getting in the way. Mary answered back indignantly for her twin – they often did this for each other – and so surprised was the housekeeper that she dropped a heavy suitcase.

"It wasn't *his* fault," said Mary. "Can't you see he was only trying to help? We always help. We're jolly useful at helping, and maybe you'll be sorry for speaking to us like that…"

"Mary," said Mother, in her special, quiet voice, "go into the other room with Dickie and Macbeth and stay there until you are called. You can be thinking of how you will apologize to Mrs Braid."

Mutinously they went into a long, low room lit by the flickering flames of a wood fire.

"Did you see her legs?" whispered Dickie. "Witch's legs, they were. All thin and scraggy. Sparrow's legs! That's what we'll call her, Mary – Sparrow's Legs. When I say S.L. you'll know what I mean … Gosh! I'm hungry."

At last old John said "Good night" and rattled away in the dusk. Mrs Morton shut the front door as David came clattering down the stairs.

"I say, you kids, this is a grand place. All sorts of secret hiding-places and mysterious rooms. Come and see."

"I'm sorry, David," said Mary, "but we can't come now … We've been rude … We're to sit here quietly till I 'pologize. We're thinking of what to say."

But Richard was not so circumspect.

"What's she like really? The old witch, I mean. We've got a name for her…"

Then Mother came in with Mrs Braid and the twins got up together.

"I'm sorry I was rude," began Mary; and "We didn't really mean to get in the way," finished her twin.

Quite unexpectedly Mrs Braid smiled. And when she smiled she looked quite different. Not a bit "witchy" and almost nice.

"Ah, well," she said. "Maybe I was a bit hasty and worried. We'll say no more, my dears, except I'm sorry, too, and hope you'll soon find old Agnes's bark is worse than her bite … And now it's time for us all to bite, I'm thinking, before yon pigeon pair is packed off to bed."

And rather awkwardly she put a hand on each twin's shoulder and gave them a gentle push towards the door.

The kitchen was a big room with a low, beamed ceiling from which hung a large oil lamp. The floor was of stone and along one wall was a big kitchen range in which was burning a cheerful fire. The table was piled with ready cut slices of brown bread, a jar of golden syrup, and each place was set with a boiled egg.

"It's that difficult to get a square meal with all this rayshunning," Mrs Braid was saying, "but Mrs Ingles

16

down the lane gets us milk and eggs, and I'm thinking you'll soon be wanting some pullets yourselves … and there's cocoa for those that likes it and tea for them as can't abide the stuff like me…"

"Thank you, Agnes," said Mrs Morton. "It's a lovely meal and not a bit like war-time. Let's sit down and start."

Mary was the first to break a long silence.

"I just can't manage that piece of cake … Dickie! It's the most scrumptious tea I remember."

After tea they were given a quarter of an hour to explore Witchend before the twins were packed off to bed.

It was a fascinating house – friendly downstairs and really "lived in". The kitchen was probably the jolliest room and full of surprises. There was an oak chest under the window. The hearth rug was made of scraps of coloured cloth all sewn together ingeniously, and a copper warming-pan reflected the firelight from one wall while on the other were two most peculiar pictures. An old calendar still hung above the mantelpiece which carried a row of exciting looking bright blue tins labelled "Currants," "Rice," "Sugar," and the like.

An uncarpeted staircase led from the kitchen, and another door opened into the scullery which had not only a sink but a copper and a bath.

"What I want to know," said Dickie, "is how we get the hot water from the copper to the bath? We shall want a hose. Bags I squirt it."

For once Mary had no answer.

In another corner was a genial grandfather clock with a loud and friendly tick and a jolly face.

When they had explored downstairs and rummaged in

cupboards and looked in the chest under the window and watched the pendulum in the clock, and given the unhappy Macbeth a drink, Mrs Morton insisted that the twins must go to bed but that they could prospect upstairs first. She gave them all a solemn warning about the dangers of oil lamps and candles, and put David in charge of the expedition.

Upstairs was more thrilling. The builder of Witchend seemed to have got in a muddle when he got to the top of the stairs. Nothing went straight. The passage had two turns in it and three odd steps. Some of the windows were almost on floor level and the boys' room had a door into Mrs Morton's. There was an exciting big room full of lumber at one end of the landing and Agnes's room didn't seem to be much more than a cupboard.

When they had been into every room and poked into all the cupboards they stood for a little at the top of the stairs leading to the kitchen. The door at the bottom was shut and they could hear Mummy talking as she helped Agnes to wash up. The flickering candle flung their shadows shakily on the walls, and Mary suddenly gave a little shiver.

"D'you know what it's all like, Dickie? I've thought of it. I've remembered."

"Yes, I do. It's like the old house on the mountain in *The Princess and the Goblin*. Do you remember how the Princess Irene went along all the lone passages and up lots of bare stairs to find her magic Grandmother?"

"'Course I do. That's what it is."

And then Mother came up with a lamp and sent them down to say "Good night" to Agnes.

They were all so tired that David for once came to bed with the others. He was a little ashamed, but suddenly found that he could barely keep his eyes open.

He had meant to put lots of his things away and make some changes in the little room he shared with Richard, but suddenly nothing seemed to matter except bed.

In the next room David could hear his mother saying "Good night" to Mary. Dickie was asleep as soon as his head touched the pillow so he put his torch on the chair behind him, blew out the candle, pulled aside the black-out and opened the window but did not even look out before tumbling into bed.

Then he was dreaming. He dreamt that he was in the garden at home in the days when Daddy went to the office every day. He was playing with Daddy and Macbeth. It was a favourite game.

They chased Macbeth down the garden until they got him into the corner by the potting shed. He might, and often did, escape them five or six times, but finally they always forced him into this corner. It was a sort of ritual and Macbeth loved it. He would tear madly round the lawn snarling and dodging, but not until he was pinned in his corner did he start to bark.

It wasn't the bark he used when ratting or rabbiting. It wasn't his watch-dog bark but a special kind of yelp. And now he was yelping loudly. Really loudly … louder and louder … David turned to ask his father why Mac was making so much noise this time, and found he was alone.

He woke up. Macbeth was still barking. Then he remembered where he was. Not at home now. A new home. Witchend in the shadow of the mountain. In the other bed Richard slept peacefully. All was quiet until Macbeth started again – an urgent, unhappy bark.

David turned over. Nothing to do with him. But perhaps it was? Daddy wasn't here now. It was his job. He'd promised.

Then from outside the house and not very far away came a different sort of bark followed by a fearful hullabaloo of squawking chickens, and this set Macbeth off again.

David reached for his torch and looked at the watch Daddy had give him last week. Twenty to three. He didn't much like the idea, but he knew he'd got to go down and stop Macbeth making such a din. He didn't stop for a dressing-gown as he wanted to get it over quickly, but by the time he was on the landing he was shivering.

He turned right for the kitchen stairs and stepped on a loose board which creaked violently. Macbeth started again with such gusto that he ran the last few steps and opened the kitchen door quickly.

The growls died in Mac's throat, and as David swung the beam of his torch round he could see the dog over in the corner by the scullery door.

"What's wrong, you silly little dog?" and with a rush Macbeth came at him and jumped up. David didn't know where the dog was supposed to be sleeping, but every time he tried to leave him on the coloured hearthrug he jumped up again and followed him to the door.

"All right, Mackie," he said at last. "I don't know what Mummy will say, but you'd better come up with me. I think you're lonely."

Mac knew. His tail wagged so violently that the whole of his little black body swayed and he fairly galloped up the stairs.

Back in his room David suddenly felt wide awake. He picked the dog up and went to the open window. The moon was going down but there was enough light for him to see the edge of the wood and the mountainside above it. Macbeth was licking his face when he first heard the 'plane in the distance. Not so many weeks ago such a sound had been frightening enough after the wail of the siren. Now it seemed out of place.

"One of our night fighters going home," he said to Mac. But it didn't sound like a fighter. It really was a bit like a German but he knew it couldn't be. Not out here. It came nearer and he leaned from the window. Just for a second he thought he saw a blacker speck against a strip of sky above the silhouette of the trees. Then the 'plane seemed to change direction and just before the last notes of the engine died away there came loud and clear from the mountain the wailing and unmistakable cry of an owl.

It was repeated three times and Macbeth growled in his arms.

David was cold now and tumbled quickly into bed. Macbeth jumped up beside him and settled down on the eiderdown. Richard hadn't moved.

The owl's cry came again.

Then the boy and the dog slept.

Chapter 2

Dark Hollow

David was late the next morning. He did not hear
Mary come in and pull her brother out of bed,
and although he was just conscious of Macbeth giving
his face a lick before going out with the twins, he did
no more than turn over until his mother came in at
half-past eight to see what had happened to him.

She teased him a little and then he remembered about
Macbeth barking.

"Thank you for going down, David," she said. "I
expect it was a fox he heard. Agnes says there are dozens
round here and that if we have chickens presently we shall
have to lock them up carefully. Hurry up and wash. We've
kept some breakfast for you."

It was a cool, clean morning when he looked out of the
window. A gentle wind swayed the tops of the larch trees
and there was no sound but their soft sighing and the jolly
running of the brook. Macbeth was sitting at the edge of
the pool looking suspiciously at his own reflection.

Although the twins hardly realized it, David knew how
lucky they were to be able to get away from London and
the raids to a place like this, and as he dressed he began to
plan some of the things they could do.

They would build a secret camp somewhere up in one

of these mysterious valleys. But they must climb to the top first and really see what it was like. He had never before been to the top of a mountain so they would be genuine explorers blazing a new trail. And when their bicycles came with the rest of their luggage, maybe they could discover the Stiperstones that Bill had told them about. And there was Bill himself to try and see if there was time. And that farm down the lane looked good too. And Bill had said something about a reservoir hidden in the hills.

He was pulling his sweater over his head when the twins came in. He could see that they were in one of their irritating "just alike" moods, and knew what that meant from previous experience.

They were both wearing navy blue jerseys and grey flannel shorts and looked maddeningly alike. When they started the day like this they would probably insist upon doing everything together and refuse to be parted. They didn't always dress alike, but sometimes, without telling each other, they would get up and put on similar clothes.

Richard began.

"Last night you snored."

David was speechless at this accusation.

"Oh, yes, you did," said Mary. "You kept me awake. Yes, you did. Hours and hours you kept me awake. *Us* awake. Me and Dickie."

David rushed at them, but they were ready for him and he was too hungry to chase them all over the house.

Downstairs Agnes was already washing up the breakfast things and gave him rather a cross look, but when he apologized for being so late she thawed and poured out his tea. The kitchen looked just as jolly in the daytime, and it was fun to have meals close to the range with a brightly burning fire.

He had nearly finished when his mother came in with the twins.

"I have been talking to Agnes," she began, "and I want you to realize that living in the wilds like this is good fun but hard work too. We're lucky to have Agnes, but it's so different from home that there's lots of jobs to do and we must share them out. You remember that Daddy spoke to you about that before he went? So I thought we had better get the work shared out and we'll all be responsible for some definite duty every day. That's what real explorers do, isn't it, David? No good getting into a muddle and into each other's way and wasting time.

"Two of the most important things in the country are things we all took for granted when living in a house in London. Water and fuel. Water first. All the water here has to be pumped. Away up the hillside behind the house is a good spring which has been piped, but we have to pump the tank in the roof full when we want a bath and that means that someone must pump for a certain time every day. It must be David's job to keep the tank full. This old range heats the water, but we must be careful not to use too much as if we have a drought the spring may run dry although the stream rarely does. You must *never* drink water from the stream unless it has been boiled. You must all promise me this. Promise?"

The twins nodded solemnly.

"And when you go exploring you must remember always to boil your water.

24

"Now about fuel. About once a year Agnes says the coalman finds his way up here. He has just been and we have enough for the winter, if we're careful. But we have to be very careful and that is why we burn wood. We are allowed to take all the *dead* wood we like from our own wood, but we shall want a big supply of logs for the winter and a daily supply of twigs and small kindling for starting fires. The twins are to be responsible for seeing that Agnes has a pile of dry kindling ready every evening. You can both help David get bigger boughs and trunks from the wood, and I will help him with the sawing. Remember to treat the wood properly. *Never* cut branches from a living tree, but collect dead and fallen pieces. Don't stamp about breaking off anything which looks handy. Learn to find your way about in the wood and make friends of the trees and help them to grow by clearing away the dead timber.

"Agnes says that the snow brings some of the larches down and that there's a year's supply waiting to be picked up.

"And while we're talking about fuel remember to be careful about fires. Never light a fire where it can catch dry wood or heather. Fire is a real danger up in these wild and lonely places, but I think David realizes this. The twins are not to have matches or to light fires unless David says so. Do you promise, twins?"

"Of course, Mummy," said Mary.

"We never would," said Richard.

"Then there's milk to fetch twice a day from Ingles down the lane. You can arrange this between yourselves, but I dare say you'll like to take it in turns. I'm sure Dickie and Mary won't want to go together every day ... and on Thursdays we shall have to fetch groceries from the farm because they don't like bringing them any further now that petrol's getting scarce. And on Fridays I believe we have to get the joint from Onnybrook, and that sounds like a job for the bicycles. And how we'll manage in the winter and when David goes back to school I don't know, but I'm sure it'll be fun... If you don't mind, darlings, I'd rather you didn't go off on any *very* distant explorations until we've got settled in because there's lots of ways you can help. Today you can start by going along to make friends with the Ingles and getting the milk, and when you're back there'll be time to make the first trip into yonder impenetrable forest! Now be off with you."

The twins hugged her until she begged for mercy and called to David for rescue. Then they remembered to ask Agnes for the milk can and disturbed her drying up and singing a doleful hymn.

"As like as two peas," she was heard to murmur. "In a pod and all."

Outside they called and whistled Macbeth in vain.

"We'll make a new responsibility," David said. "One of you kids will have to take charge of Mac till he learns sense. He'll be so excited for a bit that he may get lost. Who's going to look after him?"

"You do it, David," said Mary.

"You'd better, David," said Dickie. "We're too small."

"And he always liked you best, David."

"And you can whistle on your fingers and Mary and me can't ... not me anyhow."

It was some minutes before David was able to exert his

authority, but eventually Mary agreed to look after the dog. But they couldn't find him and so they abandoned the hunt and David led them off down the lane.

Ingles' farm was not very big, but the farmhouse of red brick was well set back from the road with a broad lawn on the right and cowsheds on the left. When they got to the gate a jolly looking man was in the yard harnessing a horse to a farm cart. He had half a cigarette behind one ear, a check cap on his head, and was wearing a brown overall. He was whistling as he worked.

David knew from experience that the twins were best able to manage new introductions. Strangers were always surprised at them and today they were idiotically excited.

Without a word to each other they went to the gate, climbed up two rungs and leaned on the top bar watching. The man had his back to them and was whistling, "There'll always be an England." He was whistling it very badly and when he stopped to search for a match the twins enthusiastically took up the glad refrain.

"There'll always be a Nengland," they carolled, and the staid old carthorse tossed his head in alarm. The man dropped his cigarette and pushed his cap to the back of his head in astonishment.

"And who might you be?"

"Good morning," said Mary. "I'm Mary Morton and this is my brother Dickie. We're twins."

"We 'spect you're Mr Ingles," said Richard. "We've come to have a great adventure at Witchend, and David's here too."

"We hope Mrs Ingles is well," said Mary.

"We've come for the milk," said Richard.

"Of course you have," said Mr Ingles with a grin, "but a rare shock you gave me singing there on the gate and me not expecting you. I was saying to the missus only at breakfast that if you didn't come along maybe one of us could find time to come up and see how you were getting on ... Come on in and let's have a look at you and see if I know the difference ... And you too, young man ... Hi, Betty! ... BETTY! BETTY!" he roared. "Here's visitors for you."

He led the way round the side of the house into the dairy. There they found Mrs Ingles who called them all "Ducks," much to David's fury, but was nice and friendly.

"Well, now," she exclaimed as she stood the twins side by side. "Just look at 'em, Alf! Did you ever…?"

"Just like two peas…" said Mary wickedly.

"In a pod," said Dickie solemnly.

Then they all roared with laughter – except David, who had witnessed the performance before.

Mary then attached herself to Mr Ingles, who suddenly bellowed, "Where's young Tom? Where is he? Now what did I tell him he'd got to do this morning? D'you know where he is, Betty me lass?"

"No, I don't," she said, "but it seems to me, Alf, the boy'll be glad there's company come to Witchend."

She turned to David. "Young Tom's my nephew from London, come to bide with us for a while. Two months he's been here and that lonely he is, sometimes he wishes he was back in what he calls 'them blitzes'. But their home has gone and his mother's somewhere else with the baby and his dad's in the war, and Alf here says he'll make a farmer of Tom maybe. But sometimes I wonder … Rur out and see if you can find him, boy. Him and you should get on together."

So David wandered out into the sunshine, and at the back of the stackyard he heard a clear and astonishingly melodious whistle. A boy – slimmer and no taller than himself – was leaning against the rick with his arms behind his head whistling one of those radio tunes that everyone knows but few can remember.

"Hullo," said David.

The boy jumped. "Hullo yourself!" he said. "Where d'you come from?"

"London," said David.

"So do I! Gosh, but I'm glad to see you. Are you living here?"

David tried to tell him, but nothing seemed to stop Tom talking. He explained that he didn't think much of it up here, and although the mountains reminded him a bit of the "pictures" there was little he could do by himself.

Then the twins found them and Tom stared in amazement.

"They're not real!" he gasped.

"Oh, yes, we are," said Mary, "ask David."

"We know who you are," Dickie began.

"You're Mrs Ingles' little nephew boy from London…"

"And you've come here to be a farmer away from the blitzes…"

"And you're not very much good at it yet…"

Tom glared.

"And that's enough of *that* from both of you." He turned to David. "Who are they?"

29

Rather apologetically David explained, but somehow Tom never seemed to get really used to them although the twins would always do anything for him.

"Well, show us something," said Mary. "We like adventures."

So Tom showed them over the farm. He showed them the cows, the chickens, the milk cooler, a colossal but gentle bull in a stall by himself, and, most fascinating of all, a baby foal with thin lanky legs and a white star on his forehead. He took them up into the hay-lofts and was about to start a rat hunt when Mrs Ingles called them and reminded them about the milk.

"We can't go very far today," David said to Tom, "but when we start exploring maybe you'd like to come along."

"What about these kids?" said Tom tersely. "Do they tag along everywhere?"

"Yes," said David stoutly. "Generally they do."

"OK by me then. I'll get away. Uncle won't mind … At least, not much…"

For the rest of the day they really did make themselves useful. The twins ran errands and helped unpack. David did some pumping and washed up after dinner. None of them suggested that they would rather be exploring. Macbeth turned up eventually, panting heavily and with a challenging look in his eye. Mary took charge of him, forbade him to go away again and tied him up in the yard where he promptly went to sleep.

After tea Mrs Morton said casually, "What about that wood for tomorrow? You'd better all go together the first time and explore. Supper at seven."

There were two things the children loved about the

country – water and a wood. Here they had both. The western side of the valley rose sharply from the banks of the stream where the larch and pine trees almost over-shadowed the moving water. Old John's description of the wood as they drove to Witchend the evening before was a good one – "Like a wedge" he had said, and so it was. Abruptly the trees stopped short at the stream, with Witchend at the point of the wedge, while higher up the mountain the wood climbed until the trees gradually thinned out amongst the heather.

David led the way. The twins followed side by side and Macbeth circled round enthusiastically. They followed the stream up the valley and paused at a wide pool.

"If we dug a bit – Tom and me could do it – and then made a dam, we could make a bathing-pool. It's pretty deep already."

"So it is," said Mary, and picked up Macbeth and threw him in. The dog gave a sharp yelp of surprise and looked back reproachfully at her before swimming to the other bank.

"Just like a little black rat," said Mary meditatively. "Isn't he, Dickie? Wasn't he sweet?"

"I'm going to swim across," said her twin. "Well, not exactly swim, 'cause it isn't quite deep enough. But *practically* swim. Wade across the foaming torrent, anyway."

And they both sat down and pulled off their sandals.

"I shan't wait for you kids," said David, jumping over the stream higher up.

But the twins weren't likely to be deterred by any such ridiculous threats. Half-way across the pool Mary stopped with the water washing past her knees.

"Parched and weary," she intoned, "the two brave travellers forced their way through the rapids…"

"Sir Richard, the leader," went on Dickie, "faint from his wounds, yet found the courage to fight off and keep at bay four ravenin' crocodiles."

"Cruelly the sun beat down upon their defenceless heads…"

"But before them lay the shelter of the impenetrable forest…"

"Where a native guide was waiting to take them to the queen of the country…"

"No, king," said Dickie. "It wouldn't be a queen."

But before the intrepid explorers could work up a quarrel they landed on the opposite bank and Macbeth shook himself all over them.

"Come along," called David. "The native guide is waiting for you."

One second they were out in the sunshine and the next in the gloom of the wood. Soft under their feet was a carpet of pine needles, but the undergrowth was thick with brambles, and David had hard work to make much progress. Only Macbeth was able to get through easily and, although Mary called him, he wagged his tail violently and with a wild yelp dashed ahead.

"We might make a camp in here," said David.

"Or a house in the trees like Wendy," said Mary.

"And blaze a trail," added Richard.

A pigeon cluttered noisily out of a tree and far away Macbeth started a breathless yelping as he found the trail of a rabbit.

And all the time they were climbing. David hoped that

they were going north-west and felt rather annoyed because he'd forgotten his compass. After a time the brambles thinned out and they came to a clearing with two big pine trees.

"Here's the place we always come back to," said David. "Scatter now and pick up all the dead wood you can find and we'll pile it up under these trees. Then we'll find the quickest way down to Witchend, and whenever we come into the forest we must pick up wood and either take it home or stack it ready for when we need it in a hurry."

He didn't really expect the twins to go in different directions. On some days they might have done, but not today! They just marched straight ahead into the "impenetrable forest," continuing in undertones the story of the dauntless Sir Richard and his companion in distress.

David worked hard and soon collected a big pile. The wood had been neglected and fallen larch trees offered stacks of fuel, but he seemed to remember reading somewhere that larch was not much good for burning.

The twins' voices faded into the distance and suddenly he was aware of the silence. For a little even the birds were still and there was not enough wind to stir the tops of the trees. He began to whistle, just to prove that he didn't mind being alone, and then after a while, heard the twins crashing about somewhere below him.

"Come on, Sir Richard," he called. "Up this way."

They soon had a good stack of kindling under the pine trees, but David made them each carry a bundle as they searched for a way down through the wood to Witchend. They found a track at last on the southern edge of the wood which led them easily down to the point of the "wedge" above the house. Although they whistled and called, Macbeth refused to appear, and Mary affirmed that she could not go to bed until he had been found.

Mrs Morton was very pleased with their efforts, but reminded them that they had forgotten the afternoon milk and that Tom had brought it up. "He says he'll be busy on the farm tomorrow, but hopes to see you soon … He seems a nice boy."

Over their bedtime mugs of cocoa the twins gave Agnes a vivid account of their adventures in the forest.

"And d'you know," Mary said excitedly, "jus' as we – the weary travellers – were forcing our way through the undergrowth searching for a bread-fruit tree, we…"

"Just as we were faint from loss of blood and zaustchun," Dickie chimed in, "there came a mighty roaring. What do you think it was, Agnes?"

"Well, now, my dears! … How would I know? And you both so weary and all … Well! Well! … Just like two peas…"

And when Macbeth barked to be let in that night at eleven o'clock, David and Dickie were sleeping so soundly that their mother had to go and let him in.

He was very penitent.

Next morning Mary went for the milk directly after breakfast. She saw Mrs Ingles, but neither Tom nor his uncle were about, so she came straight back.

It was a lovely morning. A gentle little breeze came from the south and the sun was already hot. As she came round the corner of the lane Dickie was swinging on the gate, and she suddenly knew what he was waiting to tell her.

"I know," she called. "We're going out all day. Mummy says we can. We're going to explore on our first adventure."

And so they were. Mrs Morton had decided that it was too fine to keep them about the place and that they might as well make the best of the weather.

Indoors there was a lot of sandwich cutting and packing, with David in one of his "bossy" moods.

"Come on, and don't waste time talking," he said. "Dickie, you are responsible for the compass, and here it is. Remember we may all perish miserably without it. I'll teach you how to use it when we get going. Mary! … Have you got Mac's lead? We'd better take him, I suppose."

"Of course we must take him," she said indignantly. "He'll keep the wild beasts at bay."

Mrs Morton gave them final directions.

"David is in charge. You can go where you like, and when you like now. Remember what I told you about fires and what water you drink. Be sensible and remember what Daddy will say if you spoil things by being silly. Don't go so far and get so tired that you forget the way back. If you go to the top, mind the bogs. Remember, David, that your legs are longer than the twins' and that I rely on you to be sensible. There are matches in the haversack. Watch the way you go, so that you learn the way back; and have a lovely day."

At the sight of the haversack Macbeth displayed signs of hysteria, so Mary grabbed him and put him on the lead. David was carrying the big load, but the others took their share in smaller satchels. Richard clanked along with a tin kettle fixed to his.

At the gate David remembered something else. "I will need my notebook," he said, "because we must make a map. Run back for it, Dickie, and a good thick pencil as well ... the map we make may serve many another traveller in good stead."

And at these last words he went rather red, realizing that he had begun to speak like the twins. It was difficult to live with them and not pick up some of their ways, even if you were older and more experienced.

"Aren't we going up *our* valley?" asked Mary when Dickie got back.

"No," said David. "We can explore that almost any time. We must find a new and bigger valley, and then if we can get to the top of the mountain we'll try to come back to Witchend this way. Opposite Ingles yesterday I saw a stile and a path leading round the side of the hill. We're going to follow that."

Mrs Ingles was in the yard as they passed, and waved to them.

"Tom's up the Twelve Acre with his uncle. He'd like to be along with you, but he can't today. Where are you going?"

The twins stepped forward.

"We'd like to tell you very much," began Mary.

"But we can't," continued Richard, "because we don't know."

"We're off to the great unknown…"

"'Cross the trackless wastes and through deserts and forests…"

"But we've got our dinner with us, so we shan't starve till tonight," finished Mary prosaically.

"We want to get to the top of the Mynd," said David. "Can we get up a valley if we go across these fields?"

Mrs Ingles came over to the gate and looked at them a little doubtfully.

"Up to the top you want to go? But it's a long walk and lonely, too. Does your mother know? Maybe it's all right, then, but watch for the bogs and remember the way you go, so as you can find your way back safe. Keep your dog from the sheep down here. Keep to the tracks, and don't wander off up the little gutters – that's what we call the valleys hereabouts – else you'll get lost … Yes, you can go across here till you come to a lane. Turn up it left and through a gate by a stream. Follow this right up that gutter – it's called Dark Hollow – and it'll bring you out to the top of the Mynd. But take care when you get there because it's wild and lonely and the tracks in the heather are difficult to follow."

"When we're up there," said Dickie, "when we've reached the summit will we see that old devil's chair?"

Mrs Ingles looked at him strangely. "If it's fine you'll see it over west," she said. "If you can't you come straight home, because the weather will be changing."

"Gosh!" said the twins together.

Then they said "Goodbye," lifted Macbeth over the stile, and started out.

The track led round the side of the hill, and soon the bracken was as high as the twins' heads.

"Tigers in here," said Dickie.

"Lurking," said Mary.

They came to the lane, and found the gate and the stream. Here David stopped and got out his notebook and started his map. It's difficult to make a map on a small page of a notebook as you go along, and David soon realized this and decided to do it in sections and make a big and proper one when he got home.

They let Macbeth off the lead, and he barked his thanks and took a good drink. The stream here was almost a little river. The water was running fast and it was clear and icy cold, although not very deep. Stepping stones helped them over to the track that was never more than a few feet from the bank.

David called for the compass.

"We're going to go due west now," he said. "We must mark the map and remember that as long as we follow the stream uphill and as long as this valley runs to the west we must get to the top. Are you two ready? We are really going to start."

"Maybe we'll never see Mummy again," said Mary.

"Or Sparrow Legs – Agnes, I mean," added Dickie. "Maybe we're going where no human foot has trod before," he finished triumphantly.

For a quarter of a mile the brook wandered through a sloping meadow. The bracken was close to the path which here was only wide enough for them to walk single file. They passed a cottage on the hillside, and then, suddenly, the mountain seemed to come right down to them.

The stream turned away to the left, and when they looked back the cottage and the pleasant slopes had disappeared and they were in entirely different country. Although the valley was still fairly wide the stream was already narrower and with a rockier bed. On each side the mountain came down steeply, and they could see why the valleys were called gutters. Sometimes the track wandered from the stream to avoid rocks, but it was never far away. A few hawthorns with their trunks showing wisps of wool rubbed from the backs of sheep were the only trees.

This valley was well-named "Dark Hollow."

David soon forgot how many times the path had changed direction, but when they came to their first valley on the south, bringing their stream's first tributary, he called a halt by a stunted tree.

"We'll rest now for ten minutes. Take your packs off and let's sit on this rock in the sun."

"What about some chocolate?" asked Dickie brightly.

"Save us carrying it any further," said Mary.

The captain agreed. They munched in silence for a little. Macbeth bolted his share.

David tried to continue his map, but it was difficult to remember what had happened after they had left the cottage. The compass showed that their stream was still running from the west. The "tributary" valley was very wild and lonely without even a path.

"David," said Mary suddenly, "this is a real adventure. I like it."

"The realest we've had," added Dickie. "But I hope we see that old devil."

"We must blaze a trail," said David, "to show us the way back again. We needn't always mark trees, but leave other signs like the gipsies do … we could leave a pattern of stones or bend twigs a special way … but there aren't any twigs. Never mind. We'll just cut the bark off this tree…"

"I don't suppose the tree will mind, as it's to help weary travellers," said Mary.

They had not gone very far after this before the valley narrowed and the sides became steeper. Bracken had given place to heather and bilberries. And all around them was the music of running water.

The stream ran deeper and faster and was still their cheerful guide, but little trickles from the side of the mountain made the ground soft under their feet. The path was steeper, too, and they realized at last that they were really climbing.

The twins were leading and were perhaps fifty yards ahead. David was beginning to find the haversack heavy, and was just wondering whether it might not soon be a good idea to lighten it by Mary's method, when she called out excitedly, "Come quick, David, and see what we've explored. Hurry up!"

They were hidden by a projecting rock, but when he climbed round it he found himself at the edge of a boulder strewn plateau. The hills had left it like a green saucer, and his first thought was that it was a perfect place for a camp.

Then he saw the others running towards the mouth of another valley to the right. Dickie turned to wave and pointed upwards, and David saw the cause of his excitement. This new valley ended in a miniature precipice about thirty feet high, and over it, tumbling slowly, bright in the sunshine, was a waterfall which emptied itself into a dark pool at its foot.

Dickie was hopping about on the edge.

"It's magic!" he shouted. "It's magic. It must be. It doesn't run away."

And he was right. The pool did not empty itself by another stream. The waterfall poured the water in, but it didn't run out. The pool was not very deep, but it was difficult to see the bottom for the rocks, and David supposed that the water escaped somewhere underground.

"It's witches," said Mary. " 'Course it is. That's what it is. Witches' magic. They say their spells here."

"Bags I'm not here at night," said Richard, and started to clamber up the side by the waterfall. David called him back rather half-heartedly, and then Mary started after her twin. Although David felt somehow that this was a silly thing to do, he followed them because it would be exciting to see what was at the top. They pulled themselves up by holding on to heather roots, and half-way up David wished he'd left the haversack behind. But he had to go on now, and when he was up it was worth it, for they were now in an even wilder and narrower gutter.

The stream was running fast through the heather, and behind them they could see the "rocky plateau", as Mary called it. This new valley was very tempting, but there was no path to follow – only the stream. It was here that David forgot Mrs Ingles' advice to keep to the paths. Like the twins, he felt that this was *real* exploration at last, and they set out cheerfully enough into the unknown.

Macbeth found the going heavy. His legs were too short for him to see over the heather, and he soon exhausted himself with a series of kangaroo-like hops. Mary picked him up, but progress was difficult for them all. The heather dragged at their feet and scratched the twins' knees. David's haversack seemed to weigh a ton and Dickie's kettle clanked horribly as he struggled on.

The valley widened.

"Like a desert now," panted Mary.

"Where's the stream?" asked Dickie.

"Down to the right," said David. "We're going too high, and that's why it's so difficult. Follow me and we'll go lower down."

Suddenly the ground began to give under his feet. Each step forward squelched and he turned uphill again. Then the heather thinned and gave place to tufts of tussocky rushes and patches of bright green grass. When Dickie saw such an open space he jumped on to it and then gave a shout of surprise.

When the other two turned he was floundering in black mud, but before they could help him a strange clear voice called somewhere above them, "Stand still! Don't hop about like that…"

They looked up in the direction of the voice and saw on the skyline above them a girl on a pony.

"Don't go too near him," she called again. "Tell him to stand still. I'm coming down."

Like a cat the little pony picked her way delicately down through the heather, faltered for a moment in the soft ground by the other side of the stream and then, at a word from her rider, jumped over and came quickly up to them.

Meanwhile, Dickie, looking rather white and worried, was trying to stand still, but his right leg was now covered to the knee. Mary, on the contrary, was behaving rather foolishly and hopping first on one leg, then on the other.

"Why don't you *do* something, David?" she squealed. "He's getting all swallowed up in it."

By this time David had got his knapsack off and was taking one step at a time cautiously towards the treacherous bright green of the bog. He could feel the water oozing in over his shoes.

"Take your shoes and socks off," called the girl on the pony. "You won't sink in so far."

He looked back gratefully at this sensible advice, and by the time he had followed it the girl was at his side.

"Now then," she said, "slide your feet over the bog and don't take big, heavy steps. Reach one hand behind you and hang on to me as you go. Is the little boy all right?"

Richard was so furious at being so addressed that he lurched forward and nearly lost his balance.

"Here!" he said. "I'm not a little boy."

"We're nine," squealed Mary from the background.

"Stand still, Dickie," said David sharply. "Now can you reach my hand? Steady! Now put both your hands on mine."

"When I say heave," said the girl, "we all pull, and the little boy must move his left foot just a step towards us. Now HEAVE!"

And they heaved to such purpose that there was a loud and succulent "plop" as an indignant Richard shot out of the mud and landed on his face at his rescuers' feet.

"You do look comic," laughed the girl as Dickie scrambled up. "If you could only see yourself! And I bet you smell like anything!"

But Dickie couldn't see the joke. He didn't like being

laughed at. He went very red, and although he wouldn't have admitted it for anything, he was very near tears and had to turn his back for a moment. But Mary knew how he was feeling. In a flash she was at his side and facing the stranger.

"Just you BE QUIET," she raged. "You'd look funny, too, if you'd fallen in there. P'raps you will one day. And he doesn't smell … and if he did just a bit … well, we like it. And if you don't like it I'll jump in, too, and then we'll *both* smell…"

The girl looked at the twins in astonishment. "Why, you're exactly alike," she said. "What fun!" Then she must have seen Dickie dash a hand across his eyes. "I'm sorry I laughed," she went on. "It was silly of me. Expect it was the excitement … it was jolly plucky of you standing still like that. Much more difficult for you than for us. He *was* brave, wasn't he?" she finished, turning to David. Then, "Let's be friends, shall we?" and she held out her hand.

"All right. ALL RIGHT," muttered the embarrassed Dickie while trying to scrape some slime off his face. "That's all right."

But he made an ineffectual grab at the girl's hand while Mary said, "We don't *mind* being friends, but you mustn't come and say things like that to us. Not to Dickie and me."

David was pulling his shoes on again. He laughed. "We're all being a bit silly, but let's get away from this smelly place. No, it's not you, Dickie. Only the bog! Let's go and clean ourselves up and have something to eat. I'm famished."

The girl and the pony led the way back over the stream, and they climbed up to where they had first seen her on the top of the ridge. There they took stock of each other properly.

The Mortons saw a girl of between fourteen and fifteen with a brown, laughing face, clear blue eyes, and two long, fair pigtails. She was wearing old brown jodhpurs and a bright blue shirt open at the neck. She stood with one hand on her pony's neck, smiling at them.

"Who are you? How did you get up here?"

The twins, feeling brighter at the thought of food, started their usual duet, but David interrupted and told the girl briefly who they were and where they had come from.

When he had finished she laughed. "But how lovely! We must form a secret club or something. I live here – not far away, at Hatchholt by the reservoir."

"By the what?" said David excitedly.

"The reservoir, silly! But of course you wouldn't know. Daddy looks after it, and we live up here all alone. Except for my pony, Sally," she went on. "You must all come and see it now and you can have your picnic while Daddy and I have our dinner, and then I'll show you some more this afternoon."

"But we're on our way to the top of the Mynd," said David. "Can you show us the way up? We must find it today."

"We've made a solemn swear that we will," said Mary.

"Signed in blood," said Dickie almost automatically. He was thinking of dinner.

"Yes, I'll take you up this afternoon," said the girl, "but

let's get going now. I can't think how you got up here, though. This is a stupid gutter, and it's dangerous, too, with all those bogs. Did you come up by the waterfall?"

"Niagara," murmured Dickie.

"Up the rapids ... hand over fist," said Mary.

David didn't care to admit that he'd really been silly and lost his way and the twins backed him up loyally.

"We were just exploring," he said, "and the waterfall looked fun so we thought we'd climb up and look round ... But we don't know your name, and you know ours."

"It's Peter," the girl said.

"But it can't be," said Mary.

"You're not a boy, are you?" said Richard. "Not a boy disguised and hidin' from your cruel enemies?"

She laughed. "Everyone I know calls me Peter. I hope you will, too. My full name is Petronella Sterling ... But we must go now or we'll never get home and Daddy'll be mad with me and there'll be no time left for our exploring this afternoon..." and she heaved the haversack on to the pony's back and led the way along the top of the ridge. As far as they could see there was nothing but rolling hills and little gutters all looking exactly alike. With a shock David realized how easy it would be to get lost. Although the sun was shining brightly now, and it was difficult enough to know which way to go, it was rather frightening to imagine what would have happened if they had got up here without Peter, or in the dark, or in bad weather.

They were climbing now in single file. Peter, in front with Sally, was chattering over her shoulder about what fun they would all have together and asking whether they could swim, when they reached the top of another ridge.

"Now we're nearly home," she said. "Look. There's Hatchholt and our bathing pool."

They panted up beside her and David whistled in surprise. They were looking down into a deeper and wilder valley than Dark Hollow. To their left was the gleam of water, and with a thrill he realized that they had found the hidden reservoir. The top end of the valley was a lake held in check by a dam which stretched from side to side below them. On the opposite side of the valley, built snugly into the hillside, was a trim little house. They could just see someone moving about in the garden and Peter suddenly put her fingers to her mouth and whistled shrilly. Sally, browsing in the heather nearby, pricked up her ears and stood stock still.

"That's Daddy," said Peter. "Let's wave to him so he's not too surprised when we come down." They all waved but as Mr Sterling gave no sign that he had seen them, they started off down the zig-zag path.

Peter, who was leading Sally, suddenly stopped. "Would you like to ride down, Dickie?" she asked. The twins both looked so interested at this suggestion that David said quickly: "No. *Not* both of you at the same time. Dickie first, if Peter doesn't mind."

So Dickie was helped on and for a moment it seemed as if Sally was going to protest, but Peter took the bridle and spoke to her firmly and they set off down the hill again.

"I'm Red Wolf, the Indian Chief," said Dickie.

"And I'm Tiger Lily, his beautiful princess," said Mary.

"And we're trailin' the long trail over the prairie…"

"On the track of the palefaces…"

And so they came into the valley. David looked puzzled.

"Where's the stream, Peter? There's no water down here."

"The water comes down in four big pipes," she said. "We shall come to them in a minute."

Soon they came to a rough wooden bridge and Peter showed them the pipes, now almost hidden in the bracken. They crossed and turned to the left and climbed again towards the cottage.

Mr Sterling was in the garden when they arrived and when Peter told him who they were and how they had met, he removed his hat and twinkled at them.

"Getting very crowded up here, we are," he said. "I heard tell down at Onnybrook the other day that Ingles has a lad from London too. You'll be having company, lass."

Then he seemed to notice the twins for the first time. He looked at them very carefully, produced a pair of spectacles and had another look.

Richard and Mary were just preparing to launch their usual attack when Mr Sterling shrugged his shoulders as if to suggest that he couldn't believe his eyes, and turned to the house.

"Come along in for a bit," he said, "and we'll see what we can find."

The living room was the tidiest, cleanest place they had ever seen. Everything gleamed. A table with a white cloth was laid for two places. Potatoes were bubbling in a shining saucepan on the little range and a brilliantly polished brass clock on the mantelpiece struck one as Peter came back from stabling Sally.

David wanted to ask about the reservoir but Mr

Sterling seemed too occupied with the dinner to pay much attention to him and, in any case, Peter soon took charge of the situation.

She explained that the visitors had brought their own sandwiches and that all they needed was three more plates and places at the table. There were only two more chairs, so David had to sit on a hard, black, shiny sofa and undid the haversack while the twins watched him hungrily. He was rather nervous about spilling crumbs and wasn't surprised when Mr Sterling, after dishing up the potatoes, went to a cupboard for newspaper and spread the sheets on the floor.

Mary got a drink for Macbeth and then they all settled down to an unusual meal. Mr Sterling didn't say much but once or twice David caught him peeping over his glasses at the twins who were eating like starving explorers.

At last Dickie rather rudely pushed back his plate. "Now I'm ready for that old mountain," he said, "but first of all may I please ask a question? I don't think it's a very good manners question, but it's something I want to know ... very badly I want to know it."

David and Peter both looked alarmed. Mary was unperturbed, and Mr Sterling chuckled.

"What's your question, you young limb? Ask away."

"Why," asked Dickie, "why did you call her Petronella? I've never heard of it."

"Yes. Why?" said Mary, with her mouth full of lettuce. "I've been thinking that too. We want to know."

"I've never asked you that, Daddy," said Peter. "I'd like to know too."

Mr Sterling scratched his head.

"Funny you should ask that because I don't rightly know. But it's a good name, isn't it, lass? I remember I chose it and your dear Mother, bless her, agreed it was a rare one! ... Come to think of it though, I believe I saw it on the back of a boat on the Cromer beach on our honeymoon."

"Maybe it was a pirate schooner?" said Dickie, hopefully.

"Or a smuggler's sloop?" said Mary.

But Mr Sterling didn't seem to have any further ideas so Peter explained that they were going up the Mynd and that possibly they would all be back to Hatchholt for tea.

"Do as you please, my dears," he said, "but just help tidy up a bit first and come back when you like. You're always welcome here if you keep the place clean."

So they helped wash up and then Peter suggested that they go up by the reservoir and sit in the sunshine for a little before they started on the final climb. They left their haversacks and satchels and Dickie's kettle in the house and followed her along a steep path and then up a few steps to the wall of the dam and a little red brick house which was built at the edge of the water.

"There's some sort of machinery in here," Peter explained. "Something to do with sluices and the amount of water that runs down the pipe line. Here the water is about 10 feet deep. Can you all swim?"

David nodded emphatically and the twins doubtfully.

"Practically," said Dickie.

"I can do the sprawl," said Mary.

"Crawl, we mean," said her twin hurriedly.

"Further up here," Peter went on, "I've got a little secret hiding place and a lovely bathing beach. I'll show you. Come on."

She led the way through the heather to a snug little hollow which was so well hidden that Mary, talking as usual over her shoulder to Dickie, fell in with a smothered shout of alarm. When she had picked herself up, the others were laughing down at her.

"There are lots of these hidden little dells on the mountain," Peter explained. "I know plenty. Sometimes I watch the birds and once or twice Daddy has let me stay out and watch the stars. I love stars, don't you, David? Have you read *Bevis*? It's my favourite book."

Then she showed them the way in and how she could stand upright without being seen. The sun was hot and they were sheltered from the wind. They sat down and David began to feel sleepy.

"You'll come swimming with me one day, David?" Peter was asking, and he had to rouse himself to answer her. Then she nudged him and grinned.

"Babes in the wood," she whispered.

On the other side of the dell the twins lay stretched on the short grass fast asleep. Macbeth slept too with his black head on Mary's chest.

Chapter 3

The Mountain

From far away David heard Peter say, "Come on, you lazy lubbers! Time we were on the move."

He sat up with a start. "Have I been to sleep?"

"You have," Peter laughed. "I couldn't stay quiet any longer … Do you think the little ones are too tired to go on?"

The twins sat up.

"Too tired?" said Dickie, indignantly. "'Course we're not too tired."

"Just a bit of a rest," said Mary.

"From the fierce noontide sun…" added Dickie.

"Whose rays were reflected in more than oriental splendour…" went on his twin.

"I know *that* one," said Peter. "That's something to do with the Parsee's hat in *Just So Stories* … Now we'd better start if you want to get to the top of the mountain and see the Devil's Chair … That's what the little chap wants, isn't it?"

Dickie was about to protest when he saw their new friend wink, so he just grinned sheepishly instead.

Macbeth yawned prodigiously and stretched his silly little legs. Then he looked up at Mary, with his head on one side, and wagged his tail as Peter led them out of the hollow.

She showed them her bathing beach, and then the track led them along the side of the reservoir and after a little the ground became soft again and they had to tread very carefully. At the head of the reservoir they crossed two streams but although they were still climbing they could not, as Mary said, "See over the top" yet.

Presently David said, "What an idiot I am, I ought to have kept the map. I meant to do it in Peter's dell but..."

"You went to sleep and snored instead," said Peter. "Never mind! I'll help you with it one day and we'll make a big one and put in pictures. I hate maps without pictures. We'll put in the little boy's bog, and Mary asleep with Macbeth on her tummy, and Daddy cooking potatoes ... Now, sniff all of you and tell me if you can smell anything different?"

The twins' sniffing was a little too enthusiastic, but Mary made the right answer, "It smells cleaner and colder."

They were marooned now in a sea of heather. Only when they looked behind did they realize how far and high they had climbed. There were no gutters now, no tinkling of hidden water, only sun, sky and brown heather.

"I feel about as big as a fly up here," said Dickie suddenly. "A King fly, of course," he added.

"A few more minutes," said Peter, "and you'll be up and almost able to see over the edge the other side."

They were on a wide plateau and their track joined another bridle path running north and south along the top of the mountain.

"That pile of stones marks the top of the Mynd," said Peter, pointing ahead. "Quite near there is the most secret of all my hidden dells. You'll be the first ever to see it and hide in it. Let's go there now."

Dickie was still protesting that he wanted to climb the cairn and see the Devil's Chair before he did anything else when Peter disappeared. One second she was there – and the next she wasn't! While they were staring at each other in bewilderment there was a snuffling noise and Macbeth vanished too. Then Peter's laugh came almost from their feet, and they realized that her dell was so well hidden by the overhanging heather that they were within a few feet of it without knowing. They jumped in and the heather closed over their heads. It was rather like a cave with a clean sandy floor. Peter showed them where she had dug out some "cupboards" in the sides, and they had just finished their last bar of chocolate when Macbeth suddenly cocked his head and growled.

David put his hand on his collar, and the others stopped talking.

"Quiet," whispered Peter. "Someone's coming."

"The enemy approaches stealthily," said Dickie.

"Right into the ambush," added Mary.

Peter put a finger to her lips and knelt upright so that she could peep through the heather. Then she turned and beckoned David up beside her while the twins patted Macbeth so that he wouldn't bark.

About fifty yards away a man was standing on the track. He was wearing a fawn raincoat, and had a knapsack on his back. He looked hot and tired and rather cross, and while they watched him he pushed his soft felt hat to the back of his head and began to search through his pockets. David saw him glance at the cairn of stones which marked the summit, and then he pulled out a piece of paper, unfolded it and studied it intently.

"He's lost," whispered David. "Shall we go and help him?"

"No," said Peter doubtfully. "Let's not. I've got an idea. Let's trail him and see where he's going ... I wonder what he's doing up here at this time by himself? ... On a walking tour I s'pose ... Shall we, David? Shall we follow him just for fun? It'll be good practice ... Ow!"

Her last exclamation was rather loud and the stranger looked up sharply. Peter turned round furiously to see the twins glaring at her.

"Yes, I pulled your hair," Mary said. "Beasts you are both of you staying up there in the way so that we can't see."

"Just let us have a look," demanded Dickie, in a penetrating whisper, "else we'll shout and spoil it all. Couple of PIGS whisperin' up there."

Peter and David gave up the vantage point hurriedly and the twins took their place.

"I think he looks nice – but lonely," Mary whispered.

"P'raps he's an exile comin' home at last," said Dickie.

"We'll tell you what he's doing," his twin went on. "Be quiet and I'll tell you ... He's looking at a map now. He's got a piece of paper too ... like a letter..."

"That's it," said Dickie. "He's comin' home – like the probable son in the Bible. That's what he is..."

Suddenly Mary pulled her brother down beside her and they could hear the stranger's steps coming nearer. He was whistling quietly as he passed just above their heads. They lay quiet for a little and then Peter said, "Are you all game for a real adventure? Are you ready to track him to his hiding place—"

"Lair," interrupted Dickie.

"'Course we are," said Mary. "Think we can't trail? 'Course we can. Just like Indians."

"Glad I left that old kettle behind," said Dickie, solemnly. "Red Wolf no track paleface with kettle."

"Tiger Lily put on moccasins," added Mary inconsequently.

"You know where we are, Peter," said David, "so you'd better be leader. I'll come next. Then Dickie and Mary and Macbeth."

So Peter raised her head carefully and then, after a quick glance round, beckoned David up and pointed. The stranger was about two hundred yards away now and had paused to light his pipe. Then he seemed to consult either the map or the paper again before easing the knapsack on his back and starting off at a smart pace along the track to the north.

Peter led them well. There was no cover but the heather, and although occasionally they were able to walk or trot upright, they spent most of the time on their stomachs. But the stranger only turned round once and it was obvious that he was unaware of the four Indians on his trail and the fearful fate which awaited him if he was caught.

After some minutes strenuous trailing, Peter waited for David to come up with her.

"We'll soon know where he's going," she said. "There's a track down the other side of the mountain on his left soon. If he takes that it will lead him to Appledore – a farmhouse rather like Witchend. If he goes on, he'll either have to turn down one of the gutters like ours, or walk along the top of the Mynd for another six miles ... I wonder who he is, David? ... How are the twins getting on? Not too tired?"

"'Course we're not tired," said Mary indignantly.

"Indians never get tired," said Richard.

The man was walking fairly fast, but as it was easy to keep him in sight Peter did not rush them. Once, when he seemed to pause, they fell flat in the heather and David heard the twins muttering behind him. It was becoming fairly evident that some Indians did get tired and he was just about to suggest to Peter that perhaps they might honourably give up the chase, when Macbeth yelped and Mary squealed. David fell on the dog and silenced him but Mary jumped up and pointed at her feet.

"Get down," snapped Peter.

"I won't," squeaked Mary. "I won't. There's a snake – a beastly, horrible black squiggly snake."

"It didn't bite you did it, Mary? You're quite sure it didn't? Did you see if it had a white V on its head? Was it an adder?"

Mary looked bewildered and frightened, so Richard answered for her. "No," he said stoutly. "No, we haven't been bitten, thank you, but we've been in great danger. No – it wasn't an adder. It was a cobra or ... or a bostricter! 'Bout twelve feet long it was."

"Well, whatever it was," said Peter, "we'd better get out of the heather and on the path. It may have been an adder. There are lots up here."

Mary, most unexpectedly, reached for Dickie's hand

and David began to wonder whether he was being as sensible as his father would have expected. Maybe they were doing too much. Mary's brown eyes looked rather full, and she suddenly sat down on the path.

"We've got stitch," said Dickie promptly, "and we're thirsty."

"We'd better find an oasis," said Mary rather faintly.

Peter looked rather crestfallen. "I'm afraid we've missed him now," she said. "He's just disappeared so he's probably gone down to Appledore on the other side. There are no gutters on the west side of the mountain and it's a steep climb down."

"What's Appledore?" said Mary.

"I was telling David. It's a house rather like Witchend. A lovely place but very lonely and with a big wood round it. About six months ago a Mrs Thurston took it. I've never seen her."

"What name did you say, Peter?" asked David.

"Who? Oh! Thurston, I believe. Why?"

"I'm not sure," said David rather puzzled, "but I seem to remember someone saying that name to me the other day. Do you remember, twins?"

"Of course we do," said Mary.

"It's the name the wizard black dog said at the station."

"You are silly, David! Don't you remember the lollopy black dog that banged you against the barrow and wanted the parcel?"

Peter was looking so puzzled at this strange allusion to a black dog that wanted a parcel that they had to tell her the whole story of their arrival and of the man who was so rude to them.

"I've never met him or Mrs Thurston," said Peter. "Shall we go and spy out the land for ourselves, and ask for a drink and see what happens? There's plenty of time. We've lost our victim anyway, and if the twins aren't too tired we'll go over to the edge so that you can see the Stiperstones and the Devil's Chair that Dickie wants so badly. Then, if we feel like it, we can climb down through the pine wood to Appledore and see who really lives there."

David felt that they had done enough, but the twins were so excited and so obviously refreshed by the rest, that his protest was only half-hearted. Peter, he was beginning to discover, was a very strong-willed young person but she was fun, and he was sure that they were going to be great friends. But she was so used to going about alone with only herself to please that it was difficult for her to realize that others were not as strong as she was.

So they set off again along a thin track leading to the west side of the mountain. Distances were deceptive up here, and they had been walking for ten minutes before they reached a ridge nearly as high as the summit.

"There you are, Dickie," said Peter, "there's the Stiperstones with the Devil's Chair at the top. You know what they say, don't you? When you can't see the Chair it means he's sitting in it."

"We know," said Dickie. "We've got a sailor friend who told us!"

"But thank you all the same, Peter," said Mary politely, "and we'd like to know anything else you can tell us about the old devil with the stone in his shoe. Where does he it?"

David was remembering what Bill Ward had told them about this country, but he hadn't imagined that it could be as wonderful as this. He had never seen such a view. They seemed to be standing on the top of the world and looking across a wide valley. At their feet their own mountain, the Mynd, fell away abruptly. Some of the slopes were almost precipitous, and there were dark patches of pine forest too. Far, far below them was the plain, and they could see a village with a tiny, toy church with the sun just catching the gilded weathercock on the tower. The little fields were like coloured squares on a chess-board.

The twins were silent as they followed Peter's pointing hand.

"Over there to the south is Wales," she said. "Today it's clear enough for you to see the Welsh mountains ... I forget their names. Daddy told me once, but I think Plynlimmon is the biggest. Someone told me all sorts of stories about this country – it's called the Border Country, or the Welsh Marches. Down there – you can't quite see from here – is Ludlow…"

"I know," said Mary. "There's a castle. An' bold knights come ridin' out of the Marches to me doin' my tapestry in the window."

Peter looked down at the little girl in surprise, and was just about to laugh when she saw the look in her eyes. Instead she slipped an arm round her shoulders and gave her a hug.

"Perhaps you're right, Mary! We'll all go one day. Oh! Isn't this fun? We're going to have such wonderful times I'm so glad you've come."

Richard was a little peeved.

"What I want 'splained to me is Stiperstones," he said firmly. "I s'pose that's them —" and he pointed to the north-west.

"I'm sorry, Dickie," Peter laughed. "We did look at them first, and it's really for you that we've come. Yes — there they are. The Stiperstones are higher than the Mynd, I believe. Can you see the Chair?"

Dickie couldn't admit that the black rocks crowning the highest part of the ridge looked like a Chair. They didn't — not really.

"We don't always have fine weather when the Chair is as clear as it is today," said Peter. "Once, when I was about as old as you, Mary, I went with Daddy to that village you see down there. We went to see some friends, and instead of taking the bus back round the end of the Mynd we decided to walk up over the top by Appledore — the way we'll go down presently. As we walked up through the wood I remember Daddy told me that about the weather and the Chair ... It had been a lovely day when, half-way up, I looked back and — I was a bit scared — the Chair was as clear as you see it now ... We got up here to the top and I looked back again and the Chair had gone. I couldn't see the mountain at all for the mist ... I remember how Daddy made me hurry, but before we got to the top of the reservoir the mist had caught us up and if he hadn't known the way so well we might have fallen in the water, or got lost altogether."

"What happened?" said Richard.

"Oh!" laughed Peter, "we got home all right, and I remember Daddy put me to bed and brought me some bread and milk ... He thinks bread and milk cures everything..."

"If we can't see his chair he's sittin' in it, isn't he?" persisted Richard. "I want to know. That's all I ask. I just want to know."

As he sounded rather agitated David changed the subject.

"What about a drink? That's what I want more than anything, but maybe you two are tired and we'd better go straight back? We've got to get back to Witchend after we've picked up our things at Peter's. What shall we do?"

The mere suggestion that they might be tired was always enough to spur the twins to even greater efforts, but David knew they could stand a lot, and they did seem to be rested. And he wanted to get Dickie interested in something besides the Devil's Chair.

"How long will it take us to climb up again and get back to Hatchholt, Peter?" he said. "And can you show us a quicker way back to Witchend?"

"You needn't come back to us, David. I'll show you a quick way along the top to the Witchend valley, and I'll ride over on Sally tomorrow and bring your luggage back. Come on! Let's go and explore Appledore, and see if Dickie's wizard is there … Besides, I'm thirsty, too. It won't take long to climb up again and we can have a rest on the way."

David made no further protest, but Macbeth did. He just refused to get up, but wagged his tail feebly and rolled on his back when Mary called him.

"He wants a drink like us," she said. "Poor little Mackie."

At this endearment Mac feebly struggled to his feet.

"I hope he's not going to be a nuisance," Peter said

"It's not much use having dogs up here in this country if they can't last the pace."

Richard looked at Mary, who nodded faintly.

"Goodbye," she said. "We'll be here when you come back … or if we're not, you'll know we've gone home by ourselves."

"Don't bother 'bout us," Dickie went on. "We'll be all right. If you have time, p'raps you'd bring a bottle – a very little bottle, o' course – of water for us and Mackie."

"It's not much we ask," said Mary.

"Just so as we don't die," Dickie finished pathetically.

Peter looked at David.

"What are they burbling about?"

"I think," said David, "I think they mean that they'd prefer to stay with Macbeth if he's too tired rather than come with us … You're not used to them yet, Peter. They're nearly always like this, and it's an awful nuisance sometimes. You shouldn't have said that about Macbeth. Mary won't leave him, and Dickie won't leave Mary – it's no use. We know. You can't do anything about it."

Peter went very red and looked as if she was going to say something angry. Then she swallowed hard.

"I'm sorry," she said. "Come on. Let's take it in turns to carry Mac, and I'll start."

Again the twins looked at each other, but this time there was no need of a nod. They got up, smiled sweetly at Peter, and started off down the track. Macbeth watched them with his head on one side for a moment, then yawned, snapped at a fly and trotted after them.

"Jiminy Cricket!" said Peter. "He's as bad as those twins, isn't he?"

The path down was steep and they were soon among the pine trees. The smell reminded them of the Witchend wood, but this one was much bigger. The trees were taller and there was not as much undergrowth, and the track was slippery with pine needles. The twins decided that they were Hansel and Gretel, but, apart from this rather morbid impersonation, seemed to have recovered their health and high spirits. David and Peter walked behind.

"Seems funny we only met this morning," the latter said. "I'm so glad you've come here to live. Holidays are pretty dull for me 'cause I've only got Sally really. Can you ride, David?"

He shook his head.

"I'll lend you Sally, David, and teach you to ride her, too ... I've never lent her to anyone before ... I'll tell you another thing. When I come and see you at Witchend tomorrow I'll have a big idea. Something that will last us all the hols."

"I've got some ideas too, Peter. There's lots of things I want to do here that will be better if you're with us. Then there's Tom at Ingles. He has to help his uncle at the farm, but he'd be good fun, I know..."

They were talking so hard that they didn't notice where they were going, and were really surprised when the twins jumped out at them from opposite sides of the path. Their faces were convulsed, and when David said, "What on earth's the matter?" quite naturally, Dickie sprang at him and put a grubby hand over his mouth.

"Can't you be quiet?" Mary hissed. "We're at the enemy's gate."

"Blundering along like that and spoilin' it all,"

whispered Dickie hoarsely. "Seems it would be better if we was always leaders."

"In the van," said Mary.

"No. That's behind," snapped Dickie.

Macbeth started to growl quietly, so David picked him up and slipped behind a big tree. The twins were right, for they had nearly reached the edge of the wood and could see, about two hundred yards below them, a biggish house with a thatched roof. They could only see the back from where they were standing, and although there was nobody about, a wisp of blue smoke was coming from the chimney.

Peter sniffed. "Wood fire," she said. "Somebody's at home. Yes. That's Appledore. I remember it. We seem to have missed the main path, but if we're going to ask for a drink we'd better go up to the front door, which is round the other side. What do you think, David?"

"Well, we can't very well go snooping about in the garden," said David. "And we haven't come all this way just to look, have we? I want my drink badly, and so does Mac."

So they came out of the shelter of the trees, cut across some rough and rocky ground, and joined the main track again. Appledore was bigger than Witchend, and older, too. There was a big barn and several outhouses at the back, and a well-tended garden. The house had been recently redecorated and didn't look much like a working farmhouse with gay-coloured chintz curtains fluttering from the windows. At the side was a paved yard in which a motorcycle was standing.

"Come on," said Peter. "There's sure to be somebody

at home. There's a car up by the front door. Let's go and see –" and she pushed open the white farm gate and started up the drive. There was a pond with some ducks on the left, and under the apple trees in the orchard the grass was brown and dry. Appledore lay drowsing in the afternoon sun – a lovely, peaceful old country farmhouse.

Peter raised the knocker on the oak door and knocked twice. David still held Macbeth, who had shown some inclination to assault the ducks, and behind stood the twins, side by side.

"I s'pect he's invisible," said Dickie. "Got his magic cloak on."

"'Course he can change himself into things," said Mary. "Big black dogs, f'rinstance."

"He's watching us. And listenin' too."

Peter looked round. "Shall I knock again? I believe I can hear somebody, but they don't come."

David thought he heard something move at the window above their heads, but when he looked only the curtain was fluttering.

Peter knocked again. Macbeth growled and the door opened suddenly. Before them stood the man they had seen at Onnybrook station. He was wearing a short white coat and his long arms hung loosely at his sides as he stared silently at the children.

David shivered and was tongue-tied. Macbeth barked and struggled in his arms. Peter stood back, and Dickie, the excitable, breathed a quick " Gosh!"

"What do you want?" said the man softly.

Nobody answered.

"Why do you come knocking here and disturbing the

house ? Nobody is here. Go away." On the last words his voice rose.

Peter was the first to recover

"Good afternoon," she said politely. "We're sorry to have disturbed you; but we've come farther than we ought, and we're tired and rather thirsty. Could you, please, give us a drink ?"

"Who are you?" said the man. "And what are you doing here?" Then he noticed David for the first time. "You! You are the boy who hid my parcel at the station. Go away. We do not want children here," and he started to close the door.

"I want to see Mrs Thurston," said Peter loudly, "and you've no right to speak to us like that. We only want a drink of water."

From inside the house they heard a woman's voice call sharply: "Jacob! Who is there and what do they want ?"

Peter winked at David and said louder than before: "I'm sure Mrs Thurston wouldn't turn us away without a drink. My father knew the Martins when they lived here, and they wouldn't have minded us having some water."

The man glared, and sullenly opened the door again and said over his shoulder: "Only some children pestering for a drink. I'd have them off the place if I had my way."

"That's enough, thank you, Jacob." Then to the children: "I think I heard you mention my name. Of course you can have a drink if you're thirsty. Come in and tell me all about yourselves, and who you are, and where you live, and whether we're neighbours."

She was very nice and friendly, and looked rather pretty with her dark hair parted in the middle and drawn down tightly behind her ears. She was wearing a bright red frock and red shoes, and smoking a cigarette, and was only an inch taller than Peter. She looked smart and clean and not much like the country, and the children all suddenly felt rather grubby. As usual, the twins were stimulated by the presence of strangers and responded well now that the unpleasant Jacob had disappeared.

"Good afternoon. I'm Mary Morton, and this is my brother Dickie. And that's my other brother David."

"Mary and me are twins," said Richard, "and we've come to Witchend on a great adventure while Daddy is in the RAF … And this is our very great friend called Peter, which is short for something I've forgotten, but it's about a boat."

Mrs Thurston looked faintly astonished at this somewhat complicated introduction, and then laughed.

"I can see you're twins. I was just going to have tea, and you can join me. We'll ask Jacob to cut some more bread and butter … You mustn't mind if he's a bit grumpy, but he's not used to children."

She turned to lead the way into the house, but before David could follow, Macbeth, who had been shaking and growling in his arms, suddenly yelped and jumped down. He looked most unhappy. His hackles were up, which showed he was angry, and he was growling, too, but he kept his tail down and backed away from the house. "You can bring your little dog in as well," Mrs Thurston said; but he would not cross the threshold, and when David tried to drag him in by the scruff of the neck he protested vigorously. So Mary put him on the lead and led him to the pond for a drink, but when she got near to the others on the porch again he clapped his tail between his legs, put his four feet firmly on the ground and refused to budge. When Mrs Thurston tried to coax him in he snapped at her really viciously. At last, feeling very ashamed of him, they left him tied to an apple tree, and he watched them go into the house with misery in his brown eyes.

Appledore was beautifully furnished and more comfortable than Witchend, and when they came down from the bathroom with shining faces Mrs Thurston was waiting for them in a big lounge full of soft chairs and sofas with coloured cushions. Although the day was so warm, a wood fire was smouldering in the old brick fireplace, but near the window were two low tables loaded with plates of bread and butter and jam. The twins sat together on a low stool and, wide-eyed, watched the sullen Jacob bring in the tea.

When he had gone Richard fidgeted for a minute and then said: " 'Scuse me, but is he a doctor?"

"A doctor? Why?" said Mrs Thurston.

"Well," said Dickie, "he wears that white coat. I know doctors wear coats like that. I've seen 'em."

"Oh, yes," said Mary confidently, "we know they wear white coats. P'raps he's doing you good?" she volunteered confidentially to Mrs Thurston.

"I don't know whether he does me much good, but he does look after me. He's my servant, you see, and not my doctor."

She was easy to talk to and very friendly, but she asked them lots of questions, and by the time they had finished their tea there wasn't much she didn't know about them.

She seemed particularly interested in Peter and Hatchholt, and said she would like to come over and see the reservoir one day. Then she joked with the twins and asked them how often they went to the top of the mountain.

"I've been here six months," she said, "but I haven't done much exploring because I've been so busy in the house. It's lonely up here, isn't it?"

David told her how they had only today seen the top for the first time.

"It was funny," he said, "but we did see a stranger up there."

"Oh, did you?" said Mrs Thurston. "What was he like, and I wonder what he was doing?"

David grinned.

"We trailed him for a bit till Mary saw a snake," he said. "But we expect he was just on a walking holiday. We did wonder, though, why he was wearing a raincoat on a lovely day like this, and we expected he'd come down this way because he disappeared up by the path at the top. He had a map, too … But we must go back to the top now and get home to Witchend. Thank you very much, Mrs Thurston, for a lovely tea, but it's getting late and we ought to start."

"But you don't have to climb up to the top through the wood to get back to Witchend, surely?" she said.

"It's easily the best way," said Peter. "It's much too long to go round by the road. I'll show them the way along the top to the Witchend valley, and then they'll be home in half an hour. And I must go over the top to Hatchholt, else I'll never get home and Daddy will be mad with us."

Mrs Thurston got up and threw her cigarette in the fire.

"I shouldn't dream of letting you climb up there now. You're much too tired … Oh yes, you are. Of course you are, and especially the twins. I'll take you in the car now and drop you at the end of your lane on the Onnybrook road."

Peter protested still that her quickest way was to walk over the top, but Mrs Thurston wouldn't consider it. She seemed in a great hurry to get them away, and spoke almost sharply when Peter explained that the Hatchholt valley was miles past Witchend.

"Don't argue, my child," she said. "I'm going to take you as well. Please get ready to leave at once."

They went outside and released Macbeth, who was frantic with joy at the reunion. It was much later than they thought and the sun was throwing long shadows across the grass. David was secretly glad that they were going to get a lift because he was afraid that their mother would blame him for keeping the twins out so late.

Peter whispered, "It's jolly decent of her, David, but I wouldn't have minded walking back, would you? Do you like her? I think she's really nice, but she does ask a lot of questions."

Before he could answer Mrs Thurston came out on to the porch with a tweed coat on her arm. She had just opened the door of the car when, from somewhere up in the pine wood, came the unmistakable cry of an owl.

"How strange," said Peter. "You don't often hear an owl cry like that in the daytime. I wonder why it's making that noise."

71

"Stay here, children, and don't move. Get into the car, please, and stop there till I come back. I shan't be long," said Mrs Thurston sharply, and went back into the house.

Macbeth hated the car almost as much as he disliked Mrs Thurston, but Mary took him on her lap and Dickie held the other end of his lead for safety's sake. Jacob did not appear again, but they thought they could hear him talking somewhere at the back.

"What's she want us to sit in here for?" grumbled Dickie.

"I'd like to go and watch those ducks standin' on their heads. Come on, Mary, let's go."

But just as they were opening the car door Mrs Thurston came out again, so they had to pretend they were playing and looked rather foolish. Richard looked sillier still when she asked him to get out and open the white gates for them.

As soon as he was back in the car she drove very fast down a stony, narrow lane bordered with pine trees. The twins and David and Macbeth were bumped about in the back, and although David tried once or twice to start a friendly conversation, Mrs Thurston was too pre-occupied to answer. When they joined the main road and turned left, Peter said: "We're going round the end of the mountain and just coming to the little village we saw from the top this afternoon … There's a jolly spring which comes bubbling out of the wall just here. Will you stop for a minute, please, Mrs Thurston? I'd like them to see it."

"We're too late to stop now," she said curtly, and drove faster than ever. The twins muttered mutinously to each other, but nobody spoke again until Peter said: "Here's your lane, and if Mrs Thurston drops you here you'll be all right? I'll ride over in the morning and bring your things, and I'd like to meet your mother, too."

As the car pulled up into the side of the road a tall man in uniform stepped from the hedge and grinned at the children as they got out.

"Hullo!" said Mr Ingles. "Had a good day? We was wondering how you'd be getting on. Not been lost, I hope?"

He turned to Mrs Thurston and then recognized Peter. "And you, too, Peter. Where did you find 'em? Pity young Tom couldn't join you today, but he has to work for his keep ... I was wondering if I could beg a lift down to Onnybrook, as I'm on guard tonight? Thank you kindly..." and he got in before anybody could answer.

Mrs Thurston didn't look very pleased, but she did wave to them before driving off again quickly. As they walked up the darkening lane the bats came fluttering crazily round their heads. Macbeth trotted sedately between the twins and David wondered whether Mother would be really angry. They passed Ingles without seeing anyone, and David wouldn't let them whistle or call for Tom.

At last they turned the corner by the stream, and there, leaning on their own gate, was Mrs Morton waiting for them. The twins raced ahead and were pouring out an incoherent story by the time David arrived.

"I was beginning to get anxious," she smiled at him over their heads, "but it sounds as if you've had a lovely day. Is everything all right? ... Tell me all about it at supper."

But at supper Mary fell asleep in her chair, and was furious when she was roused. And after, when the twins were both in bed, David found he was really too tired to do justice to their story. But when he was trying to tell his mother all about Mrs Thurston, several unusual things occurred to him.

"You know, Mummy," he said, "she did ask us such a lot of questions. Where we lived and what you did and whether we had anybody to help in the house, and all that sort of thing. And she was just as anxious about Peter and the reservoir … But she was nice and friendly, and it was kind of her to give us a lift. I couldn't quite see why she was so worried about the twins getting over-tired by walking up over the top again. The funny thing was that after we heard that owl hoot she was in such a hurry to get us home … But it's been a lovely day, and thank you for letting us go. We'll have to do double wood-chopping and pumping tomorrow to make up for it … I hope you'll like Peter, Mummy, and I think perhaps you'd better not tell Daddy about me being a bit silly and letting the twins climb up that waterfall and start exploring that other little valley … Dickie looked funny in the bog."

Chapter 4

The Lone Pine Club

"Just think of it," said Mary, scooping out the last shred of white from her breakfast egg. "Just think, twin – we've got all today to do things in."

"Yes," said Dickie. "And when we're not acksherly doin' them we can remember what we did yesterday ... and that's pretty good."

"What you've got to do first," said their mother, "is to go down to Ingles for the milk. And David must do some pumping, and we shall also want some wood. I'm going to make a rule for today, too ... you're not to go too far because you all had a tiring day yesterday, and I can't have Mary going to sleep at dinner-time."

"Peter's coming with our things some time this morning," David reminded them, "so we'd better got our jobs done early."

So directly after breakfast the twins went off for the milk, and David went into the scullery to pump. Between the verses of some doleful hymns Agnes told him stories of the mountain country. She told him how one winter Witchend had been cut off from Onnybrook and the world for seventeen days, and she told also a wonderful story of a clergyman who was lost in the snow on the top of the Mynd. He wandered all night in the snow-filled ravines and would have perished if he had not had the courage and strength to keep moving and so keep himself awake. "And snowblind he went, Master David, before he was found by some scared children. Twenty-two hours he struggled through the drifts, and you can see his bursted boots for yourself in Shrewsbury Museum, they say!"

When the tank was full again David went out to the gate. He sat on the top bar and was wondering whether it would be worth starting on his map today or be more sensible to wait for a wet afternoon, when he heard voices down the lane. Then Macbeth barked, and there was a clatter of hoofs as Peter came cantering round the corner on Sally. She rode hard up to the gate, and then pulled the pony up sharply.

"Hullo!" she laughed. "I couldn't wait for the twins. How did you get on, David? Was your mother cross? Daddy hadn't really noticed the time, and Mrs Thurston took me as far up Hatchholt as a car will go. Wasn't she in a hurry?"

Still chattering and laughing, she slung off the haversacks and kettle, tied Sally to the gate-post, and followed David into the house.

It may have been because Peter had no mother of her own or just because Mrs Morton loved all children, but within five minutes the two were like old friends.

When the twins came in with the milk and got in the way, Mrs Morton suggested that they explore their own valley that morning and come back presently to dinner. "And bring Peter with you," she said. "Now I've met her I'm going to treat her as part of the family ... I always wanted two boys and two girls."

The Witchend valley was much smaller than Dark Hollow or Hatchholt, but once they had passed the larch wood it soon became wild. There was no clearly-defined track by the stream, and it was difficult to pick out the easiest way through the heather.

"I've never been up this valley before," Peter said, "but I know where it comes out at the top. Few people use it, so it really is your own private valley."

"I've been thinking," David replied, "that it would be fun if we could make a real secret camp and cook and have meals up here. We've got water from the stream, and wood for the fire, and it looks as if it wouldn't be difficult to find a place which is really secret. What do you think, Peter?"

"It's the sort of thing I've always wanted to do," she said. "Let's search now. We must find a place where Sally can be hidden and then I'll teach you all to ride her and p'raps, later on, your daddy might buy you a pony for yourselves…"

"Perhaps we could bring a tent up here," David went on, "and then someone could always stay on guard."

The twins, who were ahead of them, heard this last remark, turned round, and waited for them.

"You two are always talking plans," said Dickie indignantly.

"And not telling us," added Mary. "We're practically as big as you, and as clever too."

"Of course if you want us to go off and do things by ourselves and not let you two know 'bout it," continued Dickie, "you'd better just tell us now…"

Peter looked at David who nodded, and for once the

twins were taken by surprise when they were seized and rolled in the heather. They fought and twisted like cats and Dickie was very surprised to find that Peter was quite as strong as his brother. Not until they had both begged for mercy were they told the idea.

"Just what we were going to think of ourselves," said Mary, dreamily looking up at the sky through half-closed eyes.

"It's the best idea we ever had … any of us," added Dickie generously. "Let's start now. Mary and me will go the other side of the stream and you two search this side…" and he scrambled to his feet.

"All right," said Peter. "But remember what we want. We mustn't be too far away from Witchend, but the camp must be well hidden. We must be near the stream, and we want some shelter. What else do we want, David?"

"You've thought of nearly everything, but I'd like us to be near the wood too, and it wouldn't be a bad idea to have a look-out. And we mustn't forget we shall want a safe place for our fire."

After some argument, the twins agreed to be parted and the two girls took the wood side of the stream. Both parties went almost to the top of the valley without success. Higher up it was very wild and rough and quite unsuitable, so they turned back and it was Mary who found the ideal place when they were nearly back at the wood. She was chattering away to Peter about books she liked, when she noticed a tall pine tree standing by itself about a hundred yards from the stream up the side of the valley.

"Let's go up there, Peter. It looks as if it's all gorse o

brambles round the tree, but we've searched everywhere now and I don't want Dickie to find a place first."

It was very hot scrambling up through the bracken. The nearer they got to the pine tree, the more difficult it became to find a way through and so they bore round to the left nearer to the wood. Once they paused and looked down and could see David and Richard pushing rather disconsolately along through the heather on the other side of the valley.

"We've simply got to find a camping place, Mary," said Peter, "and I'm sure this is our last chance unless we decide to go into the wood. That wouldn't be much fun anyway because we should be too far from the stream. It doesn't seem as if the boys will have any luck."

"Dickie's no use without me," said Mary tersely.

At last they reached more level ground, with the tree which was their objective about twenty yards away. Mary had been correct about the gorse for, at first glance, there seemed no way of getting round it. But they persevered until Peter found a narrow tunnel which might well have been made by a fox. She was too big to get through herself but by stooping down she could see that although the gorse was thick, there was open ground the other side. Mary took one look and then started to wriggle through.

"I'm the first white man ever to blaze this trail," she muttered through clenched teeth as a sharp thorn jabbed her bare knee. "I'm so brave that the natives don't know how to honour me ... 'spect they'll make me their Queen – King I mean, as Dickie's not here."

Flat on her stomach, Peter lay cheering her on. There were a few more desperate wriggles, several squeals and then she was through and Peter saw her stand up. For a long moment there was silence and then:

"Are you there, Peter? You're still there? I say, Peter, we've found the place. There couldn't be another camp like this in the world. Come quickly…!"

"But I can't, Mary! I can't get through there. I'm too big."

"Wait there then," Mary called, "and I'll see if I can find another way."

Then Mary's brown legs vanished and Peter could hear her moving about on the other side of the clearing. Once she called and after that there was silence. Peter rolled over on her back. It would be splendid if the girls succeeded where the boys had failed. How jolly they all were! The twins were fun, and Mary was sweet. Funny the way she'd looked when they were talking about Ludlow Castle yesterday! You might have thought she really was waiting for her own true knight to come riding home to her … David was nice too. A bit quiet, but he'd be grand helping with this camp.

She flicked a fly off her nose and sat up. The delicate tops of the trees in the larch wood were moving in a breeze she could not feel down here. There was a hum of flies in the bracken and she wondered about the time. Then she heard Mary's voice from somewhere above her.

"Petah! Petah! Where are you?"

She stood up and gave an answering hail, and then saw the little girl waving from higher up the hill.

"All right," she called. "I'm coming up. Stay where you are."

When she reached her, Mary was big-eyed with

excitement. She had a scratch down her face, blood on her knees, and her hands and arms were black. She grabbed Peter's hand and pulled her through the bracken.

"Just you wait to see it, Peter! We'll look at it first quickly, just the two of us, and then call the others." She led the way down the hill till they were approaching the tree from above and could look down into a little grass carpeted clearing, with the great pine tree standing alone like a sentinel. The going was easy, and although the bracken was as tall as herself, Mary went down confidently enough. When they were standing under the tree Peter realized what a perfect place they had found. On three sides the clearing was surrounded by gorse. Only from above could they be seen or approached. Even from the woods – a bare hundred yards away – they would be invisible.

"Well done, Mary," she said. "You've beaten us all. You saw the tree first, you squeezed through the gorse, and now you've found the only way in … I'll help you up the tree and you can see whether it's a real look-out. I think it is and that you'll be able to see right down into Witchend … Now! … Catch hold of that branch and heave yourself up … Right? What can you see?"

"Gosh! Oh, gosh!" said Mary. "I can see everything. I'm the look-out on a pirate ship. I'm on the watch-tower of a castle. I'm in the crows-nest … Petah!" she squealed. "I can see Mummy in the garden … and I can see those lazy boys down by the stream. Peter, they've stopped searching … *they're paddlin'*!"

Peter jumped for the lowest branch and pulled herself up beside her.

81

"Shout together," she said. "Ahooooy there! Ahoy!"

They saw Dickie look up and round to say something to David. They shouted again but the boys seemed to look everywhere but the right direction.

"Oh, gosh!" said Mary. "They are so *silly*. Why don't they look here? There's Mackie now. He can hear me. He's barking! I'm sure he is."

"Let's get down," said Peter. "They'll never see us and I'll tell you what we'd better do. This is your discovery, Mary, so you slip down and find them. Maybe you can squeeze through the gorse again, and you'll be down in five minutes. I should go down the side of the wood and then you won't make a track that people will see ... Tell them what we've found and ask them to go back to Witchend for matches and the kettle and anything else we shall want to start the camp. David will know. And perhaps your mummy wouldn't mind giving us a picnic lunch today so that we could have it up here and not waste time going back to the house. I don't think she'll mind 'cos she did tell me it would only be a picnic lunch at home with something out of a tin ... Will you do that, Mary? Then if you like you can stay and guide them back, or go and help them to carry some of the things. I'll stay and get things ready here and if I'm ready first I'll come and meet you ... Tell David to bring everything he can think of for making a camp. *Everything*."

Almost before she had finished speaking Mary was wriggling through the gorse tunnel again. Left alone Peter explored more carefully. Well away from the tree and the gorse, she chose a place for their camp-fire. She found three flat rocks and, using one as a hearthstone stood the other two upon edge at each side hoping that the distance between them was narrow enough to support the kettle. She gathered some twigs and dry heather to start the fire, and then went into the wood for as much kindling as she could carry. She also brought back four stout sticks which she hoped would serve as the uprights for a shelter. She grinned to herself as she remembered the twins' remark about "shelter from the cruel midday sun." But a bracken tent like this was a good idea. She had made one at the top of Hatchholt valley once and used it as a look-out. When the roof was covered with bracken it was invisible. She pulled in some heather to sit on, and then made a second journey to the wood for thin sticks to make the framework of the roof and sides. This took a long time and she had just decided that she was hungry enough for dinner when she heard voices below. She pulled herself up into the tree again and looked down into the valley. Toiling slowly along the side of the stream, in the shadow of the wood, came the three Mortons. David had the knapsack on his back and seemed to be carrying a pail as well. Both of the twins had satchels. Peter thought that the gleam of metal signified that Dickie had got the job of kettle-carrier again. Macbeth cavorted in the rear. Peter wondered whether she would try and finish the shelter as a surprise but then decided to go down and help them. But first she stood upright on a stout branch and shouted with all her strength. She saw Mary stop and point up at her and then all three of them waved.

She met them down at the corner of the wood, just as they had crossed the stream.

"Hullo, Peter," David grinned. "So you've beaten us! Mary told us lots but she's rather excited and I can't believe it's as good as she says. Is it?"

"I think so, David. Have you got everything? Have you got matches? Good, I've got the fire ready to light. I'm sure we shall want some string and some rope ... did you think of them? Oh! and you've brought a pail of extra water. That's a good idea because we are a long way from the stream and it's uphill all the way. We'd better fill both the kettle and bucket and carry them up full."

David looked at the stream.

"We ought to make a dam here so that the water is deep enough to fill the pail properly. I s'pose there's not time now, but we'll have to do it."

"Bags I help," said Dickie promptly. "We're good at dams."

Now although Mary wanted, above all things, to share her discovery with Dickie as soon as possible, he suddenly proved unexpectedly stubborn.

"Never mind the old camp," he went on. "Let's do this dam now. That will be real fun! And when we've built it we'll have dinner down here too..."

They dragged him away protesting at last and Mary led them up the hill. Not until she had taken them round the gorse bushes and pushed aside the bracken to show them her secret, did the boys realize how well she had done. When David said that they couldn't have found a better place if they had searched for months, she went quite pink at his praise.

"I've got it," said Dickie suddenly, "I've thought of a name for us and for this camp. This is Lone Pine Camp,

84

and we'll be the Lone Pine Club … Now let's have something to eat…"

Both suggestions were approved.

"You'd better be captain, David," said Peter, "because it really was your idea to have a camp although I always wanted a secret club … but I'll be camp cook if you like."

"All right," David agreed, "but you'll all have to obey orders and after dinner we'll make the rules … We've got plenty to eat and we can be out till supper if we're not too far away."

"I hope you didn't tell your mother anything," said Peter. "This must be a real secret – particularly from grown-ups who generally spoil everything however nice they are."

The twins were indignant.

"Do you think we really would?"

" 'Course we wouldn't say a word."

"We'd better all swear after," said Dickie.

"We'll sign in blood!" said Mary.

David thought that the shelter was a splendid idea and sent the twins out for more bracken. Peter soon had the fire going and then helped to unpack. The methodical David seemed to have thought of everything. There were eggs to "hard boil", several lettuces, plenty of bread, but not much butter. Cheese was scarce too, because of the rationing, but there was a pot of jam, a tin of precious sardines, a bag of potatoes, a packet of tea, a bottle of milk, and four mugs.

He had also brought a wonderful collection of odds and ends – the compass, two electric torches, a small coil of rope, and two balls of string, a scout knife, a small trowel, and a writing-pad and pencil. From his pocket he finally produced a burning glass.

"This will be useful when we run out of matches," he said proudly.

"Yes, David. That's very clever of you," said Peter, sitting back on her heels and looking over the pile. "But what do we do if there isn't any sun?"

"We use the glass when there is sun, and the matches when there isn't!"

The twins soon finished the shelter while David stowed everything away and Peter fussed about round the fire. There wasn't really much to cook, but she decided to bake the potatoes in the embers and to hard boil the eggs in the kettle. When the eggs were done they found they had forgotten spoons and a tea-pot, so they had to waste the boiling water to get the eggs out, and then put the kettle on again. Every now and then Peter tested the potatoes with the point of the scout knife and when at last they felt soft through their charred skins she rolled them out of the ashes. The kettle puffed at the same time, and the twins watched entranced as she lifted the lid and shook in some tea.

"But we can't make tea that way, surely?" said Mary.

"Just watch," answered Peter. "It's the easy way and saves a tea-pot. Hand me up your mugs and I'll fill them up."

The tea was rather strong, but they were so hungry and thirsty that they would have enjoyed anything. Macbeth had a drink from the pail and then retired into the shelter and went to sleep.

Half an hour later even Richard was satisfied.

"It's a funny thing, twin," he said. "I'm not exactly *tired*, but I am sleepy. Are you?"

"I'm full up," said Mary, "and I think Peter's the best cook ever."

"Better than old Sparrow Legs, Mary?"

"Better than … Dickie! We promised not to say that, didn't we? She's nice now."

"Yes, she's nice. She's given us a banquet and Peter's cooked it. Now the King and Queen can go into yonder pavilion and…"

"Rest from the cruel rays of the midday sun," finished Mary.

"The King and Queen will do nothing of the sort," said David. "They're going to wash up for the cook, and then they're going to fetch some more wood. I'm going up the look-out tree and then we'll settle down and write the rules of the Lone Pine Club."

For a moment or two the twins looked mutinous. Then—

"You go for the wood, Dickie, and I'll wash up," said Mary. "We'll be finished sooner."

David then hung a loop of rope from the tree's lowest branch, making it easier to climb. When he came down he reported that he could see Mrs Morton resting in the Witchend garden, but that everything else was quiet except for Dickie crashing about in the wood. At last they were ready for what Mary called a pow-wow. The sun was very hot and they were grateful now for the shade of the "pavilion". David took the writing-pad on his knee and wrote like this:

THE LONE PINE CLUB

Captain:	David John Morton
Vice-Captain and Cook:	Petronella Sterling
Club members:	Richard Morton
	Mary Morton
	(These two are twins.)

When he got as far as this he stopped.

"Before we get on to the rules of the Club, Peter," he said, "I've got an idea about a new member. Let's ask Tom Ingles. He's a nice chap and we're not a very big club yet. I don't suppose he will be able to come to every meeting because he works so hard for his Uncle..."

"Oh yes, David," Mary broke in, "let's have Tom. I think he's a lovely little boy. I love him."

"I don't mind," said Peter. "I don't really know him, but if you think he'll obey the rules we might bring him here blindfolded tonight and swear him in … All right. It's a good idea. Let's have him."

So David wrote under the twins' names:

Thomas Ingles

———————

Secret Meeting Place: The Secret Camp at
the Lone Pine near Witchend

Peter was doubtful about this last line. "I think it's too secret to write down," she said. "What are you going to do with this paper?"

"Bury it somewhere here in the sardine tin," said David promptly.

"We'll bury it in the shadow of the Lone Pine at noon," said Dickie. "That's the way to do it. We know – Mary and me do. We know all these things. We have lots more adventures than you think."

"There's another thing," Mary added. "You must put down the names of the animal members. Oh yes, you must! There's Mackie – he's a member, and I s'pose Peter's Sally is too."

"She's the beast of burden," added Richard.

The argued for a while as to how best to describe the sleeping Macbeth. Mary wanted to enrol him as the "Wild Boarhound", and was indignant when they laughed at her. Then Dickie suggested that Sally could be called "Club Charger", and David settled the matter by not enrolling either of them.

"Now, Peter," he said. "The club was really your idea so you must help us with the Rules."

The twins soon tired of rule-making, but Peter was so keen and David so strict that they had to sit still and listen. This is how the rules read when they had finished:

Rule 1. The name is as above.

Rule 2. So are the members.

Rule 3. The Club and Camp are so private that every member swears in blood to keep them secret.

Rule 4. Every member promises to be kind to animals.

Rule 5. The Club is for exploring and watching birds and animals and tracking strangers.

Rule 6. And learning how to camp.

Rule 7. Every member must obey the Captain (see above), or if not then the Vice-Captain (see above).

Peter wanted another rule which would lay down the awful punishment to be meted out to any member who broke the rule of secrecy – but nobody could agree about it.

"I don't know much about tortures," said Dickie.

" 'Cept scalping," added Mary.

"Never mind, Peter," said David finally. "These will do, and now I'll just write in the oath and when Tom comes tonight we'll all sign it."

He wrote again:

> Every member of the Lone Pine Club signed below swears to keep the rules and to be true to each other whatever happens always.
>
> Signed ....

"I'm not tired any more now," said Mary brightly, "and I think Macbeth is lookin' lazy, so we'll go and fill the kettle and the bucket."

"An' when we get back we could be thinkin' about tea," added Dickie.

David laughed and let them go.

"What are we going to do about Tom?" he asked. "How shall we get him here?"

"I've been thinking about that, David, and I've got a splendid scheme. Let's write him a note telling him he'll find something to his advantage if he goes to a silver birch tree at the edge of the wood at seven o'clock tonight and follows the string he'll find tied to the tree. We'll run the string as far as we can and then ambush him and blindfold him and lead him here and make him swear. I'll take the note when we've done it, go down to Witchend and fetch Sally, and ride down to Ingles with it. You can find the silver birch – it's on the top edge of the wood by the path and easy to find – and do the string and then we'll all meet in time for tea. I shan't be long on Sally."

David agreed and they composed a note for Tom headed "Warning" and signed with a drawing of a pine tree like this:

They were just admiring their handiwork when the silence was broken by a furious barking from Macbeth somewhere down in the valley. David jumped up.

"Don't move, Peter! I'll go into the look-out. He's not playing – that's his warning bark."

As soon as he was in the tree he saw that the twins had reached the stream. While he watched Richard suddenly pushed the kettle and bucket into the heather and went to help his sister hold back Macbeth who was struggling at the end of his lead.

"What is it, David?" Peter was whispering urgently. "Tell me quickly. I can't see."

"There must be someone coming," he answered, "but

Dickie's been sensible and hidden the kettle. Mackie's so excited they can hardly hold him back … Yes. It *is* someone, Peter … I can see them coming down the valley … I thought you said nobody ever came this way?"

"Let me up, David. I must see. I'll tell you who it is. I know everyone round here."

He leaned down and held out his hand.

"Come on then, Peter, but I hope they won't see us both if they look up … Try and stay on the lower branch and hide behind the trunk…"

One quick pull and she was up.

"Now!" she said. "Where is he?"

He pointed. "David!" she gasped. "Don't you recognize her? It's Mrs Thurston – I'm sure it is."

Peter was right. He could see her now coming down by the side of the stream. As they watched she lifted her hand and waved, and for one awful moment they thought she had seen them in their hiding-place. Then they realized that she was waving to the twins, who stood waiting for her. They watched Mary pick up Macbeth and Dickie take a quick look behind him to see if the kettle was hidden. Then she came up and put a hand on each of their shoulders, and they could see her throw back her head and laugh at some remark of Dickie's. They noticed that the twins manoeuvred themselves between Mrs Thurston and the stream, and were doing all they could to keep her looking away from the lone pine.

"Those two are *grand*, David," Peter whispered.

David nodded.

"What does she want, though? Why should she come down this valley at this time?"

While he was speaking Mary pointed down to Witch-end, and then each twin took Mrs Thurston by a hand and the three of them started off down to the house. Once Mary seemed to gesture to something on the opposite hillside, and Dickie turned quickly in their direction and made some weird sign.

Peter started to climb down.

"I'm off, David!" she said. "I'll follow them and see what they're going to do with her! Dickie meant to tell us something, I'm sure, and it may be they'll want help. I've got to get Sally anyway, and take the note to Tom. Do you agree?"

"Yes. It's a good idea, Peter. Good luck! I'll look after the fire and then go into the wood and find the silver birch and set the string guide for Tom. Goodbye!"

Almost before he had finished speaking Peter had slipped out through the bracken. From his post in the look-out he watched her make her way round the gorse bushes and down by the side of the wood to the stream. Here she looked back once and raised her hand in salute before following the others in the direction of Witchend.

David climbed down, wondering what had really happened. Either they were in for a real adventure or else the twins had been silly and spoiled the afternoon. Somehow he felt that they were being sensible.

He tidied up and put away his pad and pencil. Then he cut up a piece of turf under the tree with the scout-knife and dug a shallow hole with the trowel. He folded the secret Lone Pine document and put it in the sardine tin, which was still rather oily. Then he placed the tin in the little grave he had dug, scattered the surplus soil, and put back the lid of turf. It was well hidden and nobody would be able to find it now.

When he had made up the fire he remembered that the kettle and bucket were still where Dickie had hidden them, so he went down the hill to fetch them. As he toiled up again he realized that this water-carrying was going to be a nuisance, and he determined to search the hillside some time to see if there was a spring nearer the camp. Then he put the kettle across the two upright stones as Peter had showed him, took the ball of string and started up the hill to the top of the wood. He was higher now than in the Lone Pine, and the view was wonderful. He could see Witchend, which looked deserted, and follow the lane leading down to Ingles. Something moving in the farm-yard might be Peter on Sally. Farther away were the purple woods bordering the Onnybrook road, and far, far down in the valley was a streak of white smoke as a train crawled out of the station. He looked up and saw a brown speck hovering against the blue of the summer sky. As he watched the sparrowhawk dropped like a plummet and a minute later made off again with some little body in its claws. Then the speck in Ingles' farmyard reappeared on the lane, and he knew it must be Peter and that he must hurry. He found the silver-birch easily enough and tied the end of the string to the trunk and went into the gloomy wood, unwinding the ball as he went. Up and down through the trees he laid the trail and was reminded of the story of the awful Minotaur in the labyrinth in *Tanglewood Tales*. He worked towards the edge of the wood nearest the camp and fastened the other end to the foot of a tree well hidden in the deep thicket.

By this time he could hear Sally coming up the side of the wood and Peter singing quietly to herself. He stepped out into the sunshine, and the pony's ears went back as she saw him. Peter grinned.

"Have you done it, David? You didn't surprise me. I could hear you crashing about up here half a mile away."

"Never mind me – I want to know what's happened. Where are the twins, and what's happened to Mrs Thurston?"

Peter jumped off Sally and put one arm through her bridle and the other through David's.

"Listen," she said, "because you'll never believe it. Mrs Thurston is having tea with your mother, and so are the twins. I peeped in through the window. Dickie and Mary looked *mad*. Their faces had been washed and their hair done, and your mother was making them pass things! Oh, David! If you could have seen them!"

"I have seen them," said David grimly. "Sometimes in the hols I have to do the same myself ... I wonder if they'll escape presently? ... They know about Tom coming tonight, so I expect they'll be back. Did you leave the note? Did you see Tom?"

"I didn't actually *see* him, but I masked my face with my hankie and crept up and put the note under the knocker. I don't think he was there, but I could hear someone in the dairy ... Let's go and have our tea now."

Sally liked the camp and nibbled the short turf content-edly, while David poured the tea. When they had both finished two mugs Peter lay back and linked her hands behind her head and began to talk. She told David that she could only just remember her mother, and that for ten years she had lived with her father – the last five at Hatch-holt when he had been in charge of the reservoir. She told him that she was a boarder at a school in Shrewsbury, but that she loved the country best and all animals. She talked to him about the wild things on the mountain. She loved the stars, and told him again about these.

Then David told her about the different life in London, and of his school and of his father. An hour slipped by in this way until suddenly Sally pricked up her ears and moved uneasily. There was a rustling in the undergrowth and David looked up to see Mary's face grinning wickedly at him from the middle of a gorse bush. She wriggled out into the open and turned round to help her twin through the tunnel. It was at once obvious that they were very proud of themselves. They smirked and waited to be questioned. There was a long silence till Dickie's roving eye noticed the empty mugs.

"You beasts!" he said. "You utter pigs! You've had tea. You didn't wait for us."

"That's what it is," said Mary. "You don't really want us. Just as soon as we go away and save you all and the Club…"

"You betray us bitterly," added Dickie, "an' go and have tea without us. Greedy pigs, you are!"

"And what about you two?" broke in Peter. "Haven't you had a wopping tea? I know you have – I saw you. Ginger cake – Mary had two slices – and raspberry jam. And you'd both been washed and looked *so* sweet and clean…"

At this final insult the twins nearly burst with suppressed fury. After a little Mary said:

"Now we shan't tell you what we've done."

"We don't mind a bit," Dickie added. "We have our adventures all right, Mary and me. We won't be members of the Lone Pine. We'll just be us!"

They were pacified at last, and when David managed to stop them talking at the same time instead of in turn, they gave a fairly coherent story.

They had almost reached the stream, they explained, when Dickie saw something moving up the valley. At first they thought it was a wild pony, but while they were watching Macbeth began to growl, and then they recognized Mrs Thurston. They knew that they must keep the Lone Pine secret, so Dickie hid the kettle and they decided to try and find out what she wanted. Although the others had seen all this happen, the twins were so pleased with themselves and with the way in which they were telling the story that David and Peter dared not interrupt.

"We were very polite to her," continued Dickie. "Very best manners we did."

"An' she was just as nice," said Mary, "an' she only asked us once what we were doing, an' we said we were just out for a quiet walk with Mackie…"

"Only he wasn't quiet," interrupted Dickie. "He was awful. He hates her, and Mary an' me had to hold him in all the time … She tried to pat him, and he snapped at her, and we didn't dare let him go 'cause he might have come running up here and betrayed us all."

"Once she asked where you were, David," Mary went on.

"And what did you say?" he asked.

Dickie looked down his nose. "Gone to Onnybrook for your bike," he said.

But they admitted that they were really surprised when Mrs Thurston told them she was going to call on their mother, and asked them to show her the way to Witchend.

"You know how we think sometimes," Dickie went on. "Well, we both thought just then that we'd better get her away as quickly as we could and keep her talking and not looking up here…"

"We thought you *might* be watching," said Mary, "and I 'spose you were after what Peter said about ginger cake for tea … Anyway, you'd better tell us how much you know…"

Peter explained hurriedly how and why she had followed them and how little she and David knew, so the twins went on to explain how friendly Mrs Thurston had been and how interested in Witchend.

"When we got in," Mary said, "I managed just to 'splain to Mummy quickly not to say anything about you two, and once at tea when Mrs Thurston asked what time David would be back from Onnybrook, we felt rather beastly, but Mummy sort of looked at us and didn't say anything special."

"You see," Dickie went on, "we were wonderin' whether to come back here quickly, but it was difficult, 'cause we'd just said we were out for a walk, and then Mummy told us to wash and change and come down to tea."

"And there we had to sit, thinkin' of you two up here having a lovely tea and the two grown-ups just talkin' and talkin' and we couldn't get away."

David asked them how they managed it in the end.

"That was easy," said Mary. "When they'd finished tea – an' they finished before Dickie an' me – and Mummy was talking about Daddy and Agnes and Ingles, I just asked whether we could come and meet you, and Mummy said 'Yes' quickly and 'Don't interrupt, twins.' "

"Anyhow," said Dickie, "there's one more exciting thing you don't know about, and I s'pose we'd better tell you … an' we think you ought to be glad we saved the camp…"

"Where's Mackie?" asked Peter suddenly. "What have you done with him?"

"That's just it," said Mary. "Something very terrible an' awful has happened, and we were thinking we ought to make a new rule of the Club."

Then they both got excited again and interrupted each other, and it was some minutes before they got the rest of the story. At last Peter got Mary to admit that she and Dickie had disagreed for once about Mrs Thurston. Dickie, when they had escaped from the tea-party, maintained that she was one of the very best grown-ups they knew, and that he liked her. Mary reminded him that Macbeth was afraid of her and that for some reason that she couldn't explain she distrusted her also. They were arguing about this in whispers on the upstairs landing when they heard the living-room door open and Mummy excuse herself to go and speak to Agnes. They heard her open the kitchen door, and then, from the top of the stairs, saw Macbeth come out into the hall.

"Let me tell it, Dickie," Mary insisted. "We were just going to call Mackie and bring him up here again when

Mrs Thurston came out and sort of looked round. She couldn't see Dickie and me at the top of the stairs, but Mackie saw her, an' he looked all miserable and got under that chair in the hall and sort of growled…"

"An' then what do you think?" Dickie interrupted.

"Be quiet, Dickie! David, listen, 'cause we really saw this. When Mrs Thurston saw Mackie under the chair her nice face went all *ugly*, David, and she went up close and … and she KICKED him, David! She did! She's a beastly beast, an' I hate her…" And, to everyone's astonishment, she burst into tears.

Dickie passed her a revolting-looking handkerchief and took up the tale without further interruption.

"Mackie gave a snarly sort of yelp, and before we could do anything Mummy came runnin' out, and Mrs Thurston said something about Mackie attackin' her, and it wasn't true, 'cause we saw her kick him, and then Mummy dragged Mackie out into the kitchen again, and Mary wouldn't let me say anything to Mummy, so when they'd gone in and shut the door we went out at the back, but we couldn't find Mackie…"

"He's been driven from his home," gulped Mary. "Mummy's done it, and that woman made it all up 'cause he didn't attack her this time like she said. Anyway, I love him, and it's a rule of this club we made to be kind to animals, and we all got to go and find him…"

"Where's Mrs Thurston now?" asked David.

"We don't know," said Dickie. "We left her at Witchend, but we did hear her say somethin' about not going back over the mountain."

"He'll come home, Mary," said David, "and we'll find

him if he doesn't, so don't worry … Now we've got to build up the camp fire and get ready for Tom. Peter will put some potatoes in the ashes and we'll have tea as well, and then we'll all sign the club rules…"

"In blood?" asked Dickie.

"Yes," said Peter, "of course."

But Mary was still rebellious. She wasn't interested in Tom or even in baked potatoes, but wanted Macbeth.

"We'd better take care that Mrs Thurston doesn't come up the valley again and find us," David said. "We're making enough noise for her to hear us from Witchend. We need a look-out. What about you, Mary? Will you go up and report?"

"He's too small and lonely for me to see him from up there," she protested, "but I'll try."

They pushed her up, and rather gloomily she admitted that she could see a long way. Meanwhile, Peter filled the kettle and built up the fire, Dickie went off whistling into the wood for more fuel, while David sorted out potatoes.

Suddenly Mary squeaked. "Be *quiet*. I can see them."

David swung himself up beside her, calling as he did so: "Stop the fire smoking too much, Peter. Well done, Mary. Now show me."

She pointed down to Witchend and David saw his mother walking over to the gate with Mrs Thurston.

"Don't think she'll come up the valley, Mary. She's going home by Ingles. Tom will probably meet her."

He was right. They saw her shake hands with Mrs Morton and then walk off down the lane without looking back.

"Come down now, Mary. We don't need a guard any more, and we've got to get ready for Tom."

Although there had been no sign of Macbeth, Mary recovered her spirits and went out to meet Dickie. When they had finally tidied up, put the potatoes in the embers and tied Sally to the lone pine, David led them out towards the wood. The twins were Red Indians again, and were talking to each other in secret "gabble language." The shadows were lengthening and David hoped that Tom would not be late because he had promised to be home for supper, and Peter had a long way to ride. He found the thicket and the tree to which the end of the guiding string was tied easily enough, and then gave his orders. The twins were to hide a little way off to come along behind Tom when he had passed them. Then he helped Peter up into the tree so that she could drop on her victim while he hid behind the trunk. They were hardly in their positions before they heard Tom's melodious whistling at the edge of the wood. He was making no attempt to be quiet, and they actually heard him laugh when he found the silver birch and the end of the string. Peter was certain that if he only stopped still for a minute he would be able to hear her heart thumping, but he came blundering on through the gloom of the wood. Then the twins spoiled David's plan – Tom had passed their hiding-place quite unsuspecting and in another minute would have been at the ambush tree. Peter could actually see him as he came towards them with his lips pursed in a silent whistle and a frown on his freckled face. He was looking as if he was getting tired of a rather silly game when the twins gave two blood-curdling war whoops, jumped out of their hiding-place and flung themselves at him.

"Itchyhankunpankumbaboo," chanted Mary.

"Surrender, vile paleface," growled Dickie, "or die," and they danced round him while he roared with laughter at their antics.

David was furious, but there was nothing more to be done now, so he called to Peter and she dropped down from the tree.

Tom stared at her in amazement. "And who are you?" he said. "And what's going on round here?"

Just at this moment the twins took advantage of his divided attention and each dived for a leg and brought him down. In a flash David and Peter were sitting on him, and when he struggled violently the twins added their weight to his legs and begged him to surrender.

"Just say you do, Tom," begged David. "But hurry up, because we haven't much time. We're going to blindfold you and show you our secret camp … Will you, Tom? If you don't we shall have to stay here until you do surrender, and that would waste such a lot of time."

Tom gasped. "Tell those kids to stop bouncing on me, then, and I'll come quiet!"

So they blindfolded him with the handkerchief Peter had tied round her hair gipsy-fashion and led him out of the wood.

"Really you ought to be bound with cruel thongs," said Mary.

"We surprised you, didn't we?" remarked Dickie. "Acksherly we surprised David, too! We can do that sort of thing 'cause we're Indians of royal blood."

Tom accepted everything very well, and when they reached the lone pine and Sally whinnied a welcome to her mistress, he snatched off the handkerchief himself and looked round the camp.

"Just like the pictures," he said at last. "Only better. Who found this?"

"I did," said Mary. "Peter and me did."

"Who's Peter?" he asked. "I get all mixed up with these kids."

David explained, and Tom and Peter looked each other up and down, and decided they liked each other. They showed him everything, including the cooking potatoes and the singing kettle, and then David showed them all the secret hiding-place of the club documents. Peter poured the tea and poked the potatoes out of the ashes, and they all sat down round the fire while David read out the rules.

"We'd like you to be a member, Tom. You like the things we like. We must all stick together up here. Really we ought to have asked you first before telling all about it, but I know you'll join, won't you?"

"If you don't," said Mary, "you'll just have to stay here till you do."

"We can't let you go back to your own country with this secret locked in your heart," added Dickie.

Tom took a mouthful of hot potato and went scarlet. "Of course I will," he said. "And thanks for asking me … And I've a new rule to suggest … You haven't got a secret signal yet and we ought to have. We could use it for calling each other, or as a warning. If you wanted me on club business you could just pass me on the farm or in the lane and make the sign and I'd know and come as soon as I could. What do you think?"

"It's a grand idea, Tom. David was right when he said you'd make a good member ... But what sort of signal shall we have?"

"What about this?" said Tom. "I asked uncle what bird it was and he said it's called a peewit..." and with uncanny imitation he whistled the peewit's melancholy little cry.

Peter was thrilled. She knew more about birds than any of them, and this imitation was astonishingly good ... so good that she could almost see the little birds dipping and drifting over the fields, and crying sadly "Peee wit! ... Peeeee wit."

"It's wonderful, Tom," she said, "but I don't expect any of us can do it as well as you."

"I'll teach you," he said. "You'll soon be able to do it."

Then David heated the point of the knife in the fire, and when it was cool they each pricked the end of a finger, repeated the oath, and signed their names on the paper in their own blood. This was Dickie's greatest thrill.

It was nearly dusk now, and David said that they must go. Peter poured water on the fire to put out the embers, Mary buried the rubbish in the bracken, and Dickie took the firewood into the shelter to keep it dry. And while they were working, David told Tom of yesterday's adventures.

"Golly!" he said. "Wish I'd been there. I think I know that Mrs Thurston, and I'm sure I've seen that old Jacob. He's about on a motor-bike sometimes."

David's idea of taking kettle and bucket down with

them and hiding them near the stream was a good one, and Dickie, as usual, was given charge of these. Then Sally was freed and the little caravan of explorers set off down the hill. On the way Tom gave them whistling lessons, and soon Peter was nearly as good as her master. Down at the stream Tom asked what they had been doing all day, and they realized with a shock that they hadn't brought the history of the Lone-Piners up to date.

They were almost at Witchend by the time they had finished, but long before the end of the story it was obvious that Tom himself had something to add to it. Suddenly a little black bundle came hurtling up the path to meet them, and Mary and Macbeth fell to the ground in a rapturous embrace. The dog was so excited that when Mary let him go he dashed round and round them all, barking wildly. The uproar brought Mrs Morton to the door.

"Is that you, darlings? Are you all there?"

"Yes, Mummy," David called. "And Peter and Sally, and Tom, too."

She came out to meet them and pushed the twins indoors first. Peter said "Goodbye" and jumped on to Sally while the boys went over to open the gate for her. Tom held the bridle for a minute.

"I've been trying to tell you for five minutes," he said. "Listen. When I was just coming out of the farmyard I heard a dog barking and guessed it was Mac-whatever-you-call-him. He was chasing Mrs Thurston down the lane, and she was running away from him, and red in the face and absolutely furious. You've no idea how silly she looked! He kept dancing round her and snapping, and I was just going to see if I could get him away when she began to shout and throw stones. It was rather funny, because once Mac picked up a stone and brought it back to her. Then she tried to kick him. Last I saw was Mac chasing her down past the corner. He doesn't seem to like her."

David laughed and whistled to the dog, but he had gone in with the twins.

"Hope Mary makes a fuss of him," he said. "He's a good chap."

Then he opened the gate.

"Wait for me, Peter," Tom said. "You can canter when you get past Ingles. 'Bye David. See you tomorrow perhaps, but I don't know how long Uncle will want me. Let's have another proper meeting at the camp soon."

" 'Bye David," said Peter. "We've had a lovely day. See you soon."

He watched them down the lane, and then as he turned to go indoors there came the plaintive call of the peewit through the dusk.

Chapter 5

Fighter Pilot

At breakfast the next morning the twins realized
that their oath of silence about the Lone Pine
Club was going to be very difficult to keep. Their
mother was the sort of grown-up who had always
proved remarkably intelligent and sympathetic about
their adventures – not really like a grown-up at all –
and now they had a lot to tell her. Twice the "solemn
swear" had nearly been broken, and twice David had
kicked them under the table and glared at them so
fiercely that they were beginning to wonder if all this
secrecy was worth while. "An adventure that you
mustn't talk about isn't much of an adventure," Dickie
thought.

The odd thing was that Mrs Morton didn't seem to be
particularly curious. It was annoying in a way, but she was
a well-trained mother! Mary would have given a lot to
have told her how she had crawled so bravely through the
gorse tunnel to find the camp, and was just wondering
whether there was any way of doing so without getting a
third kick from David, when she saw him look up towards
the open window. As they listened, there came the sound
of running footsteps and the peewit's whistle.

"Who's that, I wonder?" said Mrs Morton.

"It's Tom," said David. "Excuse me, Mummy; I'll go and see what he wants. He's in a hurry."

In a minute the two boys were back. Tom was out of breath and looking rather worried.

"I'm sorry to come so early, Mrs Morton, but Uncle sent me. Auntie fell down in the dairy, and she's hurt her ankle so badly she can't walk. Uncle has gone down to Onnybrook for Doctor himself, and says could you possibly come down for a bit to be with Auntie till he comes back? He's given me some jobs to do on the farm, and wouldn't let me go for Doctor. We're very sorry to bother you, Uncle says, but he doesn't like to leave Auntie alone for too long, and sometimes Doctor is difficult to catch."

Mrs Morton jumped up. "Of course I'll come, Tom. What bad luck for Mrs Ingles! Why don't you come too, David, and then you can go on down to Onnybrook and see if your bicycles have come? ... The twins are not to go too far ... No, Dickie, it's no use looking like that. You must both have a quiet day and stay about here till I come back. You've got your jobs to do, and can certainly go and get in some wood for Agnes."

David and Tom went outside to wait.

"Funny we should have to use the peewit's call so soon," Tom said. "It's decent of your Mother to come so quickly."

The twins came to the gate to see them all off and didn't seem to mind being left behind, which made Mrs Morton rather suspicious.

"I shall be back as soon as I can," she said, "but I've told Agnes what has happened, and that you're going to help

109

her. David won't be long, and if the cycles have come you can get yours this evening or tomorrow. Goodbye."

Standing on the third rung of the gate Richard and Mary waved dutifully until the three were out of sight, and then, as one man, turned and went back to the kitchen where Agnes was washing the breakfast things. Without a word Mary took a cloth from the table and started to dry up. Dickie put the cups and saucers away. Agnes looked surprised, but continued her morning anthems. After a little while Dickie said solemnly, "I love hymns in the morning, Mary."

"Specially when Agnes sings them," added his sister dreamily.

Then Dickie knocked a cup off the top of the draining board and caught it before it reached the ground. Agnes gasped, and Mary went on:

"We do like helping you, Agnes. Specially when it's quiet in the house and we can get on quickly."

"What would you like us to do next, please?" asked Dickie. "Shall we do the beds before we go out for the wood?"

After half an hour's help from the twins Agnes felt that she might get on better without them, and it was just then that Mary had her big idea.

"I've been thinkin'," she said, "that it's a pity for us to go up into the wood and then back again right away, Dickie. I'm a bit tired today, and it's quite a long way."

"Yes, it is, Mary. I was wonderin' whether Agnes would just give us a snack jus' to take with us, and then we could gather the wood and no need to come rushin' back and disturb her 'bout dinner-time."

"I think Mummy would like us to do that so as not to get too tired," Mary went on. "We only had time to promise to help Agnes, but I know she'd say 'Yes,' and then we needn't come dashing back."

Then Dickie slipped his hand confidingly into that of Agnes, and Mary smiled up at her appealingly, and the battle was won almost before it had started. She packed them sandwiches and cake, and made them promise not to go too far.

"Tell David we've just gone explorin' up by the wood," Dickie said. "He'll understand. We won't be far away, and perhaps he could come and find us. He'll explain to Mummy."

Then they whistled for Macbeth and started off up their valley.

"That was easy, Dickie. Now we can really do some exploring on our own."

"I'm Richard Lion Heart today," replied Dickie tersely. "Goin' on a crusade. Maybe you're Blondin."

They squabbled a little, but when they came to the stream where they filled the bucket Dickie dropped his satchel.

"Now we'll make that old dam. Of course that's what we'll do."

But Mary argued that they should go up to the Lone Pine first, and reminded her twin also that they had promised to get wood for Agnes, so reluctantly Dickie was persuaded to leave the water.

Macbeth remembered the way and, as they climbed up by the side of the wood, ran on ahead. When they reached the level of the pine tree he had disappeared.

"Which way shall we go in?" Mary asked. "Through my tunnel in the gorse or go round the long way?"

Dickie was just about to suggest the longer route when Macbeth set up a furious barking somewhere near.

"Come on, Mary. He's got a rabbit. Let's find him."

But Mary was looking worried.

"Dickie," she whispered. "It's not a rabbit. He's in the camp and ... and I think there's someone there ... I heard a voice ... Listen!"

They stood tense. Then Mac started again. He was furious, and it was his "watchdog" bark. Mary was right, because they could hear somebody speaking to him. A man's pleasant voice was saying, "Don't be such a silly little dog. Here, then! Good boy, Scottie ... Here..."

But Macbeth was in his most belligerent mood, and would not be mollified by soft words. He snarled and barked again, and the twins imagined him circling round his prey.

Suddenly Mary felt the tears sting her eyes – their wonderful work of yesterday for nothing, because somebody had discovered their secret!

"What shall we do, Dickie?"

"It's our camp, isn't it? We found it. You found it – you and Peter. We've had a noath about it and we're in charge now, aren't we? It's an enemy in there, isn't it? We'll go and kill him and tell the others after ... We'll do it by ourselves just like we always do ... Come on, Mary!"

And so Richard Lion Heart went into battle, and within two minutes had led his gallant army through the gorse tunnel into the camp. The enemy showed as much surprise as the attackers, and both stared dumbfounded at

112

the other. The twins had not had time to imagine what sort of an enemy they were going to find, but they would never have guessed that he would be young, with laughing brown eyes, and in Air Force uniform with two rings on his blue sleeve, and with wings on his breast. He was sitting on the grass at the foot of the tree with a suitcase and a raincoat beside him, and looking at them in the friendliest way.

"Hullo!" he said. "Is this little chap yours? He makes a lot of noise for a small dog. D'you think you could stop him barking? I wish you would."

Dickie didn't feel quite so sure of himself now. A *real* enemy he would cheerfully have attacked, but an RAF Pilot was a different matter. Then he remembered the oath.

"You're our enemy," he said. "And you're not allowed to stay here. This is private. Nobody is allowed here except us, and it's secret…"

The officer got up.

"I say," he said, "I *am* sorry. I'd no idea I was trespassing. I was lost, and found this place by chance. I was wondering whether perhaps you'd help a chap in distress?" He looked at Dickie. "It's much easier to fly than to walk, you know. I can find my way in the air, and yet once I start walking I get in the most peculiar places…"

Mary interrupted. "Our daddy's in the Air Force, too. How did you get here? We live here now, and we don't know you."

But Dickie was not to be put off.

"You're not so much an enemy as we thought, but you can't be here. This place is ours…"

"Is it a camp?" the stranger asked. "It's a grand place for one. Looks as if you've had a fire here. Can't you tell me all about it, and then I'll tell you about fighting in a Spitfire, if you like?"

Dickie began to weaken. A chap like this couldn't be a real enemy. He seemed to know all about camps, too.

"What do you want here, anyway?" he asked.

The pilot stooped to pat Macbeth, who was now wagging his tail at him.

"I want a farm called Appledore," he said. "My aunt lives there, and I've a bit of leave and have come to see her. I came on the early train and started to walk, but I've got lost. I came through that wood, and it looked like a path through the bracken up there –" the twins looked at each other reproachfully – "so I followed it. I suppose that's my aunt's place down here?" And he pointed to Witchend.

They told him, "No."

"Is Appledore far away?" he asked.

"It's over the other side of the mountain," said Mary. "Quite a long way, and difficult to find. We know your aunt. We explored Appledore the other day."

Then he asked their names and about their mother and David, and asked where they were. When they told him he laughed.

"I suppose I'm really your prisoner," he said, "but if I give my parole not to escape or to divulge your secret here, I was wondering whether you would do something for me?"

The twins looked at each other doubtfully.

"I expect you two are jolly good trackers," he went on.

114

"You'd be fine guides, wouldn't you, to a chap lost in the jungle?"

Dickie brightened at this. He *knew* he was a good guide so he nodded modestly.

"Wouldn't you both like to guide me to Appledore? Or some of the way? Just show me the best path so that I don't waste any more time. If you like you can blindfold me so that I don't know the path out of here. What d'you say? Would you do that to help a poor pilot down on his luck?"

"Of course we will," said Mary. "The way will be rough and weary, but we'll take you, won't we, Dickie?"

This was certainly a real adventure. When they had persuaded Agnes so easily to release them this morning, they had never anticipated anything like this. Dickie had a fleeting doubt about his mother's views on the matter, but comforted himself with the thought that even if David did come to find them, they wouldn't be long away and anyway they had some provisions.

"All right," he said suddenly. "We'll guide you, but you'll have to be blindfolded for a bit and swear solemn that you'll never tell a mortal soul 'bout this place. D'you swear?"

"Would you sign in blood?" added Mary.

"I would," said the stranger.

"Very well," said Dickie. "Now we blindfold you. But what with?" And here he produced a small grubby-looking handkerchief from his corduroys.

Their prisoner proved very helpful. "I've got one in my bag," he said. "Let's use that."

They couldn't help noticing that the bag seemed very

full, but he did produce a new blue silk handkerchief which did splendidly. He knelt down while Mary tied it, and then they set off down the hill with the twins taking it in turns to lead him. It's not easy to go down a narrow track in the heather carrying a heavy suitcase and a raincoat when blindfolded, but their new friend was very good-tempered about it, although he got rather red and hot.

At the stream Dickie relented.

"That'll do," he said. "Now you can just follow us."

"And don't talk too much," Mary went on, " 'cause it's wild and desolate country, and we have to think what we're doin'."

This was a very splendid adventure, but Dickie didn't feel particularly confident. He knew they must go up their valley, because he dared not go back past Witchend and risk being seen. He remembered that Peter had told them that there was a way along the top of the mountain, and if they could find the track he knew he must go north and on past the piled stones marking the summit until they came to the Appledore path. It was just the difficulty of finding the main track at the top of the valley. A peculiar but familiar sinking feeling also warned him that it must be about eleven o'clock, but he was too near home to risk eating now. He decided to get to the top first.

Their new friend was very sensible. He seemed to know quite a lot about Indians, and tracking, and camps, and all the exciting things that could happen to intrepid explorers. He was also very interested to hear how they first met Mrs Thurston, and said that it was years since he had seen her, but that he had always promised to come and see her when he could. He asked them whether they knew anyone else here.

"Oh, yes!" said Mary. "We've got a very special friend called Peter. She lives at the reservoir at Hatchholt with her daddy who is a very tidy man."

He asked them a lot about the reservoir, and seemed to be as keen and interested in water as Dickie. He half promised to come back one day of his leave and make a dam with them.

They were talking so hard that almost before they realized it they were at the top, and the valley had flattened out into rolling moorland. Every billow of heather looked the same, and there was no trace of a path. Suddenly Dickie felt nervous, and if anyone had suggested it he would have turned back. But when he looked behind him he couldn't really distinguish which way they had come. Mary saved the situation by saying suddenly:

"Gosh! I'm hungry. Let's sit down here and eat our rations."

Their visitor seemed impatient to get on, but was easily out-voted. Dickie hoped that after food he would be a more competent leader but was doubtful, as he wasn't prepared to admit that he didn't know the way. They shared the sandwiches, and their new friend produced a slab of chocolate.

"We'd better eat this as we go," he said. "Can you just show me the path now, and then you two guides can get home before they start worrying about you."

"*That's* all right," Dickie said, "we couldn't leave you now because there's no path. We'll come along with you till we get to Peter's valley, and then we can show you the way to Appledore, and go home another way."

Mary looked at her twin in admiration. Secretly she was very worried, and had been wondering for ten minutes what they were going to do, but Dickie's plan was excellent. Once they could find Hatchholt and Peter or Mr Sterling, they would have nothing to worry about.

She looked up to see their officer watching them with a strange smile.

"Now then," he said. "Which way, my brave Indians?"

Dickie gulped and explained his predicament.

"You see," he said, "I've not 'zactly been up here before, and there isn't a real path, but I know we've got to go on walking to the right and till we get high enough to see over the other side ... Then we'll see that old devil's chair, and I'll know where we are..."

Their friend laughed. "Come on, then! We're in this together, and I don't know how I could have done without you. Let's find this Hatchholt valley first, and then you can tell me which direction to go, and you'll be safe on your way home ... I'd like to see the reservoir, too," he added.

The twins felt happier now, and Dickie began to ask the stranger about Hurricanes and Spitfires, and the fights he had been in. But like all pilots he was modest, and seemed much more interested in them and the mountain and the reservoir.

At last Macbeth found a narrow sheep path through the heather which made it much easier to get along. They were walking single file, with Dickie leading, when suddenly he shouted: "We're up! Look! There's the

Stiperstones, and there in front is that pile of stones near the place where we hid, Mary."

He turned to the others: "And if we look to the right now we shall see a little path leading to Hatchholt."

Their friend dropped his heavy suitcase.

"Well done the guides," he said. "Now I'm going to rest for five minutes and have a smoke. This case is heavy, and I'm tired." And he sat down in the heather.

Mary looked at him with a puzzled frown.

"I've been wondering," she said. "Why didn't you have old John and the car to take you to Appledore 'stead of carrying that old luggage round?"

"Who's old John?" he asked.

"He has a car at Onnybrook. Why didn't you wait for him 'stead of trying to walk and getting lost?"

"Don't worry your head about me," he said. "I came on the early train, and there was no car so I started to walk."

Dickie rolled over on his back. He was feeling much more pleased with himself now.

"Well, I wouldn't want to walk with that luggage for any of *my* aunts," he remarked.

Mary sat up and then nudged her twin sharply.

"Look, Dickie! Someone's coming ... P'raps it's Peter coming from Hatchholt?"

The officer pulled them down sharply.

"Let's trail them," he said. "Don't let's show ourselves till you see who it is."

They looked at him in surprise. He sounded serious, but was smiling as usual, and gave Dickie a broad wink. Mary put her hand on Mac's collar, and slowly raised her head above the heather.

"I can't see anyone now," she said.

"Are you *sure* there was someone there?" asked the officer.

"I think so," said Mary doubtfully. "Over there," and she pointed vaguely to the right. "I thought it was Peter."

"Let me look," said Dickie. For a long minute he crouched hidden behind a clump of heather. Then—

"There *is* someone, Mary. I can see something moving … Wait! I'll tell you … Mary, come and look and tell me who you think it is. I think I know…"

Mary squealed. "It *is*, Dickie. I'm sure it is."

She turned to their friend. "It's your auntie come to meet you. I'm sure it is. Look! It's Mrs Thurston, isn't it? But she hasn't come from Appledore. P'raps she's come up Hatchholt from the station."

"Come on!" said Dickie. "Don't you want to see her? Or shall we hide here and give her a surprise? Be *quiet*, Mackie, you bad dog … Quick, Mary, put him on the lead! He's so rude to Mrs Thurston."

Before they could say more their companion pulled them so roughly down into the heather that Mary cried out in surprise and pain. He was looking white and upset, and for a moment didn't seem to know what he was doing.

Dickie wrenched himself free. "Let go!" he said. "Let Mary go! You're hurting her."

Then he smiled and released her. "I'm sorry," he said. "This is a splendid adventure, isn't it? I haven't seen my aunt for years, and don't suppose I would know her. Will one of you look again and tell me if you're *absolutely certain* that it's Mrs Thurston? You look, Mary! You saw her first."

As he spoke Macbeth began to growl. With one hand Mary caressed him and strove to keep him quiet as she peeped again through the heather. She had no doubt now. Mrs Thurston was walking quickly towards them, and Mary easily recognized her quick brisk walk and dark head. Today she was wearing a drab belted raincoat and, as usual, smoking a cigarette. She had something slung over her shoulder which looked like a camera case.

For no particular reason Mary felt uneasy. She knew she ought to like Mrs Thurston, who had been both kind and friendly to them, but she could not forget the look she had seen on her face when she tried to kick Macbeth at Witchend. Under her hand Macbeth was shaking, too, and she was tired now and had had enough of this adventure with this nice officer. She wanted funny old David with his slow ways, and Mummy of course, and Daddy if he'd been here, and Peter, too, with the nice way she had of putting an arm round your shoulders. She thought all this in a flash and then said quietly, "I'm *positive* it's your auntie. I know it is. Let's go and meet her" – and before the others could stop her she jumped up and waved. At the same time Macbeth started to bark furiously.

Mrs Thurston stopped in astonishment. She was only about one hundred yards away, and obviously thought she was alone on the top of the mountain.

"Hullo!" Mary called.

"Hullo!" shouted Dickie. "We've got a surprise for you. Look who we've got!" And he pulled their new friend up beside him.

Now the twins could never quite agree as to what happened during the next few minutes. Mary, who was really looking at Mrs Thurston, said that for a second she looked as if she'd seen a ghost. Dickie maintained that their officer went very white and stood still. All the time Macbeth was barking madly and straining at his lead.

Mrs Thurston spoke first: "Take that dog away, Mary. He's a little beast. Keep him away from me." Then she turned to Dickie and spoke quite sharply: "What are you two doing up here today, and who is this?"

They both agreed that she looked at her nephew as if she didn't know him. Then the latter smiled, came forward and held out his hand.

"Hullo, Aunt," he said. "How are you? I'm John Davies. Didn't you get my telegram saying I'd got some leave and was coming to see you?"

Mrs Thurston shook her head.

"Too bad," he went on. "I sent it yesterday, but was afraid it might not get to you in time. I had to walk into the village from the camp, and on my way back heard an owl, and thought to myself how the evenings were drawing in ... Well, here I am, anyway, and I wouldn't be here now but for these gallant explorers who found me when I was lost and have been my guides."

Mrs Thurston laughed. "I'm glad to see you, John, and it's nice of you to come. We don't get much company up here. No wonder I didn't recognize you in your uniform, for I haven't seen you since you joined up, have I?"

Then she turned to the twins.

"Thank you for looking after him so nicely. Where are the others, though? Surely you're not up here alone?"

"Oh, yes, we are," said Dickie. "We do most things

alone, Mary and me. But we're going home now, thank you very much."

"Did you come up Hatchholt, Mrs Thurston?" Mary asked suddenly. "Is that the path? The way you came?"

"I've just been out for a walk looking at birds," she replied. "But that is the way. Just follow this track and it leads to the reservoir, and then you'll know where you are … Well, John, we must get along … Goodbye, twins…"

Now Dickie, like Mary just now, had had enough of this adventure. He was ready to go, and thought his sister would agree. He was afraid that they were going to get into trouble for disobeying orders and leaving their valley, and was thoroughly ashamed of himself. He was just about to say "Goodbye" when he had the odd feeling that Mary was trying to tell him something. The twins never attempted to explain this to each other. They just knew that it happened and that sometimes they could speak to each other without words. Now Mary was telling him very definitely that they were not going home yet, but were going to Appledore first.

"There's something we've got to find out. We must go to Appledore," she seemed to be saying. So Dickie wasn't surprised when his twin said out loud: "If you don't mind, Mrs Thurston, we'll come down with you like we did the other day. We're awfully thirsty, and we'll have plenty of time to get back this way after tea."

But Mrs Thurston didn't seem to want them. She made excuses and was quite cross when Dickie supported his sister and said, "But don't you *want* us to come and see you? We've guided this stranger to you all day and looked after him…"

"And shared our rations with him," added Mary. "And now you don't want us."

John Davies laughed, picked up his suitcase, and looked at his aunt. "I think they'd better come with us, Aunt," he said. "Much more satisfactory."

So they started back across the top of the mountain with Macbeth snarling and tugging at the end of his lead. Dickie, still a little bewildered at Mary's decision to go to Appledore, trudged along rather wearily behind the two grown-ups. Something was happening which he didn't understand, and an adventure which promised so much fun wasn't fun any more. He couldn't help noticing that Mrs Thurston didn't say much to her nice nephew, but that may have been because Mary went on chattering. Macbeth was being a fearful nuisance, too, and he felt rather ashamed of him. Once, when they had stopped for John Davies to rest, he said, "Why don't you keep that dog quiet, Mary. What's the matter with him?"

Mary looked rebellious. "Nothing's the matter with him … But I don't think Mrs Thurston likes him, and he knows it."

Mrs Thurston laughed and lit a cigarette.

"Don't be absurd, Mary! You're a very foolish child about the dog. I don't dislike him, but next time I see your mother I shall tell her that he's a nuisance. He never stops yapping. I think he's dangerous, too!"

Mary went white and her eyes filled with tears as Dickie went over to her. But before they could speak John Davies saved the situation by jumping up and saying "Never mind about poor old Mac. I expect he needs his tea as much as I do. Let's get going."

They passed the cairn of stones and the secret hollow from where they had seen the stranger in the raincoat. Then they paused a moment to wonder at the grandeur of the Stiperstones now facing them on the other side of a great valley.

Dickie pointed. "See that black rock up there on top? That's the old Devil's Chair. We'll tell you all 'bout it if you like ... Sometimes, when you can't see the Chair, he's sitting in it, and then everyone goes indoors and puts the shutters up."

John Davies looked at him strangely.

"That's an odd story, son," he said. "Sounds as if you think it's true."

Dickie didn't answer. In the clear afternoon light the black rocks looked very near. He couldn't believe the story really, because it was impossible to imagine that the chair could ever be invisible, but he didn't want to talk about it. The grown-ups wouldn't understand. They were laughing at him now.

Soon after they came to the Appledore path, and Mary and he led the way down. The others seemed to be lagging behind, so he whispered:

"What are we doin' this for, Mary? Were you really thirsty? 'Course I'm hungry now, but I generally am."

"I don't know, Dickie. I just felt we'd got to find out something ... And she didn't really want us to come ... I wish we hadn't now, but we can't go back yet."

"Mary," said Dickie solemnly, "have you thought what Mummy will say 'bout this adventure?"

"Yes, I have. Everything happened quickly, Dickie, and we couldn't sort of help it, could we? But it's a very

125

proper adventure of our own, and we'll have lots to tell the others round the camp fire."

"If Mummy ever lets us sit round it," added her twin gloomily.

They were now almost in sight of the farmhouse and Macbeth, now that he was not with Mrs Thurston, was trotting sedately in front. Suddenly he stopped, cocked his head, lifted one paw, and growled. Mary reached for Dickie's hand.

"Someone running through the trees, Dickie! *Really!* I saw him."

"This is a magic wood," said Dickie. "I don't think I like it."

Then they heard Mrs Thurston's voice behind them. "Nonsense," she was saying. "You don't understand children. I can manage them." Then, as she saw the twins still standing in the path: "What are you waiting for?"

"We've just seen a villain running through the wood," said Dickie bluntly.

"What d'you mean?" asked John. "Where?"

Mary waved a vague hand. "Well," she said, "I just *thought* I saw a man, but 'spect I didn't. There's nobody else lives round here, is there?"

The two grown-ups looked blankly at each other.

"Must have been a ghost," added Dickie.

Then, "You funny children," laughed Mrs Thurston. "How solemn you look! Now tell me. Did you *really* see anybody? Was it Jacob, do you think?"

Mary shook her head. "I don't know. Why should he want to run through the trees as if he was hiding?"

"Now, listen, twins. Just in case you did see somebody,

and just in case there's a tramp round the house, I think you had better stop here while we go and see if everything is all right."

"Thank you very much," said Dickie firmly, "but I don't like this wood, and I think we'll come too."

"We shall all be safe together," said Mary. "John will guard us, won't you?"

"I'll look after you," he smiled, "but I do think my aunt is right. Stay here for a few minutes with Mac and we'll go ahead and spy out the land. Can't be too careful these days, you know! … I'll come back for you if it's all clear."

"I'm coming with you," said Dickie stubbornly.

Then Mrs Thurston was really angry.

"You are two naughty disobedient children!" she stormed. "You will do exactly what we say and stay here until we call you."

The twins were so surprised at this outburst that they nodded. Then John actually winked at them before going on down the path with his aunt. Once Mrs Thurston turned to see if they were still there, and then, apparently sorry for her bad temper, waved before the trees hid them from sight.

Mary looked at Dickie and without further discussion they started quietly down the path after the two grown-ups. They trailed them quite well and slipped from tree to tree in the shadow of the wood. They had gone perhaps sixty yards in this way when Mary held up a warning hand and pulled her brother's head down to her mouth.

" 'Bout here," she whispered, "that I saw the quiet man running. Over there." Then she stiffened and pointed to tiny curl of blue smoke rising from the undergrowth.

"Gosh!" said Dickie. "A prairie fire! Come on!"

With Macbeth still panting on the lead they crept through the trees and there, in the centre of a circle of dry smouldering leaves, was the end of a new but still burning cigarette. Dickie stamped on the fire. "So it wasn't a ghost," he whispered.

Mary felt for his hand. "It *is* an adventure, isn't it, twin?" she said in rather a shaky voice. "I'm glad we're both here. Let's go back to the path."

Soon they reached the edge of the wood and were just in time to see Mrs Thurston and John far below. They didn't seem to be hiding or looking for anybody, but walked quickly across the garden to the front door without even looking back.

"They're very brave," murmured Dickie. "Now what do we do?"

"We'd better go back a little way and watch for John. He said he'd call us … Or? … I s'pose we wouldn't go home now, would we? Shall we, Dickie?"

He shook his head. "I don't like this magic wood either, but I'm hungry. Let's have tea first, then – then we'll be strengthened for the journey," he added brightly.

"All right," Mary said doubtfully. "But I wish David and Tom and Peter were here."

Dickie did, too, but didn't care to admit it. So they sat under a pine tree and watched and listened. They could just see the house and after a little someone opened a window at the back, but they couldn't see who it was. Then, just as they had decided that they had been forgotten, John came round the side of the house and started up the track towards them. They turned and ran back into the wood, but stopped when he called, "Come on, twins. All clear now."

They "coo–eed" and ran down to meet him.

"I'm sorry about you two," he said. "It's my fault really that you've been out all day like this. Will they worry about you? If they will I'd better come and see your mother some time and explain."

"That," said Dickie, "would be a very good idea."

Mrs Thurston was waiting in the porch, and had never been more friendly.

"All safe and sound, you see," she smiled. "So come along in and have your tea. Please tie Mac up outside, Mary, because he is rather naughty."

Mary was about to explain that there had been a man in the wood because they had seen the burning cigarette when she went on: "I want to have a good talk with John, so you won't mind having tea by yourselves, will you?" and led the way into the house. Almost before they realized it she had shown them into a little room at the back of the hall and shut the door. The window opened on to the yard, but was darkened by a rose tree clambering up outside the wall.

Dickie's eyes grew round as saucers.

"We're prisoners," he said. "Bet you we are! Gosh!"

Mary's lips quivered as she went to the door and tried the handle. It turned. The door opened.

The twins peeped out. Voices were coming from the sitting-room where they had had tea before. Men's voices mostly, and they could hear John laughing. They stepped into the hall. Another step. They didn't have to say anything to each other. They just knew that, tea or no tea, they didn't want to stay any longer in this house. They tiptoed up the hall. Opposite the sitting-room Mary clutched Dickie's arm. Her heart was going "bump! bump! bump!" and her tongue felt dry and big in her mouth. Only two more steps now and they would be at the front door … They were on the mat and Dickie reached up to the latch…

Then a quiet voice came from behind them. "What are you doing? Stop!" The man Jacob, with a tray in his hand, was standing at the back of the hall, watching them. Then Mrs Thurston came out of the sitting-room and shut the door quickly behind her.

"Thank you very much all the same," Dickie began, "but we've got to go now. We've got to go because we're late already, and Mummy will be very cross…"

"But I thought you were thirsty and wanted some tea," Mrs Thurston said. "Look, Jacob's got it for you, and it's ready now. You must have something before you go."

"No, thank you," Dickie went on, fingering the latch. "I'm sorry we can't stay, but we've just *got* to go now."

He felt the door move as Mrs Thurston laughed.

"Very well," she said. "Goodbye, and thank you for guiding John so well. Tell your mother where you've been, and say how grateful we are to you. Are you sure you'll be all right, because the car is out of order and I can't drive you home … Very well, Jacob. Don't wait thank you."

Dickie nodded. "Oh, yes! We'll go over Hatchholt way and find Peter."

Mrs Thurston opened the door for them and stood for a moment in the sunshine.

"Lucky there wasn't a tramp," she said.

"But there *was* a man," Mary said. "I saw him, and he dropped a cigarette, 'cause we stamped the fire out just now." She paused, and then: "P'raps he was the man in the raincoat on the mountain the other day. We thought he'd come this way."

"You've dropped *your* cigarette," Dickie said suddenly as he slipped out. "Goodbye."

They ran to loose Macbeth and then looked back. Mrs Thurston was still standing at the door.

"Dickie," Mary gasped. "Her face! Did you see it? It was like when she kicked Mackie yesterday."

Her twin didn't answer till they were in the wood.

"We're not afraid of *anything*, are we, Mary? Who shall we be going through this jungle? I think I'll be Sir Richard again and you be a native guide."

Mary held her head high. "We'll soon be home, Dickie. And the first thing I'm going to do is to hug Mummy and say we're sorry. I 'spect David will come to meet us. 'Spect he's up on the mountain now."

They hurried up the path and soon left the trees behind. Once Dickie turned and saw the Devil's Chair still standing gaunt and black against the skyline, and then they came to the top at last and started across the heather.

"After all, I wish I'd had some tea," Dickie said after a little.

"I'm cold," Mary complained. "The sun's gone. Hurry up, Dickie! I want to get home. So does Mackie."

Something had happened to the weather. A damp, cold wind touched them gently, and as they looked round, bewildered, the outline of the rolling hilltop wavered and grew indistinct.

Dickie turned back the way they had come, and slowly pointed across the valley to Stiperstones. The hills were there, but looked different. Softer.

"Mary," he whispered. "Look! The Chair's not there. It's gone. It's like Bill said, Mary. He's in his Chair…"

And the mist came rolling silently across the valley as if a giant was blowing great balls of soft white cotton wool.

Chapter 6

Hatchholt

As Mrs Morton, with Tom and David, hurried down the lane to Ingles, she said, "The twins were looking very innocent. Do you think they'll be all right, David?"

He thought so. Sometimes it was almost a relief to be without them for an hour or two, and he was hoping that the bicycles would be at the station so that he could do some more exploring. He was thinking that he might go through Onnybrook in the other direction and find the road that led to the Hatchholt valley.

Mrs Ingles was very upset when they arrived. They found her sitting in one chair with her swollen and bandaged foot resting on another. She was helpless and in pain.

"Alf would have you fetched, Mrs Morton," she said. "And that grateful I am to you for coming so quickly, but I reckon I shall be better soon. Young Tom can run errands, but 'tis true he's not much use in the house yet, and there's bits of cooking and that to do ... For years I've been telling Alf he should do something to the worn place in the dairy floor. And now look what's happened? Over I go this morning and find I can't stand on this leg when I tries to get up. Now I'm stuck here, and these menfolk will

133

likely have to fend for themselves for a bit, I'm thinking ... Now, Tom – don't stand there dreaming. You've got to get the cows out of the Twelve Acre, haven't you? You'd better go along with him, lad."

"Look in on your way back from the station, David," his mother said, "just in case you can be useful here."

The two boys wandered up the fields.

"That Mrs Thurston's a rum 'un," Tom said as he gave the last cow through the gate a helping whack with his stick. "You'd have laughed if you'd seen her running away from that little black dog of yours ... Shall we go up to camp again this evening? We ought to manage a meeting every day if we can, and I can teach you all to whistle like that bird I can copy ... Let's go down to the barn now and see if there are any rats..."

But David had no time for rat-hunts now. He wanted to get on, so he promised to let Tom know when they could meet again, and left him whistling cheerfully as usual.

"I'll be here when you come back," Tom called.

David set off up the lane and turned to look back at Witchend, where old John had stopped the car on the night of their arrival. What a lot had happened since then! Meeting Tom and Peter, trailing the stranger in the raincoat, and finding Appledore and, most exciting of all, founding the Lone Pine Camp. At the top of the hill where their lane joined the Onnybrook road he realized that although cycles would be useful, they would have to do a great deal of walking. It was certainly a county of hills. All the roads and lanes twisted and climbed and fell away again like crazy switchbacks. Every corner promised surprise, and rarely disappointed, and as he swung down to the village through the overhanging woods, the tinkle of running water followed him.

Once he passed a brown-faced man cutting and trimming the hedges.

" 'Mornin'!" he called. "You're from Witchend, I take it?"

David stopped and nodded. He liked these friendly people who seemed to know everything about them.

"Caught any rabbits yet?" the man went on with a twinkle. "Just let me know when your ma wants some, and I kin oblige," and he swung the keen, long-handled sickle across the top of the hedge, leaving it clean and level as a table-top.

At the station all was quiet. David was used to active and busy railway stations, and to the London termini, but down here time seemed of no account. The level-crossing gates were open and a few chickens wandered vaguely over the rails. The signalman leaned from his cabin in the sunshine and, at the far end of the platform, the old porter he remembered was watering a few brave nasturtiums clambering up the fence. The small and smelly room dignified by the name of "Booking Office" was empty, the window from which occasional tickets were issued was shuttered, and there were no bicycles. David began to whistle in the hope that someone might come and see who was breaking the peace. Nothing much happened. A butterfly hovered in the doorway for a second and a bell clanged in the signal-box. With some foreboding he knocked on the ticket window, but there was no answer. When he went out again into the sunshine the old porter was ambling towards him.

"Well, son," he smiled. "And how d'you like Witchend, eh? Not going back home yet, are you?"

David explained and asked about the bicycles.

"Bicycles, eh?" the old man repeated, as if he'd never heard of them before. "Oh! Aye! Bicycles, to be sure ... Why, yes, they've come, and a pile of other stuff besides. Must be in office, I reckon," and he led the way again into the gloom.

David was glad to have his bicycle. He looked it over carefully and untied the rags he had put round the handlebars to protect them from scratches. The pedals spun round well and the brakes worked, so he said "Goodbye" to the porter and went on to the road. He was just wondering whether to ride through Onnybrook village towards unexplored country, when he heard the clatter of hoofs, and Peter cantered up behind him.

"Hullo!" she called. "Where were you going, David? I was coming to see you."

"So was I," he said. "I mean I was thinking of coming up to see if I could find the end of your valley ... Our bikes have come."

"It's going to be hot today, and I wondered whether you would all come to us and we'll have a swim. We might ask Tom, too. I had to come round this way, as it's shopping day," and she pointed to the two laden saddle-bags.

David explained about Mrs Ingles and his mother, but was sure they would be able to come, so they decided to ride up to the farm first, then go and pick up the twins.

At Ingles they found Mrs Morton very engrossed with the kitchen range, and not much inclined to discuss anybody's plans. Mr Ingles was back again, but had gone out to find Tom and get him to work before the doctor came. Mrs Ingles had been carried up to bed.

David managed to do one or two odd jobs for his mother, but it was Peter who finally broached the subject.

"... And it's really a very good day for a swim, Mrs Morton," she said. "And we'll pick up the twins on the way and look after them, and David will bring them back this evening. Daddy will be very disappointed if they don't come, because he's got something special for dinner."

Mrs Morton raised a red face from the fire. "Very well," she said. "There's not much more I can do here, and I'm going back to Witchend presently and shall send Agnes down. Or perhaps it would be better if you asked her to come here and relieve me when you go. Take care of the twins, David. Remember they can't swim properly, although they're very enthusiastic. We packed some bathing things somewhere and you'll have to search till you find them ... No, I don't know where Tom is, and if I were you I shouldn't look for him now. He's busy helping his uncle, and they're behind this morning."

"If you *do* see him, Mummy, and if there is a chance of him coming presently, will you tell him we've gone to Hatchholt and ask him to come too?"

Mrs Morton promised to deliver the message and pushed them out of the kitchen, and they rode up the lane to Witchend. There was no sign of the twins or Macbeth, but a doleful humming led them to Agnes sitting in the sun at the back door, shredding beans.

"There now!" she said when she had heard their story. "Fancy that! Poor Mrs Ingles, and with young Tom there,

137

too. And your mother wants me to go down presently and see if I can give a hand. Of course I will, but what about your dinners?"

Patiently they explained again that they would be at Hatchholt as soon as they had found the twins, and would not be back until evening.

"Well, now," Agnes mused. "Where did they say they would be going? There was something I was to tell Master David when he came back. Young limbs they are … just like two peas and all."

At last she admitted that she had allowed them to go out and to take sandwiches with them.

"But, Agnes, did they say where they were going? Did they give you any idea at all?"

Then she remembered. "Of course they did, Master David. Up to the wood they said. Where will you be off to, I asked them, and both together they said up by the wood, and I was to tell you and you'd understand."

Peter and David understood. Both of them imagined the twins having a fine old time at the Lone Pine on their own, and wondered whether the camp would ever look the same again.

"I tell you the best thing to do, David," said Peter. "I'll ride up on Sally and bring them back – that will be the quickest way. You can't ride your bike today because we can't go all round by road, and I'll show you a new way through Dark Hollow. You look out the bathing things and with luck we'll be ready to start in half-an-hour. Agnes says they went nearly two hours ago so they may be up to anything by now."

"Yes. They're sure to be at the camp," he agreed, "or

making a dam somewhere. If you can't find them though, better leave a note and tell 'em where we are. Trouble is I doubt if they'll be able to find their way to Hatchholt by themselves. What do you think?"

Peter was doubtful too.

"I'm sure they'll be there, but if you can't find them I agree it would be silly to expect them to find their way on their own ... I know, David. I'll tell them in a message where we are and say that if they want to come they must go and ask Tom to bring them over, and then all the Club can meet. I'm sure Mr Ingles would let Tom go if Mary asks him nicely! And I'll draw a map to show them the way ... But we'll take their bathing things to save time. Lend me your note-book and pencil, and I'll be off."

So David rummaged about upstairs in drawers and trunks, and had to call on Agnes to help him before they could find the swimming suits. Quite obviously she thought they were all crazy. Water had its uses, she was prepared to admit, but why anyone should want to take their clothes off and swim in it was more than she could understand.

"And those two little ones, as well, Master David? A'plunging in the cold water up there at the rezzivoy? And your mother says you can? Well! Well! Seems all wrong to me, but different days, different ways, I s'pose ... And what are yon poor mites to put on warm after, might I ask? ... The same clothes, you say! And the Almighty knows yon bairns wear next to no clothes now! Ah well! Here be the things. Take care of yourselves and I'll be down at Ingles to your mother just as soon as I've tidied up a bit."

By the time he had put his bicycle away and rolled the costumes up in some towels, Peter was back.

"They're not there, David, but I think they've been there. The camp looks as if they've rampaged all over the place. And they're not at the stream either. I whistled the Peewit whistle and called a bit, but you know what they are. They were probably hiding a few yards away in the wood laughing at me! I've written the message and drawn the map, and fixed it to the trunk of the Lone Pine so that they can't possibly miss it ... You've found the bathing things? That's fine. Now we must hurry because Daddy will be cross if we're late, and I've got some tins of things here."

She showed him a short cut across the side of the hill to the track that led to Dark Hollow, so that they did not have to pass Ingles again. When they reached the lane at the foot of the valley, Peter turned to the right instead of going through the gate and up by the side of the stream as David had done on the day they had first met. Here she suggested that David should have his first riding lesson.

"I wouldn't ask anybody, David," she said. "Sally is the best friend I've ever had, and she knows what I want without me asking – like those twins of yours. But I'd love you to learn, and then perhaps you could get a pony and we really could go exploring then ... Just try now for a little way down the lane."

David was keen enough. He was already a little envious of Peter's skill in many ways, and her idea about a pony of their own was splendid. If he could learn to ride quickly Daddy might be reasonable about it!

But it wasn't as easy and comfortable as it looked. Firstly Sally seemed resentful of the experiment, and Peter had to speak reassuringly to her when somehow he scrambled up on her back. And once on he felt strangely insecure – Peter looked as if she were part of the horse, but he felt as if he didn't belong to anything, particularly when Sally began to move. Peter was saying something about toes up and knees in, and showing him how to hold the reins in a special way, and everything seemed to be happening at once.

"Don't look so unhappy," she laughed at him. "And don't be so stiff and uncomfortable," and she led Sally into a trot. This was terrible! He was bouncing up and down in a maddening, uncontrolled, and rather painful manner. But somehow he stuck on and after a little while began to have some conception of what was expected of him, and when his mistress told him that he had had enough for his first lesson he was almost sorry to dismount.

"Well done, David! That wasn't too bad for a start. I'll soon make a horseman of you. Do you know that riding is the most wonderful thing in the world? You can't imagine what it's like to fly along the top of the mountain even on little Sally."

And here they turned off on the left along another track, and she told him how, before the War, she was allowed to follow the hounds and how she had won several prizes at local Gymkhanas.

"One day, when I'm old enough," she said, "I want to ride in the Point-to-Points. Of course they don't have them now, but I s'pose they will again … Now we're coming to Hatchholt valley, and you can see that this is quite a quick and easy way – much better than climbing up by the waterfall and getting stuck in a bog! This is the way I've shown them on the map, and they'll have no trouble if Tom is with them and they're sensible. As soon as we get right into the valley the path follows the pipeline up to the reservoir, and you can't go wrong. Look! Here we are, and there are the four pipes leading up to home."

Sally knew her way now and was walking sedately in front. This end of Hatchholt valley was different from the others. It was very narrow and rocky even at this level, but the track was good because it had been used more often.

"How do you get food up here in the winter?" David asked.

"There's a cottage at the foot of the valley just off the main road," Peter explained, "and everything is left there for us. Daddy is keen on his garden, and when I'm at school there's not much he wants, but he goes down at least twice a week. We've got a goat for milk. Did you see her when you came before?"

David was out of breath with the climb when, after three more sharp turns, they could see the little house perched on the hillside far above them. The sides of the valley were still very steep, and Peter pointed out the hill-top and track down which they had come on the day they had first met.

This time Mr Sterling was waiting for them. He was leaning on his neat little white gate with a neat cap straight on his head and his pipe in his mouth. He kissed

Peter and shook hands solemnly with David. Then he took his glasses off, polished them, put them on again, and looked carefully at the two children.

"You're very welcome," he said deliberately. "Friends are always welcome at Hatchholt if they're tidy about the place. Very welcome."

Then he looked round again.

"I've been wondering," he went on, "whether there aren't some more to come? Two little ones, I seem to remember. One like the other. Boy and girl. Smart they were with their questions. Didn't you tell me, lass, they were twins?"

Peter explained how they had missed them, but hoped they'd be along later. But Mr Sterling didn't like this arrangement at all, and David felt a little uncomfortable.

"No! No!" Mr Sterling said. "I don't understand. Either they're coming to dinner or not. Which is it? We must be tidy in our arrangements. The potatoes are on, and there's enough for five, and you've brought the corned beef, lass?" Peter nodded.

"Yes, Daddy. But we needn't put it all out, and the potatoes we don't eat will be nice cold or fried up, and David said to me that he was sure we oughtn't to keep you waiting until the twins turned up, so we came on to let you know what had happened. It was David's idea not to keep you waiting, Daddy."

Mr Sterling looked with a little more approval at his visitor, but it was obvious that he didn't like his plans upset in any way, and that as he was cooking food for five when there were only three to eat it, the situation was serious. Just as David remembered the instance of the spread newspaper to catch the crumbs on the occasion of his first visit, Peter dug him in the ribs.

"Come on, David. I'll show you how to rub Sally down and put the harness away. We shan't want her again today as she's had her exercise. I'll show you Hepzibah, too. Hepsy is the goat."

When they were out of hearing she went on—

"Daddy's a darling, but I'm the only one who knows how to deal with him. If you want to please him just be tidy, and *don't drop crumbs on the floor*. I don't know why it is, but he hates crumbs ... Do you know, he's asked me several times about Dickie and Mary. They seemed to fascinate him. I hope he won't be too disappointed that they're not here."

When Sally had been attended to, she went into the house with the laden saddle-bags, and David could hear her explaining that if the twins *did* come there would be an extra guest in Tom. This news seemed to affect Mr Sterling seriously for David heard him say in a shaky voice, "But this is a terrible muddle, lass! A terrible untidy muddle. If young Ingles comes, we shan't have enough potatoes. I can't be upset like this when I've made all my arrangements ... You're not fair to your old daddy, Peter ... No, it's no use hugging me, girl ... I'm upset..."

Peter came out flushed and laughing.

"Best leave him alone for a bit, David. Come up and sit on the dam."

They climbed up to the wall and sat in the sun. The water was clear and clean, but as they watched the surface was continually broken by little rings of ripples.

"It's the trout," Peter explained. "The reservoir is full

of them. Daddy catches them with flies and even worms sometimes. I go up the streams and tickle them. I'll show you how to do it some time. Shall we bathe before dinner and not wait for the others?"

While they were still arguing as to whether it would be hotter later on, Mr Sterling came to the front door and waved.

"That means dinner's ready, David. It means, too, that he's not going to wait for the others and that he'll be very worried if we don't finish up all the potatoes. I don't know what we'll do if they come along presently but, of course, the twins took sandwiches, didn't they?"

"That won't stop Dickie having another meal if he's asked," said David grimly.

Mr Sterling was waiting for them.

"Everything's difficult now," he said to David, "but you're very welcome, lad. Come along in and sit down and make yourself at home."

The tiny sitting-room was gleaming. David realized suddenly that this place reminded him of a lighthouse. Last time they had come its likeness to something had puzzled him, but now he remembered.

The sofa looked just as hard and shiny, but there were flowers on the table, and the sun was pouring in through the window. The little grate was black and glossy, and the brass everywhere was twinkling, and once Mr Sterling had solved the awful problem of an equal distribution of the potatoes he began to twinkle as well. When the three plates were piled high he asked God's blessing, looked to see if David was crumbling his bread, and then relaxed.

When they had reached the plums and custard stage –

and there was no glimpse of these dainties until every vestige of the first course had been cleared away and the tablecloth brushed clean of crumbs – David felt that it was safe to ask about the reservoir.

"I wish you'd tell me about the water up here, Mr Sterling. Where does it all go, and why do you have pipes running down the valley? And what's the little brick house by the dam?"

"There are lots wonder those things, David, and very odd some of 'em are … We'll just get tidied up here and get these bits of crocks washed up, and then I'll come out and tell you all you want to know. You won't be able to swim after all those potatoes, so a rest'll be good for you."

At the mention of potatoes Peter winked broadly because she had seen David struggling to finish his generous portion.

They both helped to wash up and Mr Sterling became increasingly good-humoured as the muddle in the sink grew less. It all took rather a long time because he insisted upon washing up himself, and would not permit Peter to put the crockery away. He had a special place for everything, and did not trust even his daughter to deputize for him.

When at last everything was ship-shape Peter's father fetched his cap and his pipe, took David by the arm, and led the way out to the dam.

"This water," he began, "is part of the water supply of the great Midland cities fifty and sixty miles away. There are seven other reservoirs like this, but bigger, in the hill country round about here. Big cities need a lot of clean water, and no doubt they tell you at your school how 'tis often necessary to bring water many miles because there is not enough to be got by sinking wells and the like. No city relies on one source of water alone, but these hill reservoirs of ours are very important."

"What would happen if they ran dry?" David interrupted. "Could they get their water anywhere else?"

"They never have run dry, lad, and I don't reckon they ever will. But if they all did, 'twould be very serious indeed, for the cities can't do without us. But they never would run dry all at the same time because we never use 'em all at once. That's what a reservoir is for – to keep the water till it's needed."

"What would happen if you overflowed?"

" 'Tisn't likely we would. Water couldn't come in faster than I can let it out through these pipes. Each reservoir lets out as much as is needed at the water works. Hatchholt was an experiment though, because the flow is controlled at this end. Not all the other reservoirs have pipes and are not as high or as isolated as this one … Come in here and I'll show you the sluices…" and he led the way to the little brick house and unlocked the door. There wasn't much to see. The floor was a metal plate obviously covering some sort of well, and through it projected four iron rods each with a small wheel and a dial.

"Each of these wheels is like the handle of a tap," Mr Sterling explained. "Turn them to the right and the sluice about twenty feet down opens and the dial shows how much water is running through. Turn 'em to the left and they close just like putting the plug in the bath. I don't rightly remember that we've ever had all four open at the same time."

"Suppose," said David. "Just *suppose* that the pipes got blocked somewhere or the sluices wouldn't work and the water kept coming in and you couldn't get it out. What would happen? Would the dam burst?"

"Lord bless you, no! That wouldn't break! Water would pour over the top and run away down into the valley making a stream like that in your valley, or Dark Hollow."

Then he allowed David to open and close the sluices and watch the dials, and continued to chat amiably while Peter prowled about furiously outside. When at last he had had enough and Mr Sterling had ambled away, David remembered Peter and turned to find her. She had disappeared, so he went back to the house. She was not there either, so he collected his bathing shorts and towel and went up to the dam again and whistled the Peewit's plaintive call. There was no answer so he started to walk along the side of the reservoir, and once or twice stopped and called her name. Then he remembered the secret hollow she had shown them, and wondered if she was hiding for a joke. He was beginning to think that it was a poor sort of joke and that the afternoon was being spoiled when he saw her dart out of the heather about twenty yards in front of him. She was in a scarlet bathing costume with a bright blue rubber cap, and for a moment he wondered who it was. He called, but she didn't even look in his direction but ran straight into the water. He called again, "Wait for me, Peter. I won't be a sec," but she made no answer, dived under and swam rapidly away from him up to the dam where she pulled herself up and sat in the sun.

David ran back along the little beach, but when he was

within a few yards of her she dived in again and swam away. He was suddenly very angry and jumped down behind the dam wall, flung off his clothes and scrambled into his trunks. Instead of climbing up quickly and diving in he pulled himself up slowly and peeped over the top. Peter was now swimming lazily towards the deep end again and looking round to see where he had gone. He dropped down into hiding and, after a little, heard her pull herself up on to the wall. He waited a moment to see what she was going to do and then, as she made no further move, pulled himself slowly and quietly up. She was only about three yards away sitting with her back to him, with her feet in the water. As he watched she brushed a hand across her eyes.

With a final effort he heaved himself up beside her and said, "Hullo! Why didn't you answer me when I called?"

She jumped in surprise and then would have slipped into the water if he hadn't grabbed her arm. She wriggled fiercely and turned on him in a fury. "Let me go, you beast."

But the imperturbable David was also annoyed, so he held on.

"Don't be a silly ass, Peter," he said. "What's it all about?"

She actually gulped and there were tears in her eyes as she said in a shaky voice, "Fancy asking *me* what it's all about! There's nothing about! I can swim here if I want to, I suppose. I thought I was going swimming with you, but I made a mistake. You'd rather go messing about with old sluices and wheels and things. You'd better go and find Daddy and he'll lend you the key and you can spend the rest of the day there … I only hope the others come soon…" and she wriggled free and slipped into the water.

Without quite realizing it, David did the right thing. He stood up, breathed deep, and dived – down, down into the clear green depths. He opened his eyes and looked up through the water. Just ahead and above him he could see Peter swimming away. He kicked hard and came up to the surface. He shook the water out of his hair and puffed. "Oh, Peter," he said, "this is grand. That's the best dive I've ever had. What a wonderful place this is. Let's race to the other end."

She looked at him over her shoulder, grinned sheepishly, and said, "Right. Go!"

Peter swam very well indeed, but David was better. He had been well taught and he really loved the water, but he did the second wise thing he'd done in three minutes. He let Peter win.

After that all was well, but in spite of the sun the water was surprisingly cold, and they didn't stay in very long. The wall of the dam was hot to the touch and they lay there, full in the sun, for a little.

"I wonder what's happened to the twins, David? I suppose Tom can't come, so they've had to stay at Witchend. P'raps they'd show your mother the map, though, and she'd let them come on their own! I tell you what! My clothes are in that secret place I showed you – I'll run over and dress now, and meet you up on that ridge on the right. I used to have a look-out hut there – like the one I built at Lone Pine – and we could watch from there and see if the others are coming up the valley. It's the highest place round here, and you can practically see the summit." She ran off along the side of the water and disappeared into the heather. David was dressed in two minutes, spread his towel and trunks on the warm stones to dry, and started for the ridge she had pointed out. It was farther than he thought, but Peter caught him up before he got to the top.

"There's not much of my hut left now," she panted, "but we might re-make it. Yes, here's the place, and there are three of the stakes I put in. It's a fine spot, isn't it?"

They flung themselves down in the heather and looked down into the Hatchholt valley. They could follow the white track right down to the first turn, and David realized again how steep and narrow was this wild valley, and wondered what it would be like in winter.

"They're certainly not there," David said.

"No. Maybe they're not coming," Peter agreed. Then she turned away from him and said in a very small voice, "I'm sorry I was such a beast. I was very rude to you, and I'm sorry."

David felt most uncomfortable. He had forgotten all about this particular incident.

"That's all right, Peter," he muttered. "I was a silly ass, too. Let's forget it. We're both Lone-Piners, and we've sworn to stand by each other, haven't we?"

She sat up and faced him with shining eyes.

"Of *course* we have, David. I'd forgotten that as well as my manners. We're friends again, aren't we?"

David felt rather shy about looking at her and was, without quite realizing it, watching the opposite hillside over her shoulder. Suddenly he stiffened, gripped her arm, and pulled her down into the heather beside him.

"What's the matter?" she said, rubbing her arm ruefully.

"Look up on the opposite ridge," he whispered. "Don't let yourself be seen, and tell me if you see what I see … And put something over your hair. The sun shines on it so that you could be seen a mile away."

"But I haven't got anything," she said indignantly. "I'll be careful. Let me look," and she pulled up a root of heather and held it over her head. For a long minute she was silent, and then she whistled in astonishment.

"David! It is Mrs Thurston, but what on earth is she doing? She keeps moving about and pointing to something down here. What *is* she up to?"

"Wait a minute, Peter. We must find a place where we can be certain we can watch her without being seen. I'm so afraid she'll see your head and your blue shirt. I'll crawl down to that big clump, and you stay where you are. Don't move."

In a minute or two he had reached better shelter. They were near enough to speak to each other without being heard by Mrs Thurston a quarter of a mile away on the opposite side of the reservoir.

"Come down here slowly if you like," he called.

"I'll stay," Peter replied. "It's all right if we can talk, and I can watch her too."

David watched Mrs Thurston's dark head move against the skyline; saw her light a cigarette with a characteristic action, and then sit down in the heather. Although the sun was very hot she was wearing what looked like a drab raincoat, and so was rather difficult to see until she stood up. Once the sun glinted on something she was holding, and David realized with a shock that she had a pair of field-glasses. She was still for a long time … Just watching. It was difficult to realize where the glasses were pointed, but he called to Peter again to be careful. Then she got up and there was no doubt that she was watching the reservoir and the dam. She moved along below the top of the ridge, but still in their sight.

"David," Peter hissed. "Do you see what she's doing? She's taking photographs now. Those are not the glasses that she's holding up to her face now – it's one of those little cameras that take such marvellous pictures. A girl at school has got one … I'm positive that's what she is doing."

He was certain too. There was no doubt of it, and he suddenly felt very uneasy. There was something odd and furtive about Mrs Thurston this afternoon that he didn't like.

Then they watched her make her way round so that she was looking down on to the dam from the valley side. She was too far away now for them to see precisely what she was doing, but there was little doubt that she was also taking photographs from a different angle.

Peter scrambled down beside him. "She can't see me now," she said, "and I don't much care if she can. I'm sick of holding that heather over my face. What do you think she's doing, David?"

He rolled over on his back. "I don't know," he said shortly, "but I don't like it, and I think there's something fishy about her. Why should she want to take photographs of your father's reservoir? He told me how important all this water was to the Midlands, and she's doing nothing but spying about the place in secret. We must go and tell your father at once. And Mr Ingles is a Home Guard … I'm going to tell him. Come on!"

Peter suddenly looked serious. "You don't think…?" she began. Then, "Look! She's coming back."

As they watched, Mrs Thurston returned the same way, climbed the ridge, and without once looking behind her disappeared in the direction of the track that led to the top of the mountain. Peter got up and stretched. "She's spoiled the afternoon," she grumbled. "I suppose you're right, David, and we'd better go home and tell Daddy. Perhaps the others are there now, and we can bathe again before tea. I thought we were going to have such a lovely time."

But David was thinking over the events of the last few days, and wondering whether they really had discovered something serious. It would be silly to start imagining things, but there was something unusual about Mrs Thurston's behaviour, and it might just be that the Lone-Piners had seen more than anyone else. It was difficult up here to remember the war, but even as Peter put out a hand to pull him to his feet he was thinking of his father's face as he said "Goodbye," and he remembered too the sirens in London and the crash of the bombs in those days that seemed so long ago.

"Cheer up, David," Peter said. "Maybe there's nothing to worry about. Let's go home and have some tea, and see if the others are there."

But they were not. Mr Sterling was alone in the garden picking runner beans, and because he was not very tall he was standing on a wooden chair, the seat of which was carefully covered with newspaper. When Peter called, "What about some tea, Daddy?" he swayed violently, and stepped off into the onion bed.

"Don't startle me, girl!" he said, as he carefully adjusted the tops of the disturbed onions so that all were again pointing in the same direction. "Beans must be properly picked, and every plant left tidy. Go and put the kettle on, and cut some bread and butter."

David went in with Peter and fidgeted while she laid the table. Twice he wandered out and climbed up the wall of the dam to see if Tom and the twins were coming, but the valley was deserted and so were the hill-tops. Only the hum of insects in the heather broke the silence.

At tea David could keep silent no longer, and poured out his story to Mr Sterling. He told of their first meeting with Jacob at the station and of his peculiar, threatening manner, and also of their visit to Appledore, and of the way Mrs Thurston had questioned them and then, after the cry of the owl, had rushed them home and so prevented them returning over the top of the mountain.

"And then this afternoon, Mr Sterling," he went on, "we saw her taking photographs of the dam … and sort of spying round here and watching through glasses … And I thought – *we* thought – maybe that it was something to do with the reservoir and the water supply for the cities you told me about, and I'm wondering whether we ought to go and tell somebody about her. What do you think, sir?"

"What do *I* think young man? What would I think except that you've been reading too many books or going to the cinema? Stop worrying yourself, lad, 'bout things that don't concern you. You're new up here, and maybe don't know our ways yet. We try to keep ourselves to ourselves, and give each other a hand when 'tis needed, but we don't interfere."

David went very red.

"I'm not wanting to interfere, sir," he said. "And if you don't think I need to say anything to anybody, I won't. But we've been to her house, and I can't see why she should take photographs of Hatchholt. Why should she?"

Mr Sterling chuckled. "How do you know she was a-taking pictures of us? She was taking pictures of birds I'll be bound. Many a stranger has come up to the mountain to watch birds and take pictures of 'em. I met your Mrs Thurston once, lad, and she told me why she'd taken Appledore. She's interested in birds and wild things, and that's why she's so often about on the mountain ... Why, she told me herself, boy, so must be so! Cut yourself a piece of my best cake and welcome and forget the woman."

David grinned ruefully, and followed this advice.

"But I wish those youngsters of yours had come along," Mr Sterling went on, "I've seen some strange things in my life, but nothing as like as those twins." And then, with an effort, he dragged his mind back to the exciting present. "And your swimming," he went on, "how did you get on with spoiling my fishing? My Peter's a bonny swimmer, and I doubt if you could catch her."

Peter looked at David under her lashes as he said, "No, sir – I couldn't. She's too fast for me."

They helped to wash up, but somehow David couldn't settle down to much else, and was feeling very uneasy when Peter tried to persuade him to go swimming again.

"I don't think I will, Peter," he said. "I'd love it really, but I'm worried about the twins, and think I ought to get back. Will you walk down the valley with me till we get to the turning?"

She didn't try to keep him so he said, "Goodbye and thank you" to Mr Sterling, who told him to come again soon and bring the little 'uns, and they started down the track by the pipe-line.

"We must swim all we can while the hot weather lasts," Peter said. "Will you all come tomorrow and really try and get Tom? We can go to the Lone Pine when it's cooler, and we can have a fire … I'd love to see Mary doing what she called the sprawl … Oh, and David … why did you tell Daddy that you couldn't catch me swimming? You know you can race me."

He went very red. "No, I couldn't. You're jolly good. You beat me this afternoon."

"I've never seen a better swimmer than you, David," she said, and her eyes were shining.

When they came to the turning, David broke a long silence. "Look here," he said. "We'll come tomorrow, if we can. We'll come this way, and you meet us about twelve. We'll bring sandwiches and Tom too, if we can get him. 'Bye, Peter. See you tomorrow."

She was still standing looking after him with a puzzled frown on her face when he stopped and came back to her.

"Peter!" he called. "Here, wait a minute! Don't mind me asking, but do you think your father is right about Mrs Thurston? Honestly, do you think I'm silly about her, and had better forget all about it? Do you *really* think so?"

157

"I don't know, David. I think she's all right, really; and Daddy did tell us about her bird-watching."

"You *do* think I'm crazy then? Why don't you say so if you think so?"

She shook her head miserably. "I don't think you're silly, David. I just can't understand it all. Why don't you forget her? … It's getting cold. I shivered then."

She looked back towards the top of the valley, and then gripped his arm. "The sun has gone … we're going to have Mynd mist. You'd better hurry home, David. Shall I come with you or can you find the way now?"

"No need for you to come, Peter. Of course I can manage. Straight down here into the lane where I tried to ride Sally, and then turn right till I come to the track round the hill to Ingles or go a little further and cut through to Witchend. It looks as if it's worse at the top."

"Yes, it is, but I could find my way blindfold. It's just that Daddy will worry … Very well. Goodbye, Captain. See you here tomorrow if it's fine enough for a swim, and if not I'll ride over to you," and she grinned, saluted him, and turned back into Hatchholt.

David hurried on. It was cold now, and the hilltops were hazy, but he reached the lane without difficulty. All was very still. Even the birds were quiet, and the world seemed to be waiting for something unknown, and when he put a hand to his pocket the tweed of his jacket was damp. Then the road grew indistinct, and the cold white mist came rolling silently down from the hills. He passed the track to Ingles knowing that he must go straight home now, but just before he reached the short cut which Peter had shown him that morning, he stopped in surprise.

Faintly, yet unmistakably, there came the sound of an aeroplane. It was difficult to guess its direction, but suddenly the heavy air throbbed fiercely as the machine passed nearly overhead and David spared a thought for the unfortunate pilot caught in such weather, and wondered how he would find his way back to his aerodrome when all he could see was a flat soft surface of billowing cotton-wool. He wondered, too, how he would avoid the hills if he couldn't see them. As he hurried along the path by the sodden bracken, the noise of the engine died away, and when at last he came to their own familiar white gate, the silence was complete again.

As he raised the latch of the front door he called out cheerfully: "Here I am, Mummy. Hope you weren't worried about me. How is Mrs Ingles, and what have the twins been up to?"

Mrs Morton came out of the living-room at the sound of his step, with her usual happy smile of welcome. As he spoke, the smile faded and she said quickly, "Aren't the twins with you, David?"

He shook his head.

"But they *must* be. You're not playing a game with me, David old chap? They're not hiding outside in the mist, are they?"

"But, Mummy, I thought they were with you. We left a note for them saying where we were and telling them to come with Tom. When they didn't come I supposed that he couldn't bring them, and that they'd be here."

His mother's face was very white.

"Come here!" she said, and led the way into the kitchen. "Agnes, the twins are not with Master David.

Tell me quickly, what they said to you this morning."

Agnes told what she knew, and David added again Peter's news about the camp, and the message she had left for them.

"Listen, David! You must go as quickly as you can to Ingles. It's just possible they may be there, or that Tom is bringing them home through the mist now, although Agnes has not been very long back. If they are *not* there, ask Mr Ingles what is the best thing to do. Let me know quickly, but find him first. He'll help us. Go on your bike if you can see and if it will be quicker, but *hurry*, old man, and find them for me."

David gave his mother a quick hug and went out again into the mist. He felt sick and afraid, but somehow couldn't believe that the twins were actually lost. It just couldn't happen, but this was a real chance for the Lone-Piners to prove themselves. The fog was worse now, and as he could no longer see the big gate he knew it would be useless to cycle. He wondered what it would be like when it was dark, and had the sense to run back for his torch. Then, for a minute, he stood by the stream and called and whistled the Peewit's cry. But the latter was a forlorn and feeble little effort, and his voice seemed to come back to him muffled and thwarted.

Twice in the lane he stopped and called again: "Dickie! Mary! Where are you, twins? Can you hear me?"

But the only answer was the slow drip, drip of moisture falling from the trees.

Chapter 7

Appledore

Alone, on the top of the mountain, with the heather already damp and cold against their bare knees, the twins stood hand-in-hand as the mist slid like a silent, silvery ghost around them. The Stiperstones vanished even as Dickie whispered, "He's in his chair, Mary."

There seemed nothing to say, and Mary fought back the horrid tight lump in her throat, and tried hard not to cry out as her twin's fingers gripped her own fiercely. Then she put the shivering Macbeth on his lead and looked back where she believed Hatchholt to be. But although in this direction, the mist was not quite as thick, the track was only just visible. For a moment she felt that she must run blindly down that little path ... on and on until she found something or someone who would spirit her away from this beastliness and put them all safe by the wood fire at Witchend. And when she thought of Witchend and Mummy and David and Agnes the lump crept up into her mouth almost, and the tears scalded her eyes. She groped in her knickers for her handkerchief, but Dickie had one ready for her. His voice was funny, too, when he said, "Are you frightened, twin?"

"Not ... not 'zactly *frightened*, Dickie," Mary gulped. "Just something in my throat. This old fog, I 'spect."

161

"I am," said Dickie. "I don't think you're saying truth, Mary. I hate it."

"Well," said Mary. "I couldn't let you be it by yourself. P'raps I am a bit too."

This cheered Dickie considerably. "*That's* all right, then," he said. "If we're both frightened it's not so bad. What shall we do?"

If Peter had been there she would have recognized again the same look in Mary's eyes that she had noticed when they spoke of Ludlow Castle. Her father knew this look well, too, and loved it. Always when he saw it he would wonder in what strange world his little daughter was wandering, and whether her dream would come true. And so when Dickie, quite naturally, asked her what they were going to do she brushed her hand across her eyes and held her chin high and looked hard into the mist before she said:

"I don't know yet, Dickie, what's best to do, but this is the biggest adventure we've ever had, and I know we've got to be *specially* brave … Think what we've got to tell the others now, and 'member that Mummy and Daddy will ask if we've been brave…"

"Yes," said Dickie. "An' Daddy and David'll ask us something else, too. They'll want to know if we've been sensible … Come on, then, Mary! Let's be brave … Let's make another swear that whatever happens we won't cry once … Now I'm Sir Richard…"

He felt for her hand and squeezed it again. Then he shivered and could feel Mary shaking too.

"Dickie," she said after a little. "I don't think it's a good idea just to stand here. Which way shall we go?"

Then Dickie was sensible.

"If we try and go to Hatchholt it's a long way, and we shan't know whether we're going the right way 'cos this part of the mountain is so big. Let's go back to Appledore. It's not far, and we'll know we're right because it will be downhill soon through the wood ... I 'spect that Mrs Thurston's a witch, but John would help us, and I think that's the best thing to do."

"Come on, then," said Mary. "I'm hungry too."

"Gosh!" said Dickie. "So am I. We didn't have any tea after all, and now she'll have to give us supper, p'raps."

So, slowly and carefully, with Dickie in front, they went back the way they had come. Even in sunlight the little path had been nearly invisible with the heather so high, but now, when they could only see a few yards ahead, they kept losing it altogether.

"Much better be Red Wolf, the Indian Chief," said Mary, when Dickie fell over a root and brought her down with him. They found the path again, but for a second Mary had a frightful feeling that they were facing the wrong way, and going back towards Hatchholt. It was rather like the feeling when you wake up suddenly in the night and cannot remember the position of the door or the window. They walked on like this for what seemed like hours, but was only five minutes. Macbeth was a misery, and although he wagged his tail feebly when addressed, the spirit seemed to have gone out of him. Once he pulled Mary away to the right, and she followed him without thinking. Dickie went on ahead. Suddenly she realized she was alone and shouted wildly, "Dickie! DICKIE! Where are you? I'm lost!"

But he was only about ten yards away, and waited for her.

"Better hold on to each other," he said.

Whether or not they did keep to the track they had used on the way up they never knew, but after a little while they felt the ground sloping downhill under their feet. "We've done it, Mary. We're real path-finders and trackers all right. All we got to do now is to go on downhill, and we'll find that old witch and have some supper."

Mary's teeth were chattering. "C-c-c-come on then. Let's hurry, Dickie. I feel beastly."

And this is where they went wrong. There was no proper path to follow, and although by going steadily downhill they soon reached a few trees, they could not tell whether they had been there before. Macbeth seemed to try to lead them sometimes, but his trail usually finished up in a briar bush or at a rabbit-hole. Mary and he were in front of one of these excursions which led them steadily downhill when, out of the white fog, something large and black loomed out at them. She stopped so suddenly that Dickie blundered into her.

"What is it?" he whispered.

Whatever it was it remained still and silent shrouded in the fog. For the last hundred yards there had been no trees or brambles, and this great bulk was particularly frightening as the twins stood under it. Mary let go Macbeth's lead without realizing it, and the little dog sauntered ahead without fear or enthusiasm.

Then Dickie laughed. "Gosh! We're chumps, Mary. Don't you see what it is? It's a rock!"

And so it was. A big outcrop of rock bursting out of

the hillside and hanging forward over the close turf which was dry in its shadow. Mary sat down with her back to it, and pulled Macbeth on to her lap.

"Come on, Mackie! We're all wet and cold and dirty, so it doesn't matter. Let's keep each other warm … You come too, Dickie! Let's have a rest."

Dickie was ready. He didn't say much, but snuggled down beside his sister, and without a word they put an arm round each other and shared a little of the other's warmth. Mary had stopped shivering when Macbeth's ears cocked, and they heard the sound of an aeroplane. It was the first sound besides their own steps and voices and the drip of moisture which they had heard since the fog came down on them. The plane came nearer.

"It's very low, Dickie. It's coming here…" And with a mighty roar it seemed as if it passed only a few hundred feet above their heads. Then it seemed to circle and come back again.

"He's lost, Mary. That's what it is. He's like us and doesn't know where he is. Wish I was up there, though."

Again his words were drowned by the roar of the engines as the lost pilot tried to find his bearings by picking out a landmark. They heard him for a few minutes longer, and then the blanket of fog closed down and muffled the distant throbbing.

Under the rock the two children and the dog waited. They were warmer and drier now, but getting very hungry. For once Dickie refrained from mentioning his appetite, but he was so hungry that it hurt. Every now and then Macbeth looked up and licked Mary's face, but nobody had any suggestions. It was getting darker now –

not really dark, but the whiteness of the fog was turning grey. Dickie was wondering what he ought to say or do, and was struggling very hard to keep back his "swear" about a tear, when the silence was broken strangely again. From far away, somewhere below them where the wood must be, came the cry of an owl.

"Tu-whoooo! Tu-whit. Tu-ooooooo!" it called.

"Perhaps he's lonely, too," said Mary.

The call came again. Nearer. Then, by some odd chance, the mist began to clear a little and, as the children listened and watched, they could see the shape of trees at the edge of the wood below them.

They stood up. "It's going, Mary. The fog's disappearing."

"It isn't really going, twin, but it's moving. What a funny old owl. It's quite near."

And while they listened the first owl's cry was answered, loud and clear, quite close to them. It seemed to come from a little higher up the hill and behind the rock. Macbeth barked, and at the same time they heard someone crashing about in the undergrowth somewhere in the wood below them. Dickie was just going to shout when a man came out of the trees, put his hands to his mouth, and hooted like an owl. Macbeth barked again, and the stranger looked up in surprise. Then the children saw that the man was Jacob from Appledore, and, much as they disliked him, they ran down the hillside towards him while a cold, dank wind eddied some more mist into the clearing.

Mary reached him first. "Please, Mr Jacob," she said, "please take us to Appledore. We don't know where we are, and we can't get home over the top 'cos the fog is too thick."

Then Dickie and Mac arrived, and Jacob looked at them all as if he hated them.

"Why do you children not go away and stay away? Always you are a nuisance. Go away. This is private."

"But you can't just go and leave us here," said Dickie indignantly. "You just can't beastly-jolly-well do it! Can't you see we're lost – and cold *and* hungry," he added more brightly.

But Jacob was in a hurry, and was also very angry. He began to back away from them across the clearing.

"Go home!" he shouted. "You are not wanted in this place. You will get into trouble. Go away, I say."

Dickie ran after him.

"We're not going to stay here all alone in this beastly fog, and don't you think it."

"No," Mary chimed in. "No! Don't you dare think it. We're coming with you wherever you go till you take us home – or back to Appledore. You can't make us stay away from you."

By now Jacob was almost spluttering with rage while the twins were rapidly recovering their spirits. Anything – even Jacob – was better than being alone on the mountain!

"Come here," Jacob shouted angrily, and made a sudden grab at Dickie, who dodged him easily enough. At the same time Macbeth went into battle and snapped viciously at the man's ankle and then circled round him warily, growling and snarling, before Mary grabbed his lead and pulled him away.

"Don't you dare do that again," she said breathlessly. "Don't you try and hurt us. Dickie and me is brave today, and we're just going where you go till you take us somewhere safe."

Then Dickie spoke up. "And another thing. What were you hootin' for? Have you gone mad or something? Pretendin' to be an owl!"

"Just a silly old man," added Mary scornfully. "Hootin'! Not much like an owl, anyway!"

Jacob's fists were clenching and unclenching at his side, and he was actually hopping first on one foot and then on the other as the twins retired just out of the reach of his long arms. Then the silence was broken first by a sharp bark from the dog, and then by the sudden loud hoot of an owl from somewhere near.

"We heard that just now," said Dickie. "Seems to be some funny people about today in this wood."

At this Jacob actually produced a sickly smile.

"And so you heard the owl cry before, little ones? And where was it you heard it? Over past that rock, you say? Listen! Jacob will take you back to Appledore, and perhaps he take you home later and you forget the adventure in the wood, eh? Now you wait here till Jacob comes back. He goes to find the owl in the nest. That is why he make the owl noise – to catch the early bird on the nest. Ha! ha!"

The twins gazed at this transformation in astonishment. Jacob, smiling and trying to be pleasant, was almost more unpleasant than Jacob in a rage. Then the owl cry came again, and he started off quickly towards the other side of the clearing. The fog was thicker now, and he would soon have been out of sight if the children had not run after him.

"That's all right," Dickie said. "We'll come with you and see the owl on his nest. If you go away now maybe we'll lose you."

"There's another thing we heard," said Mary.

"What was that?" said Jacob quickly.

"A big 'plane. Right over here."

"Practically knocked our heads off," added Dickie.

Then Jacob seemed to make up his mind. He put his hands up to his mouth and hooted, and the answer came back to him at once from higher up the wood. Then he turned and looked oddly at the children. "Come," he said. "We will go and find this bird," and he led the way uphill through the trees. Twice again he called, and twice came the answer through the fog. And as they toiled uphill he talked loudly to the twins, almost as if he wished their voices to be heard.

Then came a new voice from just in front of them. "Help!" someone was calling. "This way, please, whoever you are. Where are you?"

And so they found the owl – the mysterious bird on his nest. Under a rock a white-faced man in a raincoat was lying. He was young and pleasant looking, and smiled when he saw them. One foot was stretched out awkwardly, but the twins' eyes opened wide in amazement when they saw beside him, half trailing from a tree, a muddle of strings, straps and billowing silver-grey material. Before they could speak he said: "Hullo! Did you hear me call? Was it one of you hooting like an owl?"

"Yes," said Jacob quickly. "I hoot like an owl. These

children – they are lost in the mist and I find them. You have hurt yourself?"

The stranger nodded. "Ankle twisted. Rather painful. I suppose I'd better tell you who I am. I bet you'd like to know, wouldn't you, young man?" he added, turning to Dickie.

"Yes – we would," Mary answered shortly.

The man looked at her and grinned.

"Yes. We're twins," said Dickie. "Just alike. We do the same things."

"And this," continued Mary, "is Jacob. He lives at Appledore, and he's taking us back there 'cos we got lost on the mountain in the fog."

"Is that place your home?" the man asked.

"Oh, no! That's where Mrs Thurston lives."

"I see. D'you think she'd look after me till I get this ankle right?"

"Now I know what that is," Dickie broke in excitedly. "It's a parachute! You've fallen out of a 'plane."

"You're right, son. That's just what I've done, and now I've got to let you into my secret, but you must promise faithfully not to tell anyone. Do you both promise?"

"We swear," said Mary solemnly.

"Very well. I'm a British officer, and it's one of my jobs to test parachutes in all kinds of weather."

"That must be pretty difficult," said Dickie.

"You must be very brave," added Mary.

"Oh! I don't know about that, but it's nice of you to say so. Anyway, we hope we're going to drop in Germany one day, and there are all sorts of points which have to be watched and tested. We thought we'd try coming down i fog today, and you can see what I've done. I've twisted my ankle. Beastly 'chute caught in the tree."

"It's a funny thing," said Dickie thoughtfully, "but we're always finding people."

"What do you mean?" Jacob asked sharply.

"Well, there was a man we trailed the other day up on the mountain. And then just this morning we found John Davies in a secret place, and this afternoon somebody was runnin' about in the woods down by the house. There's always people about this place."

"And owls," added Mary.

Jacob looked surprised. "It is not so. You think you see them, but you don't. It is a fairy story. Silly."

"D'you think we don't jolly well know what we see…?" Dickie began, but the man on the ground interrupted him.

"Never mind that now. Just help me get this 'chute folded, old chap. My ankle is hurting me, and I'm hungry and cold, and I'd like to get going, but I can't walk without help." He turned to Jacob. "If you'd just help me up and let me lean on you and take the weight off the foot, I think I could manage if it's not too far."

"Not very far," Jacob said.

The twins folded the 'chute; it was of very thin, silky material, but was extremely difficult to fold neatly, particularly as Mac created a diversion by getting mixed up in it. Then with Jacob's help, the man somehow heaved himself up and they noticed that he had a heavy knapsack on his back. When he saw them looking curiously at it he explained:

"We have to test the 'chutes with extra weight because

171

if we were in action we'd be carrying guns and ammunition and all sorts of things."

"Better if I carry it for you," said Jacob.

"Thank you," said the stranger, "but I think not. Too much bother to take it off now. Let's get on. I'm hungry."

"Gosh!" said Dickie. "So am I. Faintin'."

The fog was still as thick, but Jacob led the way down to the big clearing again, past the rock under which they had sheltered, and then into the wood. Progress was slow because the stranger could only hobble a few steps at a time, and the twins noticed how he winced when his twisted foot touched the ground. Nobody talked much, and even Macbeth looked dank and unhappy. Jacob paused once or twice, and how he was able to find his way through the gloom and fog was a mystery they never solved. But he did guide them well, and it was not many minutes before they were on the path again, and it was only a matter of sticking to the track. The twins were now so tired that Mary hardly knew what she was doing. She could feel her eyes closing and her head nodding, but seemed to have no control over her feet. Every now and then she clutched at her brother to save herself from falling.

"I'm so sleepy, Dickie," she whispered. "What d'you think they'll do to us?"

"I'm so hungry. Oh, gosh, I'm hungry! I don't care what they do, Mary, just if they give us some supper."

So they staggered down to Appledore, and in the garden Jacob said to the children, "You go to the front door and I let you in. I take the officer this way at the back. It is quicker."

Dickie pinched his sister's arm to wake her and said firmly, "No, thank you. We'll come with you if it's quicker. I'm hungry and Mary's sleepy – an' if she's too sleepy to eat her supper I can manage hers too. Don't leave us out here in the cold. We'll come with you."

"You will do what I say…" Jacob began, but the officer interrupted him:

"Come along, and don't argue. I can't manage much more of this hobbling. Let's try the front door."

Grumbling and muttering, Jacob went round to the front and banged on the knocker – once, twice quickly, and once again. Then the door opened and everybody seemed to talk at once. The twins, from behind, saw Mrs Thurston in her red frock step back in surprise. The usual cigarette was smouldering between her lips. Then Jacob started to explain, and the stranger began to thank her for her hospitality, and Dickie spoke louder than anyone, so that they all turned to listen to him.

"And please hurry up and let us in, 'cos we're tired and hungry, and we've had the biggest adventure. We've been lost on the mountain and the old Devil was in his Chair, and the fog came, and we heard the 'plane, and then this officer hooting like an owl…"

"And what do you think, Mrs Thurston?" added Mary, now more or less awake. "Did you know Jacob tries to hoot like an owl too?"

"He's not too good," said Dickie.

"He wanted to find the owl on his nest," Mary went on.

"Come in quickly, and don't talk so much," said Mrs Thurston sharply. "It must be nearly black-out time. You children are a nuisance. First you come and then you run away, and now Jacob tells me he found you wandering about in the wood."

She closed the front door behind them and stood with her back to it as the stranger was led by Jacob to an easy chair. Dickie thought he could hear men's voices near, but as he now had a most unusual pain in his stomach, and as the pain was accompanied by enormous rumblings, his mind turned to other matters.

"We're very hungry," he said slowly and distinctly.

Mrs Thurston blew a stream of smoke up to the ceiling and looked down at the bedraggled little boy and girl standing side by side. Her eyes were hard, and Mary shivered as she looked up at her through the smoke.

"We want to go home," she said. "Please take us home or tell Mummy we're here. I don't want anything to eat. I just want to go home…" and on the last words her voice broke a little.

"Oh, no!" Mrs Thurston shook her head. "Oh, no! I can't take you home. You've come back here and now you must stay."

"But *please*…" Dickie began, and then suddenly she smiled, shrugged her shoulders, and dropped her cigarette end on the stone floor and trod on it.

"Come along," she said. "Never mind about going home now. Dickie's hungry. I know he is, and so is Mary really. I'll get you some supper and we'll make plans presently," and she led them down the hall to the little room from which they had escaped earlier in the day. On the way the man in the chair grinned at them.

"Thanks for finding me," he said. "I'll give you a bit of my parachute as a souvenir before you go."

174

"Thank you," said Mary politely. "We shall like that."

Mrs Thurston switched on the light and closed the door. Dickie moved to the table when he saw that the tea had not yet been cleared away.

"You are both a great worry to me," Mrs Thurston began, "but you had better stay here now and have something to eat while I go and look after the poor wounded officer. Jacob shall bring you a hot drink, and I will come back and see you presently."

Almost before she was out of the room Dickie had started on the bread and butter.

"Come on, Mary. We'll feel better when we've had something to eat. Gosh! I just can't wait."

But Mary was shaking with weariness. She didn't feel hungry now, and all she wanted was her little bed at Witchend. She wanted to snuggle down and draw her knees almost up to her chin and forget everything and be warm. She was feeling funny, too – not really ill, but sort of swimmy. When she looked at Dickie his face wavered to and fro, and she couldn't really be sure of what he was saying.

"I want to go to sleep, Dickie," she heard herself answering. "Leave me alone. I'm cold, too."

So she sat down on the rug in front of the dying fire and rested her head against a chair and was asleep in three seconds. Dimly she remembered being lifted into the chair by Jacob, who made up the fire, and it seemed hours later when Dickie shook her awake.

"You've just got to have this, Mary," he was saying. "You're being silly. Wake up and have this while it's hot, and I'm eating all the bread and butter and there'll be nothing left for you. Old wizard Jacob brought it, and jus' now he came and put you in the chair. Gosh! I feel much better."

She yawned and stretched and suddenly felt hungry, too. The hot milk was just what she needed, and now the fire was blazing up merrily and for a little they both forgot where they were and what had happened. Mary was the first to remember.

"Dickie," she said as she sat back on her heels and held out her grubby little hands to the flames, "what are we going to do now? It's dark outside and Mummy doesn't know where we are. Do you think they'll come and find us?"

"I don't know, Mary. Maybe we're prisoners again. We're always being captives or explorers. It's jolly excitin', but I don't think the others are going to be awfully pleased about us."

"We've *got* to go home, Dickie. Mrs Thurston will just have to take us. We'll make her."

"What's that I've got to do?" came a voice from the door. The twins looked up to see her standing there with her red frock and shoes and a cigarette between her fingers. Although her voice hadn't sounded horrid, she wasn't smiling when they turned round.

"Thank you very much for our nice supper," Dickie said, "and thank you for the hot drink and letting us stay here. My sister has had a nice rest, and now please we'd like to go home."

"But you can't possibly go home. Don't be ridiculous children."

"We've got to go back to Mummy *at once*," Mary said

and she hoped her voice didn't sound as trembly as it felt. "Mummy will be just *desprit* about us. Please take us now, and we're very sorry if we've been a bother."

Mrs Thurston came in and closed the door. "Now, both of you listen to me very carefully and stop talking nonsense. You cannot possibly go back to Witchend tonight. It's dark now and still foggy, and the car is out of order."

"Please," said Dickie, "please, couldn't you take us?"

"It's Mummy we're so worried about," Mary went on. "You see, she doesn't know where we are."

"Of course I can't take you," she said sharply. "I've got this officer to look after, and then my nephew has come specially to see me…"

"…Why, John would take us, Mrs Thurston! I'm sure he would. We took him this morning, and now he's had a rest from his suitcase he'd take us home. Please ask him to come now and tell him the way we have to go."

"Oh, no. He can't go tonight, and neither can Jacob … No, you must get used to the idea of spending the night here – there's a bedroom upstairs for you. You shall go home directly after breakfast in the morning … Now, I was wondering whether you would like to tell me all about your adventures in the wood and on the mountain this afternoon? You must have had some real adventures before Jacob found you. Perhaps you saw and heard someone else besides the English officer. Did you?"

The twins looked at each other quietly. Then:

"Thank you very much, Mrs Thurston," Mary began, "but we must be going now."

"We'll just go along by ourselves. We'll go down the

lane and into the road, and we shall be all right," Dickie went on, and made a dash for the door.

Mrs Thurston smiled as he tugged in vain at the handle.

"It's locked," he whispered. "She's locked it, Mary."

"Let us out," Mary stormed. "How *dare* you lock us in? I'll call for John. He'll help us … John! John! It's us here again. Come and help us!"

Mrs Thurston flung her cigarette in the fire, jumped up from the arm of the chair on which she was sitting, and pulled Mary away from the door. Her face was white with anger. "Be quiet, you naughty, disobedient little girl. Be quiet!"

Dickie opened his mouth to call for help, too, but the look on Mrs Thurston's face frightened him, and before he could do more she swung him away and then held them both at arm's length.

"Now listen to me and be sensible children. You cannot go home tonight. The fog is still bad and there is nobody here who can take you. You certainly cannot go by yourselves, as it is too far, too dark, and too dangerous. In the morning, early before breakfast, Jacob shall go to your mother on his motor-cycle and tell her you are safe and sound and will be coming home soon. You are to go to bed now, and you are not to call out to *anybody*. Not to anybody. Do you understand?"

The twins looked at her and gulped. She looked so angry that for a moment they were afraid. Her red lips were set in a hard line in her white face and her eyes looked big and dark. She held them each by a shoulder, and her fingers gripped so hard that they both winced. Try as she would, Mary could not keep the tears from her eyes, but somehow she stopped them from falling. And Dickie was the same. They felt very small and lonely after all their adventures, and there didn't seem to be anything they could do, but suddenly Dickie remembered his mother and how she would be worrying. He still felt guilty about leaving Witchend and going with John in the morning, and as Mrs Thurston's fingers were still hurting his shoulder he unexpectedly twisted out of her grasp and made a dash for the door and shouted, "John! John!"

Then Mrs Thurston lost her temper. She pulled him back roughly and slapped him hard across the mouth. Dickie's face went white, but he stood still and quiet, watching her – a tired but brave little boy facing a grownup he couldn't understand. But not so Mary. Someone had once said of the Morton children – and of the twins in particular – that they often squabbled over details, but if anyone had the temerity to criticize them "the ranks closed"! Now it was Mary's turn again to defend her beloved twin.

She was so angry that the tears streamed from her eyes without her realizing that she was crying. She could see the red marks of Mrs Thurston's fingers across the white of Dickie's cheek, and she could see, too, how his lip was trembling. She forgot her mother and Witchend, and the Lone-Piners, and everything except Dickie and Mrs Thurston.

"You utter beast!" she said. "You hit him! Yes, you did. You great beastly bully! I'll tell everybody 'bout you. Everybody I see I'll tell you hit Dickie. He didn't do anything … we only want to go home … No! I won't be quiet. I'll shout and scream till somebody…"

At this Mrs Thurston raised her hand again, but before she could strike Mary, Macbeth, who had been sleeping the sleep of exhaustion under the table, took a share in the proceedings and jumped out at his enemy, growling fiercely. Mrs Thurston had forgotten him and backed to the door, taking the key from her pocket.

"Hold him back, Mary!" she said quickly. "Keep him off!" Then she turned to Dickie. "I'm sorry about that, Dickie," she said. "You shouldn't have made me so angry. I didn't mean to hit you, but you were so disobedient and naughty. Now will you be sensible children and go quietly to bed, and I promise you shall go home in the morning?"

Mary, holding Macbeth, looked up at her steadily.

"It's no good you being sorry now," she said. "You hit him … look at his face! All right. We'll go to bed now if you won't let us go home. But we're not friends, and I hate you … I think you're a horrid witch. Yes, I do. You're a witch, and I b'lieve you're a spy!"

There was a long silence while Dickie fingered his cheek. Then Mrs Thurston laughed shortly and turned the key in the lock.

"Come along," she said. "Perhaps you had better leave the dog down here."

"I won't," said Mary tersely. "He's comin' with us wherever we go in this house," and she picked up the growling Macbeth firmly.

There was no sign of Jacob as she led them across the hall and up the stairs. Mary had the dog under one arm, and was also holding Dickie's hand, so that progress was not very fast. At the top of the stairs they turned to the right down a dark passage and then to the right again, and came to an open door. Mrs Thurston reached across to close the door, but the twins were close enough to see everything. The room was brightly lit with a lamp. On a bed at the side of the shuttered window was lying the English officer. He was in his shirt-sleeves, with his bandaged ankle stretched out in front of him, but his sound leg was resting on the floor. Seated in a chair at the side of the bed was another man, who looked up sharply at the sound of their steps. The twins recognized him instantly as John Davies, although he had a different, slightly startled look on his face. They had been looking at a piece of paper which was resting on his knee, but just as the twins smiled at him and were ready to speak, Mrs Thurston closed the door quickly and urged them forward. At the end of the corridor she opened another door.

"Wait there," she said, "while I light the candle."

Macbeth wriggled out of Mary's arms and turned an inquiring eye up at the twins. Then a match spluttered and the room came to life as the candle burned up and threw strange flickering shadows round the walls.

"Here's your room," she went on. "Get to bed quickly," and she brushed past them and closed the door behind her. Dickie tried the handle at once, but the door was locked. He shook it fiercely and almost hysterically until Mary pulled him away.

"That's no use, twin. She's got us. Are you frightened, Dickie?"

"Not really," he said. "I'm mad with her and worried 'bout Mummy, but I don't think I'm really *frightened*. Are you?"

She shook her head.

"We're real prisoners this time," she said. "*This* is our biggest adventure, Dickie … Did you see John?"

He nodded.

"Did you see that paper?"

He nodded again.

"What did you think it was, Dickie? The paper, I mean."

He sat on the bed and slipped his shoes off without untying the laces.

"Like a drawing … or a map."

"And there was something else, Dickie. Did you notice what I noticed? Did you hear?"

He looked puzzled for a moment.

"Wasn't anything to hear, was there?"

Then they stared at each other without speaking, and Dickie's second shoe dropped to the floor.

"Of course," he went on. "Of course there was something to hear. They were talking all the time…"

"'Course they were," said Mary slowly. "But they weren't talking English."

Chapter 8

Ingles and Appledore

When David left him at Ingles, Tom was very bored. He would have liked to have gone down to Onnybrook too, but knew that he must stay at the farm at least until his uncle returned with news of the doctor. He leaned on the farmyard gate and whistled. He whistled everything he could remember and watched David up the hill until he was lost to sight under the trees at the top. A goldfinch settled on the hedge and listened with his head on one side. Then he answered and for a minute boy and bird whistled to each other. A rabbit ventured out of the bracken on the hillside opposite, and behind him, in the house, he could hear his aunt and Mrs Morton talking.

Oddly enough Tom's thoughts were far away. He was thinking of his old home in a North London suburb – of the tarry smell which would come from the roads on a day like this, and of the big friendly red buses that swayed past the end of his road. He knew how much he owed to his Aunt and Uncle – nobody could have been kinder to him – but Ingles wasn't home and these hills were not the same as the steep slopes of the Northern Heights where the straight roads of houses climbed up the hills that looked down on London. It would soon be the football season but he'd get no games this winter. And Dad had gone to the war, and his mother and the baby were somewhere down in Somerset and he'd got to be a farmer! Then he thought of David and the twins and grinned to himself. Maybe they'd all have some fun and excitement yet. He was glad they had come. The Lone Pine camp was grand and he liked Peter too. Funny kids all of them – especially the twins!

So he sauntered back across the farmyard in the sunshine and went in to see if he could do anything to help. Mrs Morton was upstairs making the beds so he ran a few unnecessary errands for his aunt who was the sort of person who hated to see anybody doing nothing and was in a rare state of annoyance because she was temporarily helpless herself. At last he heard his uncle's motor-cycle and went out to open the farmyard gate. The doctor had been found at last and brought along in the side-car. Evidently Mr Ingles had been shouting at his passenger for the whole of the journey and he continued in the same strain although the noisy engine was now at rest. "THIS WAY, DOC.," he bellowed. "Hope she's where I left her … OH, THERE YOU BE, YOUNG TOM! GOT THEM COWS OUT? … Go and try your hand at trimming hedges and don't trim your arm off with sickle while doctor's here! … COMING NOW, BETTY LASS…" and the bewildered and rather frightened-looking doctor was led into the house.

Tom wasn't very interested in hedging. He'd tried it the other day and found to his surprise that it was a very skilful job, so when he went to the barn for the sickle he didn't search very hard for it. Twenty minutes later his uncle came shouting out of the house with the doctor, thrust the latter into the side-car and roared away with him. Back in the house his aunt was much more comfortable.

"It's not so bad as I thought, Tom," she smiled. "And he's a clever man is Doctor Griffiths for he's bandaged my foot beautiful and the pain has nearly gone. Says I'm not to use it but if you'll get me a stick maybe I could get about a bit … Didn't your uncle say you'd better be hedging? Better get on with it afore he comes back." This seemed sound advice so Tom went up to the Twenty Acre again and practised with the sickle. He watched the road for David but his friend did not come back, and when Mr Ingles returned he had time for nothing except work.

Mrs Morton went home to Witchend after dinner, and after tea Tom was free at last. He was still bored for, unlike the Mortons, he had never been particularly good at finding his own amusements and was still unable to adapt himself properly to life in the country.

He wandered out into the lane wondering what had happened to the others. It was funny of David not to come back this way and give him a call. He had promised to look in. And the twins hadn't been along either. He was just trying to make up his mind to stroll up to Witchend before his Uncle had finished milking and wanted him when he noticed something glinting in the ditch. He went back and picked up a little round tube of gold-coloured metal about three inches long. He fiddled about with it and found that it was a lipstick. He was just about to throw it back again when something else caught his eye and he stepped down into the narrow ditch to search more closely. Within a few minutes he had found a powder compact to match the lipstick, a half-full carton of cigarettes, a florin, a blunt pencil and a folded square of paper. Tom was naturally curious and had no hesitation in unfolding the paper and, slipping the trinkets into his pocket, he sat under the hedge the better to examine his find. The first thing he noticed on the paper was a crude drawing of an owl in the top right-hand corner. Under the owl were some pencilled figures, but he couldn't make head or tail of the rest of the sketch – if it was a sketch! Dotted lines wandered over the paper and a peculiar triangular symbol was marked with a red cross.

What on earth did it all mean?

Tom turned the paper up the other way, but except that the owl was now upside down he was no nearer the answer.

"Golly!" he said to himself. "I'd better go and find the other Lone-Piners. This is a real secret, but I s'pose I'll have to take these bits of things down to the policeman at Onnybrook. Perhaps there's a reward out and we can all share it? But I'd like the others to see them before I go. It's what young Dickie would call Treasure Trove I s'pose."

He looked at the treasures again, but it was the paper with the clumsy drawing of the owl which intrigued him. And suddenly he remembered to whom these things must belong. It was at this very time last evening and in this very place that he had seen Mrs Thurston running down the lane chased by Macbeth. The lipstick and the pencil – and the paper too – must have fallen from her bag without her knowledge. Tom whistled and ran his fingers through his hair.

"By golly!" he said. "We can take 'em straight to her and ask her for a reward maybe. Of course they're hers. I bet she's wild! But what does this paper with the owl mean? P'raps it belongs to someone else."

So he looked again and then guessed what it must be. It was surely a rough map of some sort, and the dotted lines were paths or tracks. But the triangle with the red cross beat him and so did the blot which *might* perhaps be intended to represent a house or haystack and from which the boldest of the dotted lines started.

He began to run up the lane to Witchend with the paper clutched hotly in his hand. Then he stopped and turned back. Better see his uncle first.

Mr Ingles had finished milking and was enjoying a cigarette by the gate when he got back to the farm.

"Well, my lad," he smiled. "What are you losing breath about? No need to run if you can walk, and work's near finished for the day now … Weather looks funny … don't like the look of it … Mynd mist maybe. Where are those Morton youngsters, d'you know? Hope they're not on the mountain."

"I don't know where they are, Uncle. I was just going up to Witchend to find them but I thought I'd better show this to you first. Look! Isn't it a map? I picked it up with these other things in the ditch up there, and I reckon I know who they belong to."

Mr Ingles removed his cigarette, and with an indulgent smile held out his hand for the paper, while Tom brought out his treasure trove again.

"Who did this?" his Uncle asked. "One of those twins I should reckon looking at this old owl!"

"I never thought of that," said Tom ruefully, "but I bet these other things belong to Mrs Thurston over at Appledore. She was running down here last night with Morton's little black dog after her, and I reckon her bag broke open and everything spilled out … I s'pose I'd better take 'em all back to her in the morning … Maybe young Dickie or Mary did do that drawing, but it was near the other things in the ditch and I thought perhaps you'd better see it, Uncle Alf."

Mr Ingles looked at his nephew and then back to the scrap of paper in his hand.

"How d'you know that Thurston woman was running down the lane last evening?"

" 'Cause I saw her, of course," said Tom indignantly. "I watched her and she ran like fun with that dog snapping at her. Once she stopped and tried to kick him, and he thought she was playing a game, and began to dance round her … I'll take the paper up to Witchend and ask those twins whether they did the drawing."

"Just a minute," said Mr Ingles quietly. "Not so fast, young fellow. Let me look again … Seems to me I've seen something like this before … sort of familiar it is … and yet … I don't know that it wasn't done by one of those youngsters…"

And then, with a slap on his knee, he roared—

"I'VE GOT IT, YOUNG TOM. 'TIS A MAP, I'M SURE. This is the top o' the mountain, and that red mark is Hatchholt reservoir, I reckon…"

Tom didn't know the top of the mountain, but he remembered what the others had told him about it, and he remembered too the adventures they had had with Mrs

Thurston at Appledore. He decided to tell his uncle the whole story and risk the anger of the others at the breaking of the Club's vow of silence, for Mr Ingles was looking very interested. So he told everything as quickly as he could.

"... And David said they got out of her car at the end of the lane and that you were waiting there and went down to Onnybrook with her and Peter," he finished.

"So I did, Tom. That's so, and a rare hurry she seemed to be in now I remember it. Hadn't got much to say to either of us." He looked up at the sky as he spoke. "Mist's coming down, lad. See how the top of the Mynd has disappeared. It's going to be a dirty night ... But let's have another look at the paper ... There are figures here under the owl but I can't rightly see what they are ... Let's get inside and light the lamp."

So they went indoors and caught Mrs Ingles hobbling about with a stick and trying to get their supper. They bullied her into her chair again, and Tom finished off the table while his Uncle lit the lamp. For once Mr Ingles was very quiet while he peered at the paper. Tom had never seen him look so stern and worried before, so he wasn't really surprised when he got up quickly from the table, folded the paper carefully into his pocket-book, and said, "Reckon you've found something important, young Tom. This is a map of the Mynd all right, and it looks as if the dotted lines lead from Appledore to Hatchholt. Those figures show tomorrow's date, and I'm going off now to telephone my Home Guard officer and tell him what we've found ... Betty, me dear, you mustn't mind me going off. Tom must stay and be company for you, and I'll be back as soon as I can – but don't wait up for me, and take care of your foot."

Tom ran for his uncle's old trench-coat hanging behind the door, and went out into the yard with him. In a few minutes the mist had thickened and was now eddying down from the hillsides into the lane. The mountain was nothing but a shadowy bulk, and the white gate wavered in the fading light as Mr Ingles started up his motor-cycle. He called back something to Tom as he held the gate open, but the boy couldn't hear him properly and so waved vaguely as he disappeared into the fog.

Back indoors he made up the fire but couldn't settle down to anything. He felt annoyed that he had to stay in and not be with his uncle – after all, he had found the map – and upset that he'd seen nothing all day of the Mortons. At his aunt's directions he blacked out the house and then fetched some paper with the intention of writing to his father. He was just biting the end of his pen when Mrs Ingles looked up from her book and said, "Someone's coming, Tom. I can hear running in the lane. Slip out and see who it is."

Tom closed the door carefully behind him and stood in the dark listening. His aunt was right. The fog was playing strange tricks with the sound – sometimes the footsteps seemed far away, and then, suddenly, at the gate, they stopped and a breathless voice called, "Tom! Tom! Are you there? I can't find the gate. Where is it?"

David! He ran across the yard towards the voice.

"Here I am. Wait a sec. I'll find you."

Then he saw the dim glow of a torch as David groped down by the hedge.

190

"Gosh! I'm glad to see you," Tom said. "What's happened to you all day, and what's wrong now? Better come in."

But David was so breathless that he could hardly speak, and he actually put a hand on Tom's shoulder as he led him back across the yard. At the door he gasped, "Is your uncle in, Tom? I want him badly."

"No, he's not, but you must come in. I've got something exciting too."

The light dazzled David and at first he didn't see Mrs Ingles in the chair by the fire, but when the latter saw the boy she forgot her ankle and stood up.

"Lawks!" she said. "What's wrong with the boy? Sit down, lad, and get your breath back. You're white as a sheet."

"Where's Mr Ingles?" David said. "I must find him. The twins are lost."

"Now take it easy, boy," she said, sitting down suddenly. "Those two can't be lost. Just tell me slowly what has happened. Alf isn't here just now – he's gone down to Onnybrook. Take it easy."

David suddenly felt sick. He was tired and hungry and out of breath and not a little frightened about the twins. He remembered his mother's face just now when she had sent him out for help, and he thought of what his father would say when he heard the full story.

"Tom. Get the boy a glass of milk and something to eat," he heard Mrs Ingles saying, and when he had got his breath back and had a mouthful of cake he felt better. He told his story quickly and well, but not until he had explained how he and Peter believed the twins to be at

Witchend all the time, did he add a word about Mrs Thurston.

"We watched her taking photographs of the reservoir," he said, "but Mr Sterling thinks she was taking pictures of birds, and it didn't matter. But I think it does matter, and I think there's something fishy about her wandering about up on the mountain like she does and being so peculiar to us at Appledore, and I want to tell Mr Ingles about her … But the twins are the most important … We've got to do something quickly. Mummy said I was to find him and ask him what to do … She said I was to find him first…"

Mrs Ingles spoke quickly, "Don't you worry, David. We'll find them if the whole county goes out to search. I think you'd better go quickly up the lane and if you meet Mr Ingles you must stop him and tell him everything just as you told me. He'll take you back to Onnybrook, I shouldn't wonder, but you do what he says and you'll be all right … Now you be off if you've finished your milk! Tom – you'd better get yourself a coat and scarf and go with him."

Tom ran to the stairs, and then came back.

"I can't leave you, Aunt Betty. I promised Uncle I'd stay here."

"Nonsense. Run along with David. He needs your company. I shall be all right."

But Tom wouldn't give way. His Uncle had put him in charge of Ingles and he didn't like to leave. David understood how he felt and helped him out.

"That's all right, Tom," he said. "You stay here and I'll go and look for Mr Ingles and tell him you're waiting til we come. Thank you for the milk, Mrs Ingles. I feel fine now. I'll find him," and before they could argue any more he went out again into the dark. The mist was not quite as thick now, and the ray of his torch picked out the white bars of the gate. He hurried up the lane and, in ten minutes, was at the top of the hill and there the weather was much better, and once as he looked up he caught a glimpse of the stars. Then, far away below him, he caught the faint "phut-phut" of a motor-cycle engine and after a little the shielded headlight rushed up the hill towards him. He stepped out into the middle of the road and waved his torch shouting, "Mr Ingles! Is it you? Stop, please!" It was Mr Ingles, and he drew to a stop a few yards from David and pushed up his goggles.

"What's the matter with you, young man? Why, it's David Morton, isn't it? What's wrong?"

Again David told his story, but as soon as it was clear the the twins were missing Mr Ingles pushed him into the side-car, turned and raced back down the hill. David didn't care much for this journey. His driver was reckless and excited, and seemed to have little conception of the danger of taking corners with the wheel of the side-car off the ground! David was bumped from side to side in the restricted and uncomfortable space, and was sore and battered when they drew up outside a red brick cottage in Onnybrook.

Before he realized what was happening he found himself in a tiny, dimly-lit hall with an old-fashioned telephone projecting from the wall. An enormous red-faced man in his shirt-sleeves had opened the door, and was viewing his visitors with astonishment.

"It's Alf Ingles and a young gentleman!" he said finally. "And what brings you here might I ask?"

David was still a little confused by Mr Ingles, the man of action. Up to now he had known him as a genial, happy-go-lucky farmer with a majestic voice and infectious laugh. Now he spoke quickly and decisively and didn't smile at all.

"George," he said. "This boy is from Witchend. His young brother and sister are lost, and maybe on the mountain in this fog. We'd better be getting a search party. Take him in and listen to what he has to tell you and get busy. I want the use of your 'phone to ring up Captain Ward of Home Guard."

Then David realized that he was in the local police station – but only because of the telephone in the hall and a policeman's helmet on the sideboard in the front room. But George was friendly enough and put the boy in a big, creaking chair near the fire, and while Mr Ingles' voice rumbled on in the hall David told his story once again. The constable made him repeat some of his statements and then solemnly put on a pair of braces and removed a belt, but without making any helpful verbal suggestions. David began to feel very tired again, and was exasperated by this inaction.

"But aren't you going to *do* something?" he asked peevishly. "My mother is very worried, and we must go and tell her what we're going to do."

"No 'urry," said the law ponderously. "Don't get excited now. Can't do nothing till I've telephoned to Ludler. Can't telephone till Alf comes off it."

David appreciated a certain logic in this argument, but

before he could reply Mr Ingles rang off and came into the room.

"Tell you what, George," he said. "I'm going straight off to Appledore to see if those kids are there. They might be. While I've gone you'd better get some men together – just in case. David—"

"I'm coming with you, Mr Ingles," the boy said quickly, "and I think we ought to go back to the farm and Witchend first of all to let them all know what we're doing."

Then came another interruption – a thunderous knocking on the door. George muttered and grumbled and pulled on his uniform jacket, and went out into the hall. David thought he recognized the voice that greeted the constable, and wasn't surprised when their sailor friend of the train came into the room. He shook hands with Mr Ingles and then looked with astonishment at David.

"Why! It's David Morton," he grinned. "What are you doing here, and how are those twins of yours? Bit soon to get locked up in the police station, isn't it? Why haven't you been to see us yet? You said you would, and I've only got three more days. I came to have a friendly word with old George, and I've run into a murder or something. What's it all about?"

Mr Ingles told him quickly.

Bill looked sternly at David. "You haven't been silly, have you? I warned you about the mountain, didn't I?"

David felt miserable. It wasn't really his fault that the twins were lost, but when he came to think of it they had been rather foolish to leave Witchend this morning without knowing where the twins had gone. As soon as Peter came back from Lone Pine they ought to have searched.

"Never mind," Bill smiled. "I guess it wasn't your fault. I can see you're a sensible chap. Don't worry. We'll find 'em … You go and do your telephoning, George, while we fix something up."

And when the policeman had gone into the hall the two men made their plans. Bill did most of the talking.

"I'll get a search party together in half-an-hour. Fog's clearing a bit, and we'll go up on to the Mynd right away. The moon will be up by twelve, but we'll call at Hatchholt first just to see if by any chance they've found their way there."

Here David interrupted to tell them the time he and Peter had left Mr Sterling.

Bill nodded. "Maybe the fog came too quickly for them to get as far if they were on the mountain, but we'll look in and warn them. We'll get all the horses we can."

"If you'll do that, Bill," Ingles broke in, "reckon I'll do what young David suggests and run back and see the missus and Mrs Morton before going to Appledore … I'm looking forward to seeing our nice neighbour, Mrs Thurston, and I've got my instructions about her."

When they went out through the hall George was still talking into the telephone.

"The young party concerned," they heard him rumbling, "the young party maintains that he saw the woman Thurston…" and then they closed the door and what the "young party" really did maintain remained for ever a mystery.

Outside, Bill sniffed the air. "Plenty of it about yet," he said, "but it's getting better. Reckon it'll go as quickly as it came. Now, David! Keep your pecker up and tell your mother you've met me and that we'll find those two young cautions for sure … Don't worry, old chap. I'll find some of us who know that mountain like our own back gardens. So long! You'll have to come up Hatchholt after us if you find them at Appledore, but I shall send some up the Witchend valley as well."

He saluted and went off down the road with a curious rolling gait while Mr Ingles started up his noisy engine again. He didn't say much as they drove up the hill, and David noticed how grim he looked. Again the mist was thinner at the top of the hill when they turned into the Witchend lane, but if Mr Ingles hadn't known the road so well they might well have come to grief. As David climbed out stiffly to open the gate, he said, "Mr Ingles, will you please let Tom come with us now? Mrs Ingles wanted him to come with me before, but he wouldn't 'cause you said he was to stay in charge."

"Did he? He's a good boy. Yes, he can come if the missus is better, and doesn't need him."

When they got in, the kettle was singing ready on the hob and Tom was making the tea almost before he had time to ask, "Any luck, David?"

While Mr Ingles was drinking his scalding tea and explaining everything to his wife, the two boys got into a corner.

"You're coming with us to Appledore, Tom. I asked him if you could. And in the police station that sailor, Bill Ward I told you about, came in and he's going to get a search-party … Now we're going up to see Mummy and tell her what's happened."

Mrs Ingles protested so vehemently that she could be left that her husband gave way and within five minutes was driving the two boys up the lane. Mrs Morton heard them coming and, with Agnes, came out to meet them.

"Stay there, boys," Mr Ingles said tersely, and left them at the gate. They couldn't hear what he said to Mrs Morton but after a little she came over to the side-car, smiling bravely, and said, "Sure you're not too tired to go, David? Sure? Daddy wouldn't blame you if you came in now."

David shook his head in horror.

"Very well," she smiled. "Thank you, Mr Ingles, for all you are doing. I shan't go to bed. Good luck – and find my two for me, won't you?"

The next twenty minutes were more of a nightmare than a thrill to the boys. Tom travelled in the side-car while David clung to the belt of Mr Ingles' coat and bounced cruelly up and down on a hard cushion on the carrier. The fog was clearing now as Bill prophesied, and they roared past Ingles and up the hill with a fearful clatter. When they turned into the Onnybrook road David was nearly flung off, but Mr Ingles had little concern for his passengers, and the miles slipped by as they sped round into the shadow of the mountain. After one or two attempts to sit up in the swaying side-car, Tom gave up the idea and lay back. Every now and then he could see the stars through the overhanging branches of the trees, but when they turned off the road into the rough track that led up to Appledore the dark was intense. Mr Ingles had to slow down here, and when at last he stopped his engine they seemed to be surrounded by trees. He pushed back his goggles, switched off the headlights, took each boy by an arm, and led them over the pine-needles into the wood.

"Now listen carefully," he said quietly. "I'm not going to run the bike right up to the house. In a few minutes we'll push her as far as the gates and, if we can, hide her in the trees. One of us must stay with the bike just in case anybody is about, but I don't want them to know we've arrived till we can knock at the door. Tom, I think you're the chap to stay while David and I go and ask if the twins are there. It looks more natural if David goes with me. If you hear or see anything suspicious while we're inside, better sound the old horn and we'll soon be out to help … Now, David! Be just like yourself when the door is opened, and if you're not sure what to say, let me do the talking. Don't act suspicious – after all, we've nothing really to be suspicious about – and don't say anything about that photograph business. She doesn't know you saw her … Are you both ready? Come on, then, and push the bike. I'll use my torch and not the headlights."

They were farther from the house than they had thought, and it was so dark and the track so bad that they were all out of breath before they reached the gate. A light breeze whispered in the tree-tops now that the mist had gone, and only the thudding of their hearts broke the silence as they pushed the motor-cycle off the road under the pines. Tom got into the side-car again and whispered, "Cheerio! Don't be too long. If you come in a hurry or call, I'll switch the headlamps on. If I want you I'll sound the horn, but don't worry about me. I'll be all right."

"You're a good lad, Tom," his uncle whispered. "Don't you fret. We'll soon be back."

Then David heard Tom mutter something that sounded like, "Up the Lone-Piners!" but before he could answer Mr Ingles put his fingers on his wrist and led him off into the darkness. For such a large man he was extraordinarily quiet and light on his feet. He unlatched the white gate without a sound and propped it open. "Might want to come out quickly," he grinned. They walked on the grass, avoiding the gravel of the drive, but not even at the front door could they hear anything suggestive of life in the house. Then David saw a chink of light from the shutters on the right of the porch, and Mr Ingles lifted the slit of the letter-box and put his ear to it. Then he straightened his back and knocked twice with the heavy iron knocker. "There's someone there," he said in a normal voice. "I can hear voices."

Then David heard footsteps and voices, too, but nobody came to the door. Mr Ingles knocked again, while David felt sick with excitement. His heart was banging away and his mouth felt dry as if it was the last day of term! He was just about to try and look through the letter-box himself when the door opened suddenly a few inches.

"Who is there?" came the voice of Jacob.

As if by accident, Mr Ingles put his boot in the gap of the door and said quickly: "Let me in, please. I want to see Mrs Thurston urgently. Hurry up – you're breaking the black-out."

"There is more than one of you there. Who is the other?"

200

"Come along, man! Hurry up! This is only a lad I've brought with me."

"What do you want?"

Mr Ingles raised his voice. He was getting annoyed.

"I'll tell you what I want," he began, when he was interrupted by Mrs Thurston's voice from inside: "What are you doing, Jacob? Open the door at once and let the people in."

They were both dazzled by the light of the lamp on the hall table, and Mrs Thurston was able to take good stock of them before they could speak.

"Good evening, David," she smiled. "How are you? It's very late for you to be out on the mountain, isn't it? Has the fog gone? ... I don't think I know your friend. Is anything the matter?"

Before David could reply, Mr Ingles stepped forward. "Maybe you don't remember me, Mrs Thurston; my name is Ingles – farming down the Witchend road. You were so good as to give me a lift down to Onnybrook other evening ... but you were in a big hurry..."

She looked at him keenly before she smiled and held out her hand. "Of *course*, Mr Ingles. How very rude of me! How do you do? Will you come in and sit down and tell me why you've come up here at this time of night? Have you walked far?"

David opened his mouth to answer, but Mr Ingles nudged him.

"We won't sit down, thanks; and we're sorry for disturbing you, but we hoped that the twins are here. Are they?"

"The twins?" She looked puzzled. "You mean little

Richard and Mary Morton? Here? Oh, no! They're not here. Why should they be?"

"They're lost," David blurted out. "And we thought perhaps they'd found their way here in the fog. We've lost them since this morning. Are you *sure* you haven't seen them, Mrs Thurston, please? We shan't know what to tell Mummy, if you can't help us!"

Mrs Thurston looked up at the man enquiringly.

"It's true," he said bluntly. "We'd hoped they would be here. If they're not, we've no time to waste, and I reckon we'll get on. Sorry to have troubled you."

"But tell me some more," Mrs Thurston said. "Isn't there something I can do? And what are you going to do now? Where could they have gone? When did you miss them, David?"

He answered the last question first.

"I've been at Hatchholt nearly all day, and Mummy has been looking after Mrs Ingles, but they went out fairly early this morning with sandwiches, and have disappeared ... Then there's been this fog..." And he gulped a little at the thought of his mother's face when they returned without news.

"We'll get back quickly," Mr Ingles went on, "and help with the search parties."

"Search parties?" Mrs Thurston queried. "Is that necessary? Oh, I am sorry. I'd no idea you thought it as serious as that. I suppose you think they're on the mountain?"

"We do," said Mr Ingles grimly. "They may have been wandering about in the fog for hours ... Come on, lad. We must get going."

David moved to the door through a haze of unshed tears. He knew it was babyish, but he couldn't help it, and suddenly he felt very tired and miserable.

"Surely you haven't walked?" Mrs Thurston was asking.

"No. We came on my motor-cycle."

"How odd!" she said. "I didn't hear you ... Now I wonder what I could do?"

"There's that man of yours," said Mr Ingles. "Perhaps he'd go out and search a bit between here and top of mountain? Could he do that? In an hour or two he'll meet the other parties coming up Witchend and Hatchholt. We'd go that way, too, but I've promised to take this boy back to his mother. What do you say, ma'am? Would you help in that way?"

For a moment she seemed slightly taken aback. Then:

"Of course," she said. "I'm sure Jacob would go. If they turn up I'll take care of them till morning. Unfortunately my car is out of order, so I can't run them back to Witchend. But tell your mother, David, that if we do find them we'll take care of them and return them safe and sound in the morning. Good luck to you both! Don't worry! They'll turn up. Be sure to call on me if there is anything else I can do," and almost before they realized it they were out in the dark again, for she hadn't waited for Jacob to let them out.

"Stand still a minute till your eyes get used to it," said Mr Ingles. "And don't make a noise – listen!"

But they heard nothing beyond the distant slam of a door. As they made their way back to the gate David felt too unhappy to speak, and was surprised when Mr Ingles said: "Does your sister wear hair-ribbon?"

"I don't know," David said dully.

"Don't be silly, lad. Just think. Does she? Bright green ribbon?"

David looked up. "Yes, she does sometimes. Just a little bit. Why?"

"I reckon yon woman's a liar. There was a bit of green ribbon at the side of the bottom stair. I hope she didn't see me looking at it. I reckon she knows more than she's told us … but we'd better start the bike up because she'll be waiting to hear us go."

Suddenly through the darkness came Tom's urgent voice: "Here I am. This way. Any luck?"

"Quiet a minute till I start her up. No, young Tom. No luck really. She says she hasn't seen them, but I'm not so sure. Get her out in the road again."

They pushed the combination out on to the track, and both the boys squeezed into the side-car. Mr Ingles started the engine, let it race for a little till the hideous clamour came echoing back at them from the woods, and then started down the track. Twice Tom poked his uncle in the back and whispered hoarsely: "Stop, Uncle! Stop please!" But Mr Ingles drove for nearly half a mile before pulling into the side and stopping his engine.

"Reckon we're out of hearing now," he said. "Who was it hitting me in the back?"

"Me," said Tom. "I wanted you to stop. Did you hear anything when the bike started?"

David shook his head. "Don't think so. I'm jolly tired anyway!"

"P'raps I was wrong, then. But I thought I heard tha

little dog of yours bark. I s'pose it wouldn't be, but that's what I thought … just when the engine started."

Mr Ingles looked interested. "That settles it, then. We're going back to have another look round. This time we'll all go and chance leaving the bike. It will be too long to push her up the hill again … I don't like that woman … She talks too easy … Hope she thinks we're on our way home now…"

They left the motor-cycle at the side of the track and turned up the hill again. Tom, not nearly so tired as David, and feeling much more bored after his cold and lonely vigil in the side-car, hurried ahead with his uncle. David plodded along behind. Dull of him not to have seen the ribbon, but of course it may not have been Mary's. And he hadn't heard Mac either, but Tom had seemed fairly confident. If only they could find the twins … Only this morning he remembered, his mother had said that they looked particularly innocent and were probably up to something, and he'd felt a bit relieved that he was going off without them for once. Now that they'd gone he realized how much he missed them. Funny kids they were, but it was grand the way they stuck up for each other. Then he remembered Mrs Thurston this afternoon by the reservoir, and the way in which she had just spoken to them. She seemed somehow to be two different people. Sometimes she was pleasant and friendly enough, and then she would spoil everything by kicking little dogs! He was still thinking about her when he walked into Mr Ingles, who whispered under his breath: "Look where you're going, boy. Stand still and listen."

They stood so still for an endless minute that the weary

David was swaying before Mr Ingles led them forward again.

"I'm going to explore at the back," he breathed. "You two stay in front here and keep your ears open. Don't move far even if you hear anything, and I'll come back to you when I've explored."

When he had slipped away into the darkness the two boys crept nearer the front door.

"Are you sure about Mac, Tom?" David whispered.

Tom was shaking with excitement. "I'm not so sure now," he replied. "I hoped you'd hear him, too, but the bike was making such a din. P'raps I was only guessing, but it seemed as if it was that short bark of his, and it was sort of muffled."

"Would it be a good idea if you whistled the peewit call?" David suggested.

And Tom, anxious to play some part in the proceedings, was just about to give his rendering when David put his hand over his mouth and hissed, "Silly chumps we should be, Tom. I don't suppose they whistle at night…!"

"Maybe not, but if those twins are there they'd like to hear us."

"I've got a better idea. I've just remembered that I saw a crack in the blackout of that window when we were waiting for Jacob to come to the door … Let's go over and see whether the shutter is loose and whether we can see into the room."

When they got to the porch the slit of light was still showing, so they crept over the damp grass and, by bending down, found that they could both get a restricted view. David went first and was so astonished at what he saw that he forgot Tom until he was prodded violently in the back and had to make room for him. The room into which they were spying was new to David, and although he could not see it all his attention was held by three men standing round a table. One of the men was Jacob, but all three were busily engaged. Unfortunately it wasn't possible to hear what they were saying and what they were actually doing was puzzling enough. Each man had before him a large rucksack, which he was filling with square packages piled in the centre of the table. There were also some coils of wire and a number of unusual looking boxes and cylinders. One of the strangers were consulting a list and another something which David guessed to be an engineer's blue print.

There was no sign of Mrs Thurston or the twins, and David was wondering whether to go back and call Mr Ingles when Tom's foot slipped and he lost his balance. Luckily David caught him as he fell forward and prevented his head from banging against the window. They were so alarmed by this narrow escape that they scuttled away from the window on to the grass under the trees.

"You silly ass," David muttered. "Why did you do that?"

"I couldn't help it. My foot had gone to sleep ... I say, David, what *are* they doing? And who are those chaps?"

Before David could answer, Mr Ingles loomed up out of the dark, and, taking them each by an arm, led them over towards the gate.

"Just a minute," he whispered. "Wait till we're out of

earshot ... Now then. I can see you've found something. Are those kids there? I couldn't discover anything at the back except that all the rooms, including what must be the kitchen, are dark."

David told him quickly what they had seen, and he said: "Stay here, Tom. Come over and show me the window, David. I want to see this for myself."

Left alone again, poor disgruntled Tom jabbed his hands in his pockets and did what he usually did when he was on his own – he did it without thinking – he whistled. Fortunately he whistled what had been in his mind a few minutes earlier – the peewit's lonely little call. Twice he sent out the Lone-Piner's call for help and the answer came unexpectedly. From somewhere near, but very muffled, came the short, warning bark of a dog. Tom, suddenly realizing what he had done, stiffened in anticipation. Would the others hear? And would someone in the house be warned? And was the dog Macbeth? It might not be!

Then David was at his side.

"Tom! That was Mackie. I know it was. They're somewhere in the house. I'm sure of it. Let's tell your uncle to go and bang on the door, and we'll jolly well go and get them out."

"Where is Uncle?"

"I left him looking through the crack. He'll be back in a sec. Here he is..." and he started to pour out an excited story till Mr Ingles stopped him.

"Be quiet, David! Wait a minute, else you'll have them all out here wondering what the noise is about. We've got to go straight back to Onnybrook. There's not a minute t spare. We've found something important and I must get you kids out of the way…"

"But they're here, Uncle," Tom interrupted. "We're sure of it. I heard the dog bark."

"Nonsense," said his uncle. "You're tired and imagining things. Come on. We must be off at once."

David stood firm. He suddenly felt better and was as confident as Tom about Macbeth.

"Mr Ingles," he pleaded, "we just can't go and leave them … I'm *sure* they're here. I know that was Mac's bark and I know Mary would never leave him. They're in this house somewhere and we must try now and find them. Please!"

Mr Ingles hesitated. He had his own ideas now as to what was going on in this house, and he knew he'd got no time to waste. He had not heard the dog, but both the boys seemed confident, and if there was a doubt he could hardly leave without making sure. If the situation was as serious as he feared, he dared not leave two young children in this house, and yet they might be wasting precious minutes on a fruitless search. Then he thought of Mrs Morton, who had been so good to his wife today and he remembered, too, the way in which Mary had slipped her hand into his and the saucy way she had looked up at him on that first day he had seen them in his own farmyard. He had always wanted a daughter.

"Quickly, now!" he whispered suddenly. "Think, young Tom. Where do you think the dog would be?"

Tom scratched his head. "Indoors," he said at last. "Not here in the front. Seemed a long way away. Shall I whistle again? Maybe he'll bark back."

"No, not yet. We'll search the back of the house again. Come along," and he led the way quickly round the side of the house. At the back was a paved yard, where David blundered into a water-butt. Here it was darker than ever, and Tom said, "Haven't you got a torch, Uncle? Let's look and see if any windows are open upstairs."

"I didn't look for that before, Tom. Good idea. Here goes," and he swung the narrow beam up the wall. They watched the little spot of light travel over the ivy until it picked out a stone ledge. Mr Ingles raised the torch a few inches and the light was reflected back from glass. A window – and one half of it just open. He switched off the torch and in the darkness Tom whistled softly again the peewit's call. His uncle gripped his arm in surprise and annoyance, but Tom was justified, for from the window above there came Mac's throaty growl.

"Oh, gosh!" David whispered, "he'll bark. How are we going to stop him barking? Listen and see if the twins are there."

But there was no other sound, and then David had a big idea.

"Lift me on your shoulders, Mr Ingles, and I can reach the window. I'll keep Mac quiet if I can speak to him and if you'll give me your torch I can see if they're in that room. If we're not quick maybe he'll bark again."

"All right, boy, but look sharp. We've got to get back soon. Off with your shoes … Now help him up, Tom."

David was fairly solid, and even Mr Ingles swayed as he strained himself upright. David held out one hand for the torch, while with the other he grabbed the ivy. He was high enough to see into the room. Oddly enough, he fe cool and collected now and had forgotten how tired he was, but he did wonder what he was going to see when he switched on the torch. He could just slip his right hand in through the open window, and said very quietly. "All right, Mackie, old boy. *Quiet Mackie!* Down, boy! Quiet!" And even as he found the switch he heard a faint "thud, thud," which he knew was Macbeth's tail wagging.

This is what he saw. In the far corner of a small and sparsely-furnished room was a bed against the wall. Stretched across the bed, fully clothed and fast asleep, were the twins. They looked grubby and tired, but otherwise unhurt. Sitting on the end of the bed, his eyes glinting like emeralds in the light of the torch, was Macbeth. His ears were cocked and his tail beating a frenzied tattoo on the blanket.

"Here, boy," whispered David, and the little dog flopped off the bed and tried to jump on to the window ledge. David put down the torch inside and used his hand to scratch Mac behind the ears.

"Good old boy," he whispered. "Go find them. Wake them."

Mac was making little crying noises in his throat now. He didn't quite realize what was expected of him beyond the fact that he had to restrain his joy. It was all very difficult for a dog who had been through as much as he had. He hated this house and the woman downstairs, but everything would doubtless be all right now. Up till this moment all the humans he had met entered a room through the door, and now here was his young master arriving in a most peculiar way! And he was trying to make him understand something. How silly these humans

211

are sometimes! Why can't they just talk sense?

"Go wake them," David was saying. "Go on, boy! Quick! Wake them," and then his head disappeared and there was a scrambling noise from outside.

Actually, David had forgotten the other two in his excitement, and couldn't hear Mr Ingles' urgent whispering. Not until his ankle was pinched did he withdraw his head from the room. Mr Ingles tottered ominously as the boy grabbed at the ivy. "Come down, boy," he muttered. "And stop fidgeting about. Come down and give me a rest." There seemed nothing for it, so David transferred his weight to the ivy for a moment, and then Mr Ingles grasped his waist and helped him down.

"Now. Are they there?"

David told them quickly. "Now you must hold me up again, and we'll wake the twins somehow, so that they can open the window wide enough for me to get in and help them. I can't manage now. They're so fast asleep that I'll have to shout to wake them. I know them! I was trying to make Mackie do it, and I believe he would have done it if you hadn't made me come down ... I say, Mr Ingles, how are we going to get 'em out?"

Tom was beside himself with excitement.

"Jiminy Cricket, David," he kept muttering. "What a do! We'll have to let 'em down on a sheet."

But Mr Ingles was worried. If they were discovered now and he was prevented from getting back to Onnybrook he would be guilty, he believed, of neglecting his duty. He was wondering whether, now that they knew that the twins were safe, if he dared leave them here till the morning, when he intended to return in very different company. These people were hardly likely to do any harm to two small children. Then he wondered and remembered Mrs Thurston's shameless lie.

"Very well, David," he said quickly. "Up with you again, and do your best. But keep cool and *you must be quiet. Not a sound from any of you.* Get into the room sharp as you can, and if you're strong enough, lower the kids one at a time from the window, I can lift them down. If you can't manage that you'll have to let them down on a sheet. *But be quick, lad, and be quiet.* Now up with you again…"

When he shone the torch into the room again, David saw Macbeth on the bed. The dog turned to look at him, wagged his tail and started to lick Dickie's face.

"Good boy," encouraged David from the window. Dickie stirred in his sleep, rolled over and buried his face in the blanket. Mac thrust his cold nose into the boy's neck and whined softly. "Dickie," David called urgently, shining the torch on him. "Wake up, Dickie; it's us!"

And then Mary sat up in the light, blinked and said loudly, "Hullo!"

"*Quiet, Mary!*" David hissed in anguish. "Be quiet. Come over and open the window."

Mary pushed her hand through her curls, clutched Macbeth and slipped off the bed.

"Oh! David," she said, "it's you. Oh! David, is Mummy cross? Is it time to get up?"

"Don't be silly," David snapped. "Open the window."

This seemed to wake Mary up, and she promptly did as she was told. In a second David had pulled himself over the sill and could feel his sister hugging him hard round the legs. Perhaps it was because it was dark that he did a very unusual thing – slipped an arm round her shoulder and dropped a clumsy kiss on the top of her head.

"We've been brave, David," she was whispering. "True, we have."

Dickie was sitting up in bed now.

"I'm very frightened," he was saying to himself. "No! I'm not really, but who is it?"

"Don't be an ass, Dickie," said David, grinning in the dark. "It's me. We've come to take you home."

There was a thud as he slid off the bed.

"You just jolly well ought to tell us when you're comin'," he muttered. "Just wait till you hear our adventures. You'll be sorry you weren't with us. Mary and me have done everything…" But the last of his recital was checked by David's hand over his mouth.

"Mr Ingles is outside, Mary. He'll hold you as I let you out of the window. Will you hold on to my wrists tight as I lower you? Can you manage?"

"Yes, David," she said quietly. "Just what you say."

He leaned from the window and flashed the torch down.

"Put that out!" said Mr Ingles urgently from just below him. "Here I am. Tom found a big box in the yard and I'm standing on it. Now! The first one quickly."

Almost before he had finished speaking Mary slid over the sill into Mr Ingles' strong arms, and was lowered easily to Tom, who lifted her to the ground. Then Dickie, protesting all the time, "I *can* manage. Jus' let me alone, David. I done bigger things than this yesterday – or today, whenever it was…"

214

Then David passed Macbeth down before Mr Ingles gave him a hand for the last time. In the yard they stood still for a minute before creeping in single file to the corner of the house. They were just about to cross the grass to the gate when Mr Ingles put out his arm and pressed them back against the wall.

"Quiet," he said under his breath. "Don't move."

He had heard the front door open, and now came the clear and unmistakable voice of Mrs Thurston.

"The moon will soon be up," she said. "The wind has dropped and the mist has gone…"

A man's voice rumbled an answer, but they couldn't hear what he said. Mac growled softly till David checked him. The woman laughed. "They're all right. Don't you worry. I'll look after them … Come! There's plenty of work to be done…" and then the door slammed and all was quiet again.

David felt Mary shaking as she leaned against him, and Dickie was muttering, "Beast and pig! I hate her!"

"Now," said Mr Ingles, and led them across to the gate. "Walk quietly. I'm going to take you on my back, Mary. We'll be quicker that way. If Dickie can't keep up with us you chaps must take it in turn to give him a lift. Mac will have to walk."

And so they escaped from Appledore. Once Mary, whose head had been resting against Mr Ingles' shoulder, looked back. The stars were bright and clear and the rim of the rising moon was just peeping above the dark line of the mountain behind them. The horror of the grey clinging mist and the darkness of the night was forgotten. She was safe again and would soon be home. Mr Ingles smelt funny, but nice. He smelled of cows and the farm-yard. His hair was crisp and black at the back of his head, but he was warm and comforting. She sighed contentedly and was very cross when she found herself being pushed into the side-car with David while Tom and Dickie had to manage on the carrier. And then everything was vague again. A lot of noise and bumping as they started, David's jacket against her cheek and, at last after a long, long time, the voice she loved best in all the world welcoming her home.

Chapter 9

Hatchholt

After David had left, Peter turned back up the Hatchholt valley in the thickening mist. She could have found her way blindfolded, so she had plenty of opportunity of thinking over the day's adventures. But mostly she was thinking of David. Her cheeks burned as she remembered how beastly she had been to him in the reservoir and how decent he had been to her. And that brought her to Mrs Thurston and her strange behaviour. She was still angry with her for spoiling her afternoon, but puzzled over David's suspicions.

The mist was very thick now and she was just crossing one of the rough plank bridges over the pipe-line when she heard the throbbing of an aeroplane. She stood in alarm as the plane came rapidly nearer, until it seemed to be actually roaring up the valley. Straining her eyes upwards, she thought she glimpsed a rushing dark shadow in the grey fog, but soon the noise of the engine died away and she trudged on up the hill, knowing that her father would be fidgeting about her. But David had sown a doubt in her mind over Mrs Thurston. He had been so serious, and although he had been polite enough to Daddy when he had insisted that she was bird watching, she knew that he hadn't believed him. But almost the last thing he had said to her was his angry accusation that she had thought him crazy and she began to wish that she had gone back with him so that they could have talked more of their afternoon's adventure. But somehow the longer she thought over all that the Lone-Piners had found out about the mysterious inhabitant of Appledore, the more she began to think that David was correct in his suspicions. It was just because she hadn't *wanted* to believe this that she had not taken it as seriously as David. She was beginning to feel very unhappy and was wondering what she could do to help and how soon she could explain to David when she realized that she was home again.

Mr Sterling was very glad to see her.

"Always gallivanting about, my girl! And look at you now. You're wet through. Run up and change your clothes and give your hair a rub, and by the time you're ready I'll have some bread and milk for you."

So Peter, very down in the dumps, did as she was told for once without arguing. She didn't really like bread and milk, but knew that her father would worry all night if she refused, and when she had changed and washed and come downstairs again and saw him bending over the bright little saucepan on the edge of the fire, she suddenly felt a warm rush of affection for him. How lovely and cosy Hatchholt was tonight, with the cold fog outside and just Daddy and herself here in the warm! She went over and hugged him.

"Daddy, darling," she said, "you're an old pet to me. I'll eat up the bread and milk if I can sit here on the floor and dry my hair at the same time."

He beamed at her over his spectacles, and when he had poured the contents of the saucepan into a basin and added some sugar, sat down so that she could rest her back against his knees. As she shook out her hair, he spoke.

"Was the mist very bad as you came up? How far did you go with the lad, and will he find his way?"

"Yes, Daddy. I'm sure he will, although it's very thick out there now."

"He's a nice lad," Mr Sterling went on. "A good-mannered lad, who's been taught to listen politely to his elders. And I think he's got a good headpiece on his shoulders, too."

Peter finished her bread and milk and put the bowl down in the hearth, from where her father promptly picked it up and took it into the scullery. Peter heard him washing it up while she rubbed her hair dry, and when he came back she decided to talk to him again about Mrs Thurston. She told him everything they had found out, reminded him again of the afternoon's activities and of David's suspicions.

"I know you think David was being silly," she finished, "but I've been thinking about it all, too, and now I believe he's right, and … and, Daddy, I believe we ought to tell the police."

Mr Sterling remained unmoved at this outburst, but he didn't laugh at her.

"You're both as bad as each other," he said. "You read too many books and get ideas into your head … And suppose we could get hold of that old slow-coach of a policeman in Onnybrook? Suppose we could? What would you tell him? That you saw Mrs Thurston taking photographs of the water for one thing, and that she kicked the Morton's little dog for another? Forget about it, lass, and worry your head about something worth the worry."

But Peter had made up her mind now.

"I'm sorry, Daddy, but I think you're wrong. She's up to something mysterious, and somebody ought to be told about it. I wish the fog would go and I'd saddle Sally and ride down to Onnybrook. The moon will be up soon."

Mr Sterling was horrified at this suggestion.

"Well, if you wouldn't let me do that," his daughter went on, "I'd like to ride to Witchend. I wish I knew what was going on there, and I wish I knew what had happened to the twins. I believe David was very worried about them, too. I haven't remembered them much today, but I'm sure that they had been to…" and just in time she remembered that this was a secret. "Anyway, I wish we weren't so far away tonight. All the others are together, and even Tom at Ingles is near, and I'm stuck up here and don't know what's happening." She got up and wandered to the door. Outside the fog was still as thick, and because she didn't feel like bed and because she felt so fidgety, she got out the draughtboard. They played several games, and Mr Sterling won them all. He didn't usually win every game, but Peter obviously couldn't keep her mind on her moves tonight, and wasn't a match for him. Mr Sterling took a childish delight in winning any game, although he was most punctilious in the playing of it. Although it was late, he really was surprised when, having set out the men for a final game, Peter suddenly pushed the board off the table, scattered the draughts and stood up.

"I'm sorry, Daddy darling," she said, but not very convincingly. "That was beastly rude of me, but I just couldn't help it … No, I couldn't. I just had to do that. I keep thinking about the others, Daddy, and about Mrs Thurston. And I'm very tired now…"

Mr Sterling looked at her seriously, but didn't scold. "If it will make you easier, lass," he said, "we'll go down to Onnybrook tomorrow and you can tell your story … or I'll go to the village if you like and you can ride over to Witchend after early breakfast and greet those two young rascals for me. They'll be there, I'll be bound."

Peter's eyes filled with tears as she bent to pick up the draughts.

"Oh! *thank* you, Daddy. Will you really do that? I'm so sorry I've been beastly and rude … I was to David, too … I don't know what's the matter with me today, but I feel something is going to happen … Perhaps I'll go to bed now after all."

So when she had tidied up and lit her candle she kissed her father and went upstairs. Her bedroom was tiny, but it had a dormer window jutting from the roof and facing down the valley. Before undressing she left the candle on the landing, closed the door and opened the window. To her surprise the mist had nearly gone and she could see the stars. Clear against the velvety blackness of the night the Great Bear straddled the sky and, as she leaned far out into the fresh, keen air, she thought she heard the sound of distant voices. She held her breath, so that not even her breathing would break the silence. Just as she felt she could hold on no longer – it was like coming up from a dive – she distinctly heard voices again, and now they were nearer. And there was another familiar sound, too … the clink of a horse's hoof on a loose stone.

She waited no longer, but raced down the stairs.

"Daddy! Come quickly! There are men and horses coming up the valley!"

This was too much for Mr Sterling. He had had a lot of shocks, disappointments and upsets today, and this ridiculous outburst was the last straw.

"The fog's got into your wits," he said sternly. "Go to bed and go to sleep and stop talking nonsense." But before he had time to finish Peter opened the door and slipped out into the dark.

The voices were near now. Once a man's laugh. There didn't seem to be anything secret about the approach, so Peter ran to the gate and called, "Hullo! Who's there, and what do you want?"

There was a pause, and then a voice she recognized said: "That's Sterling's girl, I'll be bound. Wonder what she's doing up at this hour?" Then he called, "Hullo, there! Is that young Peter?"

She ran down the track to meet them, and sure enough it was their old friend Bill Ward with two other men – one of them mounted on a chestnut mare which she knew came from a farm the other side of the Onnybrook road.

"What's wrong, Bill? What's brought you up here at this time? What's happened?"

"Now, don't you start worrying till you have to, Peter. Where's your father? I'd like a word with him. Are the Morton twins here, and have you seen them?"

"No, I haven't," Peter said quickly. "Not all day, and we looked for them this morning at Witchend. Daddy is indoors, but never mind him. He didn't believe I could hear you, and I don't expect he'll believe you when he sees you. Tell me what's happened."

The man on the horse spoke for the first time: "Tell her, Ward. Maybe she can help – and perhaps her father can, too."

"Lead on, then, Peter. We've got no time to waste. The Morton twins have disappeared and we've no idea where they are. Alf Ingles and young David seem to think that they might have wandered to Appledore, and he's gone round on his bike to see. If they're not there we can be pretty certain they're on the mountain and have probably got lost in the fog. We've got three more chaps searching the Witchend valley, and they're going to meet us on the top, and together we can cover a lot of ground. Don't you worry, Peter. We'll find them."

She gripped his arm fiercely. "Do something *grand* for me, Bill? We're friends, aren't we? We always were. Please, *please*, Bill, let me come with you. I've got my pony Sally still, and you know how I know the mountain. I could really help, I'm sure."

They were at the gate now and the big man dismounted.

"If she's got a horse, let her come. We'd better hurry, though. Moon's coming up."

When Mr Sterling heard the twins were missing and that they might be lost on the mountain, he said just three words – "Wait for me." In three minutes he returned strangely disguised in rubber boots, a long nondescript raincoat and a little tweed hat with two trout flies stuck in the band.

Bill looked at him a little doubtfully. "It's jolly good of you, Mr Sterling, but we'll be out for an hour or two. Won't be too much for you, will it? Young Peter wants to come."

Mr Sterling actually snorted in disgust at the suggestion that he was an old man, but all he said was: "If those youngsters are on the top in the mist they'll be cold and tired now. We'll put some more coal on the fire and make the place a bit snug for them ... Now, let's be going."

Meanwhile, Peter had slipped on her jodhpurs again and saddled an indignant and sleepy Sally. Mr Sterling carefully locked the front door and put the key under a flower-pot, and the search-party set out again. The moon was up now and they could see quite a long way, but not until they got to the top did Bill order them out into a long line, with the two horsemen at each end.

"Go slowly," he said, "and search the hollows particularly carefully. Keep in touch with each other and we'll make for the Witchend valley first and meet up with the others. Remember that if the children are up here they may well be so exhausted that they've gone to sleep somewhere. George and Peter mustn't go too fast, but you can both search a much larger radius, as you're mounted. I'll stay in the middle of the line. It wouldn't be a bad idea to call and whistle just in case they are asleep somewhere. Right; spread out. Your pony is fresh, Peter, so you take the far side. Good luck!"

So Peter touched Sally with her heel and the little hill pony picked up her heels and was away. The heather was bathed in white moonlight, and the night was now very still as she galloped over towards the cairn on the summit. Peter had forgotten how bored and lonely she had been, for this was one of the greatest adventures she had ever had. Pity David wasn't here, too. She pulled Sally in a little and looked back at the others. Bill Ward waved an arm as if to indicate that she could search behind the line as well, so she turned the pony and trotted back a little way towards the track to Appledore. Twice she stopped and shouted, "Dickie! Mary! Where are you?"

And she whistled the peewit call, too, but the sound didn't seem to carry very far. Occasionally she could hear the others calling, and far away she could see the big man on the horse circling behind the line as she was doing. Because Sally was fresh and fast she rode back a little further until a rise hid the others from sight. The night was so lovely that for a moment she sat in silence and watched the stars. Then she remembered why she was here, and called and called again. And this time she was answered. From quite near a man's voice called:

"Hullo! Are you calling me?"

Both Peter and Sally jumped in astonishment. About sixty yards away, just off the track, was a man who raised his arm in salutation as they looked in his direction. Peter hesitated, and he started to walk towards them. As he came nearer she saw that he was wearing a tweed jacket and light trousers under a raincoat and was carrying a heavy knapsack on his back. He took off his hat as he approached and gave her a cheerful grin.

"What's wrong?" he asked. "Can I help you? Or are you just having a private ride in the moonlight and shouting to yourself for joy?"

225

Peter flushed. "No," she said, "I wasn't doing either. We're searching for two children on the mountain 'cause we think they got lost in the fog. Have you seen them? Twins – a boy and a girl about nine. I do so hope you have."

He shook his head.

"I'm sorry. Are there some more of you? Surely you're not doing this on your own?"

"No. Bill and Daddy and the other men are back there, and we're going to meet another search-party."

He nodded. "I see. Perhaps I could help … Strangely enough, I'm lost, too. The mist was too much for me. I'm looking for a place called Hatchholt. Do you know it?"

"I ought to," smiled Peter. "I live there. Who are you?"

"You wouldn't know my name. It's Evans. I'm on a walking holiday and started this morning to walk the length of the Mynd. I've got a map and made up my mind to go down a valley where there's a reservoir called Hatchholt and try to get to Onnybrook for the night. Then the mist came and I didn't know what to do, so I stayed still in a hollow in the heather up there somewhere. After a bit I must have gone to sleep, and when I woke up the mist had gone and I heard you calling." He held out his hand with a friendly smile. "There you are. That's my story. Let's be friends and let me help you find these children, and then perhaps you can give me a bed for the rest of the night or some shelter in your barn."

His friendliness was difficult to resist, and he was really very charming. Now that he was close Peter saw that he was older than he had seemed at first, and he would certainly be a great help to the search-party. So she took his hand and said: "Right ho! My name's Petronella Sterling, but everyone calls me Peter. And this is Sally. Let's go and find the others. If you'll follow along after me I'll gallop back and tell them and then you can join the line."

As she breasted the rise she turned and waved her hand to her new friend and galloped back to Bill. He saw her coming, and sensing that her haste meant news he halted the others and waited for her. When she had told her story he scratched his head.

"We can do with him, Peter, but I'm a bit worried. If he's come along the top from the other direction he would have passed the Appledore track, and if the twins had seen or heard him they'd have called for help. Looks as if we've narrowed the search a bit, but we'll wait for this chap, and I'll have a word with him."

Evans, when he arrived, was as helpful as he could be, but he hadn't anything much to add to the story he had told Peter.

"Of course," he said to Bill. "I might have passed the children, but, you see, I wasn't looking for them. I've never been up here before, and after this afternoon's experience I doubt if I'll ever come again. I suppose you gentlemen know only too well what the fog is like up here. I know now, and I don't like it!"

The others grinned at his way of putting it, but Bill added: "Anyhow, Mr Evans, you've been lucky. Very lucky. The fog cleared in an hour or two tonight. Sometimes it lasts for days, and I doubt you'd have found your way down … But we've these children to worry about. I'm anxious, and we'll be glad of your help. Why don't you dump your knapsack down where you can find it again easily? You don't want to carry it round with you, surely?"

"Oh, that's all right, thanks," Evans said hastily. "I don't mind a bit, and I'm used to it now. It's heavy, but it balances well."

So they started off again, calling and whistling and searching, but without success. Now that the excitement was wearing off Peter began to feel terribly sleepy and had to make terrific efforts to keep awake. Fight as she would, she began to sway in the saddle, and twice she dozed off for a few seconds.

After half an hour's progress their shouts were answered by the other party, but when they met they could see by their gloomy faces that they had had no luck either. Bill was very serious, and called them all together. He was just about to speak when he glanced at Peter. Even as he watched, the girl slumped sideways in the saddle, and he jumped forward to catch her as she fell. Drowsily she looked up at him and murmured: "Sorry, Bill. I'm so sleepy I don't know what's happening."

He laughed and shook her gently.

"Only one place for you, my girl. Bed. Don't you think so, Mr Sterling?"

Mr Sterling, who by now was almost as weary as his daughter, nodded.

"Never ought to have come," he muttered. "Disobedient girl. Always gallivanting … Certainly she must go home."

"Someone must go with her," said Bill, and then to the others: "She's better out of the way now, for I don't like this business at all ... Mr Sterling, sir! We're much obliged for all you've done, but maybe you wouldn't mind taking her back yourself. I'm thinking we'll have to search the other side of the mountain and the Appledore woods, and you won't mind me suggesting that you're not as young as you were."

Mr Sterling looked up with battle in his eyes. Then he glanced at Peter who was again half-asleep in the crook of Bill's arm.

"You're right, young man. You're right. I'd only slow you down ... but I'm worried about those little ones."

"May I suggest, sir," went on Bill, "that you keep a good fire going with plenty of hot water and then, when we find them, we'll bring them down to you and know they'll be in good hands."

Mr Sterling straightened his thin shoulders.

"You can, Mr Ward. It's a sensible tidy suggestion. Come on, my lass. Home and bed for you," and he steadied her on the saddle as Bill swung her up as if she had been a baby.

Then the newcomer spoke up rather apologetically. "I'm awfully sorry," he said, "but I wonder if you can manage without me. Actually I fell into a hollow hidden by the heather when I was wandering about in the fog, and I'm afraid I turned my ankle. I hoped it would be all right, but it's painful now, and I don't think I'll be much use to you ... If Mr Sterling would be so hospitable as to allow me to sleep at Hatchholt till the morning I'll be very grateful. Frankly I don't feel fit for much more. I seem to have got chilled, too, in that beastly fog, and I can't stop my teeth from chattering!" He finished with a nervous little laugh, and there was an awkward silence until one of the men produced a pocket flask and passed it over to him. Then Mr Sterling made rather unenthusiastic noises which appeared to signify doubtful approval.

"Hrrrm! Ahem! Not much accommodation, Mr Evans. Hrrrm! ... Shake down on the sofa if you like."

Mr Evans's thanks were almost embarrassing, and the party then split up. The six men from Onnybrook stretched out again in a line headed towards Appledore – a line which would first go again over the ground already searched. Bill went across to Peter.

"Cheer up, old lady!" he whispered. "We'll find them, never fear. And thanks for your help, Peter. You've been grand ... Now go back to bed. That's where little girls should be."

Ever since she had known him he had teased her like this so she just grinned rather sleepily, gave his hair a tug in response, and turned Sally's head towards home.

"Be sure and let us know how you get on," were Mr Sterling's last words as they said "Goodbye." It was getting much colder now, and Peter still had difficulty in keeping awake. Her father kept a hand on Sally's bridle but the pony had been born on these very hills, and was sure and confident and never put a foot wrong.

Mr Evans may have hurt his ankle – he certainly couldn't hurry – and he may have caught a chill, but neither misfortune prevented him from talking. Peter didn't hear half of what he said, but he seemed to be telling Mr Sterling his life story, and she gathered that he had been in Wales and was now a master at a big school near Birmingham. But her father seemed tired and dispirited too, and it was rather a gloomy little cavalcade which wound its way slowly down to the reservoir. Peter felt better for being home and, in spite of Mr Sterling's protests, insisted upon unsaddling Sally herself. When she came in, blinking in the strong light of the lamp, her father was bustling round murmuring something about "A cup of tea for us, Mr Evans, and bread and milk for my little girl when she's in bed."

The stranger was helping to make up the fire, and had put his heavy knapsack under the table.

"I don't want any bread and milk, thank you, Daddy," Peter said. "I'm too sleepy. I'll just go to bed. Good night, Mr Evans, and thank you for helping us."

She didn't even remember getting into bed, and was furious when her father woke her ten minutes later with a bowl of bread and milk. Dimly she realized that he was forcing her to have it, and even feeding her himself as if she had been a baby. But it was warm and comforting, and when the spoon clinked against the empty bowl she lay back on her pillow, put her arms up, and pulled her father's face down to her. His moustache tickled as she kissed him.

"Thank you, Daddy. I didn't want it, but it was lovely ... Oh, Daddy, what do you think has happened to those two? They're such darlings, Daddy. Such fun. Nothing could happen to them, could it...?"

But she didn't hear his answer for she was asleep again. Downstairs the two men chatted for a little and then Mr Sterling made up the fire, found two blankets for his guest, whose lot it was to sleep on the shiny black sofa, and left him.

When Peter woke the sun was shining through the window on to her pillow. She stretched her legs and turned over blissfully. How lovely it was to be warm and cosy in bed! Then she heard somebody whistle – not a tune but the sort of whistle you use to attract somebody's attention. She opened her eyes again in annoyance, and began to remember some of the excitements of last night. She supposed the whistler was Mr Evans. Then she realized that it came from outside, and while she was making up her mind to do nothing but go to sleep again, a soft friendly voice called, "Anybody awake up there?" and the voice certainly did not belong to Mr Evans.

"Oh dear," she thought. "Only last evening I was grumbling because nothing happened here and the others were getting all the excitement. Now something is happening here again, and I'll have to get up."

The whistle was repeated as she ran over to the open window. The floor was cold to her feet and the air fresh and keen as she leaned out and saw three men in khaki grinning up at her.

"Good morning, Juliet," said one. "Speak to me from your window, I pray thee."

"Hullo, Peter," said the sergeant softly. "Sorry to disturb you so early, but the Home Guard's come to see you, and I didn't want to wake the house. Now don't shout, but tell me as quietly as you can – have you seen or heard of any strangers up this way, either last night or this morning?"

"Oh, gosh!" breathed Peter, copying Dickie without realizing it. "Oh, gosh! What adventures we're having." She knew the men; they were all from Onnybrook or the next village, and the one who had called her Juliet in his cheeky way was employed on the Ward's farm away down by the river. The sergeant was an old friend and drove the Onnybrook grocery van.

"Yes!" she whispered. "Yes – we've got one. He's downstairs."

The three men looked at each other and then up at her. "Where did you get him?"

"On the mountain last night," she whispered hoarsely.

"Come down and tell us all about it, Peter, and wake your father up, too. *Where's* your stranger, did you say?"

"He's in the sitting-room. We've only got two bedrooms, and I'll have to go through his room to get to the door ... Shall I come quietly and creep through without waking him?"

"Yes. Be quick, Peter, and be quiet. Don't wake your father, after all, for a minute. Come out here first."

Even as Peter drew back from the window she saw the three step quietly to the door. Her hands were shaking with excitement, but she couldn't have been wider awake as she scrambled into her old dressing-gown. Her bedroom door had the sort of latch that clicked when you pressed it, and it seemed as if minutes instead of seconds passed before she was able to raise it soundlessly. She crept down the stairs with one hand on the rail. The house was so quiet that she could hear her father snoring his gentle snore in the other room, but there was no sound from the sitting-room. The stairs led directly into this room, but were screened at the foot by a curtain. The curtain was closed now and when she reached it, she hardly dared to move it for fear of what she might see. For a moment she listened intently, but there was not even the sound of breathing. She moved the curtain an inch, and then another, hoping that the rings would not clink on the rod. Then she peeped in. The black-out was still up, and the only light came from the stairs behind her, so she moved the curtain another few inches. There was enough light now to show that there was nobody in the room. Two blankets had been flung untidily on the floor, and the heavy knapsack had disappeared, but for a moment Peter wondered whether Mr Evans was in the scullery washing. Then quickly she ran across to the door and felt for the bolts. They had been drawn back and the door was unlocked, so it seemed as if their guest had left early. She flung back the door and noticed the grim look on the faces of the three men outside.

"He's gone," she said. "The door was unlocked. His knapsack has gone too … unless he's in the scullery."

"Show me the scullery," said one of them quickly.

Peter pointed to the door and two of them stepped inside and went into the inner room where Mr Sterling did so much of his work.

"No luck," said one, as he came out. "The bird's flown I'm thinking. Better tell us all about it, Peter, and ask your father to come too. Sorry to be such a nuisance, but it's important."

"And better put some slippers on, Juliet," called the cheeky one, as Peter went to call her father. "Or would you like to borrow my boots?"

She paused to put out her tongue at him, realizing to the full that she was behaving in a very unladylike manner.

Mr Sterling was not responsive. When Peter told him that three Home Guards had arrived and were looking for Mr Evans, who had mysteriously disappeared, he just said, "I don't believe you, girl. Go away."

Then she shook him, and said he was to come at once or should she ask the others to come up? At this he sat up in alarm.

"Are they tramping all over my kitchen in those great boots?" he demanded petulantly.

"Not yet, Daddy," she said tactfully, "but they will if you don't come," and this achieved its purpose.

"I'll be down," he said. "Very well. All about nothing, I expect, and another upset, but I'll come."

"He's just coming," she said, when she got back. "But tell me why you want to know about Mr Evans? He was awfully nice. I liked him. And he helped us search for the twins on the mountain."

Peter's Romeo looked up at this. "But you don't know that news, do you? The twins are safe and sound and in their beds at Witchend. Alf Ingles and those two lads — their brother and young Tom — brought 'em back from Appledore."

"Daddy! Daddy!" Peter shouted up the stairs. "The twins are safe. David found them. I knew he would."

They could give no further details but while they were waiting for Mr Sterling Peter told them quickly how she had found Mr Evans. They listened carefully to her story, and when at last her father appeared the sergeant said, "Look here, Peter. I've got a suggestion. We've got a lot to talk to your father about and may be some time. Why don't you get dressed and ride over to Witchend, and see those twins? I should think you'll all have a lot to talk to each other about, won't you?"

"What about my breakfast?" said Peter indignantly. "I'm jolly hungry!"

The sergeant looked pleadingly at Mr Sterling. "Would you mind, Mr Sterling? Frankly I think it would be an excellent idea if she could manage to go over to Witchend as soon as possible. I'm sure they'll give her some breakfast."

"I don't know what all this is about, but the girl can go if she wants to, I suppose."

"I don't want to," said Peter firmly. "I want to stay here and find out what the mystery is about – but I'll run up and dress first if you like."

She was as quick as she could be and even skimped her teeth a bit but when she came down the four men had their heads together sitting round the table.

"I don't believe a word of it," her father was saying. "It's impossible! Couldn't be done. You're as bad as one another with your crazy suspicions."

When they saw Peter they stopped talking and Mr Sterling looked up.

"Peter, my dear," he said. "I want you to do what I ask you and not argue about it. Ride over to Witchend and see how they all are. I want to know about those two especially and of course Ingles or Mrs Morton will give you breakfast. You can stay as long as you like, if you're not in the way."

Peter was so surprised at his firmness that she replied

quietly, "Righto. I'll go! But you might tell me what's it all about."

"We'll tell you everything soon enough," the sergeant said, "but we know you could be more useful over at Witchend this morning. Goodbye, Peter, and thanks for waking up so quickly this morning and telling us what you have."

" 'Bye, Juliet," said the saucy one, and blew her a kiss behind her father's back.

She was so thrilled and happy at the news of the twins that she forgot to be annoyed at this summary manner of getting her out of the way. Just as well perhaps to talk the mystery and adventure over with the others instead of waiting about here with the grown-ups. So she saddled Sally and set off down the valley in the sunshine.

At the plank bridge she turned and saw her father walking with the three men up to the dam. He was pointing, but when she waved to them there was no response. They were busy about something, but it was all very mysterious.

Chapter 10

The Reservoir

Peter was unusually excited as she set off on Sally down the Hatchholt Valley. It was a glorious morning and as she trotted along the track she was thinking that all their recent adventures were connected in some way and that today many of the mysteries might be solved. It seemed ages since she had seen the others and the news that the twins were safe was a great relief. She had grown very fond of those two with their impulsive loyalty and odd understanding of each other, and she smiled to herself as she pictured the way in which they would interrupt as they told their story of the greatest adventure that had ever happened to them.

She turned right at the corner where she had said "Goodbye" to David in the mist last evening, and cantered up the lane to Ingles. On the way she passed two more Home Guards on their bicycles. At the farm the smoke was rising straight and lazily into the already hazy air, and Tom's unmistakable whistle welcomed her as she rode into the yard.

"Hullo!" he grinned. "You're up early. Had any adventures? We have!"

"Adventures? Wait till I tell you, Tom. I hear the twins are safe. Is that right?"

"Right it is. We rescued 'em!"

"Who's we?"

"Me. And David. And Uncle helped a bit too."

Peter swung to the ground.

"Don't be so irritating, Tom. Are you going to tell me or must I ride up to Witchend and hear the story there? And where's Mr Ingles this morning?"

Just as Tom was relenting and had told her that his uncle had gone off with the Home Guard to Appledore, Mrs Ingles called from the back door.

"Come along in, Peter, my dear, and tell us what you've been doing with yourself. You're up early this morning."

When she heard that the girl had intended to go on to Witchend for breakfast, she insisted that she sit down with them, and across the table Tom told her briefly of the night's adventure. Peter's eyes shone as she heard of how David had climbed up to the window and how the twins had been rescued and then she told in turn, as quickly as she could, of their search of the mountain, of their meeting with Mr Evans, of how he had disappeared in the night, and of how the Home Guard had called her out and sent her down there.

Mrs Ingles looked up at this.

"Ah well!" she said, "Maybe the chaps thought you'd be better off down here amongst all your friends ... Now that I can get about with a stick and as the day seems topsy turvy already, you'd both better help me wash up and then you can go up to Witchend together to see how they're getting along. I'm right glad to know that those two little 'uns are safe ... And what a wicked woman that Mrs Thurston be, to be sure? That house, with its outlandish name, never brought any luck to anyone to my knowledge. Appledore, indeed! Sounds like the South to me … Never mind, my dears. Those chaps of ours will sort it all out, I'll be bound. Your uncle's gone off like a schoolboy this morning and never in his bed all night. Soon as he brought the others home, off he dashes to Onnybrook or somewhere … Come along now. No use gossiping here if you want to get on…"

It was over an hour before the children could get away for there were many odd jobs to be done and Mrs Ingles found it difficult to hobble around. But she must have noticed the anxiety behind their willingness to help for she still insisted that she could be left as she could now look after herself. Tom was a little worried about leaving her and Peter felt mean about going up to Witchend without him, but they got away just as ten o'clock struck from the grandfather clock in the hall. The sun was very hot as they walked up the lane with Peter flicking the flies from Sally.

"Gosh, Peter," Tom said, "don't I wish I was up with Uncle at Appledore. Wouldn't I like to know what's happened up there? I asked him what they were going to do, but he wouldn't tell me … Let's call a special urgent meeting of the Club this morning and compare notes … David'll want to hear about you and the others searching on the mountain … Perhaps the twins will still be in bed though. They were asleep when we lifted them out last night … 'Course we don't know yet what really happened to them yesterday. They started to tell us but were too tired and even then they interrupted each other … They're funny kids all right."

Now they were at Witchend's white gates and Peter tied Sally to the post. The heat was rising above the wood and over the pool a cloud of flies hovered. On the grass in the shade lay a little black dog. When Peter called his name he raised one ear and beat his tail upon the ground – and that was all.

There was nobody else in view, but from the open window came the babble of voices. "Surely not, darling?" they heard Mrs Morton ask incredulously.

"Yes she did, Mummy. D'you know what she did…?" chimed in Mary only to be interrupted by her brother—

"Could I *possibly* have another egg, Agnes *dear*? That's the sort of food you need after bein' a prisoner."

Tom and Peter laughed and then the boy put his fingers to his mouth and whistled, loud and long, the peewit's lament. Peter, who could also whistle this way, copied him fairly successfully, and the voices ceased and David looked out and waved.

"It's Peter and Tom. How are you, Peter? Come in. We've got the twins back safe and sound."

Mrs Morton met them at the door and slipped her arm through Peter's.

"And what have you been up to, my dear? I can't sort it all out yet but everybody except Agnes and me seems to have been having wonderful adventures. All that we could do was to sit about and mope! First Mrs Ingles sprains her ankle, then the twins were really rather disobedient and silly and went off without telling anybody, and got lost in the fog so that the whole county had to go out and look for them. Ever since they woke up this morning they've been eating and talking, and I don't know where I am."

"We said we're sorry about not telling Agnes where we were going," said Dickie.

"An' we did think we ought to help that Air Force pilot resting in … in … in the place we were in," added Mary.

"An' we love being home again, Mummy."

"That beast of a woman hit Dickie…"

"Just as I was goin' to fight through to get old Jacob…"

"An' we did promise not to cry once…"

"Stop! Stop, twins!" their Mother called. "We don't want to hear any more now. Come and sit down, both of you, and have another cup of tea."

Then Agnes appeared with two boiled eggs and slipped one in front of each twin murmuring, "There now! Starving, you must be. Poor mites a'struggling in the fog."

Then everyone started to talk at once until Mrs Morton put her hands over her ears and shooed them out of the room into the sunshine. Macbeth got up, stretched, and came slowly over to the group in the porch. The twins, taking alternate bites from a slice of toast and marmalade, sat on the step and continually interrupted the others until Tom said, "Let's go up to Lone-Pine. Auntie said I could go off for the day, and then we can really compare notes properly. Besides, the Club ought to meet. It's in the rules that we should."

Then he turned to the twins and rather surprisingly said, "And you kids just keep quiet for a bit. Anyone would think you were the only people had any adventures. What about Peter? Not even David knows yet what she was doing in the night, hunting all over the mountain for you."

At this unexpected tribute, Peter went pink with

pleasure and the twins were so astounded that Mary dropped the remnant of toast, marmalade side down, in the dust. For once they had nothing to say.

David grinned. "Quite right, Tom. Better mention it to the grown-ups though, or shall we leave these kids behind?"

But this was too much for the twins.

"David," said Mary in shocked tones. "David *dear*. You wouldn't *do* that? You wouldn't dare! Why you just don't know only the teeniest bit of all our adventures…"

"Let 'em go by themselves, twin," said Dickie in a strangely unnatural and strained voice. "We don't really want to go with them. We went by ourselves yesterday to have our own private adventures. We'll make our own Club. Maybe a … a … a Soltry Oak club of our own," he finished triumphantly.

But when Peter looked over at the little boy his eyes looked suspiciously moist for all his defiance.

Then Mrs Morton came out and helped everybody by saying, "Now what are you all going to do today?" just as if the twins had never been lost. She was like that. They all knew that she was the very best and most understanding mother anywhere. Already she made Peter feel the same and she had only known her a few days.

David looked at her gratefully.

"Well, Mummy, we did think of just going off for a bit on our own. The twins have promised to behave and be sensible and do what they're told, and we promise not to go too far, and to come back to lunch. Do you mind if we do? There's such a lot to tell."

"If the twins have promised –" they both nodded

violent and enthusiastic agreement – "and you promise me not to go wandering about on the top of the mountain today or to go near Appledore, you can be off. We shan't have dinner till two o'clock as we're so late with breakfast. I'm trusting you big ones, so be sensible, won't you? If Mary falls asleep in ten minutes – and I expect she will – you must bring her straight home … Are you going to take Sally, Peter? If not you'd better put her in the shade."

Peter took this wise advice gratefully. "I'll ride her, thank you, Mrs Morton."

David ran in for his notebook and pencil, and was surprised to see that Agnes was standing just inside the hall.

"Missus," she said in sepulchral tones. "Missus, surely you're not going to be letting them out again. Not the two mites, missus?"

Before his mother could answer, Dickie took advantage of the situation. "Maybe we'd better take a little something to eat with us," he said quickly. "Yesterday we were fainting three times with hunger."

"When we were fighting our way through that forest to rescue that man that fell out of the aeroplane…" Mary chimed in, but by then David had returned and was asking them what they were talking about. Mrs Morton reassured Agnes, rather unexpectedly hugged the twins, and whispered, "Look after each other, my two!" and went indoors. Macbeth consented to join the party, so they set off up the little valley with Peter leading on Sally.

"Shall I bring the kettle?" Dickie asked, when they got to the place where one day they hoped to build the dam.

"Yes. Fill it," said David. "We don't want hot drinks, but we might like cold water."

Sally climbed up by the edge of the wood easily enough, and when they reached the camp at last, Peter tied her in the shade. They all sat under the tree for the sun was fierce and, truth to tell, they were all very tired, and Peter yawned several times as she began her story for David. She told him how Bill and the others had come up Hatchholt in the dark, and of how she had joined the search party and found Mr Evans. When she got to the part where the Home Guard called her out of bed to ask if she had seen a stranger, David interrupted: "There never was such a place for strangers. I've seen more strangers here in a week than for months at home."

"I know, David. That's all part of the mystery I'm sure. I've never seen so many either. It's all to do with this Mrs Thurston, and I'm very sorry about last night, when I thought perhaps Daddy was right about her bird-watching. I'm sure now you were right … I'm always saying 'I'm sorry' to you, David, aren't I?"

"Well, get on with the story," Mary broke in, and smiled sweetly. "Never mind about being sorry to David."

"Sometimes even we make a bit of a mistake," was Dickie's contribution.

But when she told how their guest had disappeared by the time she had crept down the stairs, David whistled with surprise.

"Gosh, Peter!" he said. "It was jolly plucky of you to come downstairs like that on your own."

"Oh no, it wasn't," Peter said. "There wasn't anything really to be afraid of. I just had to be quiet and be certain

245

not to wake him up. I didn't know he wouldn't be there ... I wonder where he's gone, David? It was rude of him to go off quietly like that ... But I'm sure he couldn't be anything to do with Mrs Thurston ... At least, I don't think he could ... What do you think, Tom?"

Tom shook his head.

"I reckon he was. I reckon everyone we don't know round here is a spy or something. I reckon everyone has gone mad except us. What were the Home Guard chaps doing up at your place this morning? They asked you if you'd seen any strangers, didn't they? 'Course they did. They're searching them all out, and Uncle has gone to Appledore to get old Jacob and Mrs Thurston, I'll be bound. That's where the fun is going to be. Gosh! I wish we were there again, don't you, David?"

"Yes, I do. But we can't go because we've promised, so it's no use worrying about that." Then he turned again to Peter. "Who suggested you coming down here so early, Peter?"

"Why? The Home Guard fellow did. Seemed to want me out of the way."

Tom and David looked at each other. "P'raps something is going to happen at Hatchholt?" said David.

"But what could happen there?" said Peter indignantly. "It's just that those men are looking for somebody and came up that way. Daddy's there too. Nothing could happen. What do you mean, David? You're always imagining something."

David flushed. "Maybe I am." He turned to Tom. "What do you think, Tom? Shall we go up and see?"

Peter suddenly realized that she was being snubbed.

She still did not find it easy to accept leadership from anybody else, and although she was sorry that she had been rude again to David, she resented the way in which the two boys made their plans alone if she didn't happen to agree with them. Peter still had a lot to learn about team work, but this time she had the good sense to swallow her pride, and when Tom jumped up excitedly she listened to him without comment.

"Jiminy Cricket!" he almost shouted. "That's it, David! Of course that's what we'd better do. You're right. That's where there'll be some fun, I'll be bound. Let's go up to Hatchholt and spy out the land."

David turned to Peter.

"Will you come too, Peter? You're the one who knows the valley best?"

Before she could answer, the twins, who had been lying in the shade of the bracken at the edge of the clearing, sauntered over. "We heard you," Dickie began. "Always the same you are, making plans an' adventures without us."

"What we want to know," Mary went on, "once and for ever we want to know is whether we're in this Club or not?"

" 'Cause if not, not," finished Dickie triumphantly.

David grabbed them each by an ankle and pulled them down on top of him, and the three Mortons fought and struggled until Tom and Peter dragged the twins away.

Dickie protested vehemently.

"Let me go, Tom! Jus' let me get at him ... That's how I was going to fight old Jacob."

Mary pushed the hair out of her eyes. "And that

reminds us," she said breathlessly. "We've never told Peter all our adventures … nor Tom, properly … We'll have to go with them, Dickie, anyway, till we've told our adventures."

"I s'pose so, twin … We've got to tell 'em to *somebody*, and it might as well be them."

David sat up. "It's agreed then. We'll pack up here for now and go to Hatchholt. We promised not to go on top of the hill, so we'll go down past Witchend again. Coming, Peter?"

"Rather, David," she said quietly. "Of course I'm coming," and she went quickly over to Sally so that he should not see her face. He was always being so *decent* to her.

So they all had a drink of water from the kettle, tidied up, and whistled Macbeth out of the wood. Once over the stream at the foot of the hill Peter lifted Mary on to Sally's back and with Dickie on her other side was subjected to a cross fire of anecdotes which made her head reel. But it was perhaps from what Mary did *not* say that she got the best idea of how they had felt when they found themselves alone on the top of the hill with the mist swirling round them. She noticed that the little girl shivered slightly in the sun as Dickie boasted of how he had led the way down to the Appledore woods. Of their discovery of the man with the parachute and of Jacob hooting like an owl they made little, and were far more obsessed with being locked in by Mrs Thurston.

"An' d'you know, Peter!" Mary went on in awe-struck tones, "D'you know … that beast hit Dickie … She did … and then Mackie…"

But by now they were passing Witchend again, and before Dickie was able to interrupt with his story of what he had intended to do to Jacob, Peter changed the subject by inviting him to take a turn on the saddle. The two elder boys caught them up, but as neither Mrs Morton nor Agnes could be seen the little party went on down the lane to Ingles. Tom ran ahead to see if his aunt was all right, and if his uncle had returned, but he soon caught them up again.

"No news," he said. "Uncle isn't back, and Auntie says she's managing very well, and what have I come back for?"

On their way across to the Hatchholt valley David came up to Peter. "I say, Peter," he said, "it was mean of you to tell Tom all your adventures first. I think you might have waited for me. We always seem to be starting to tell each other something, and then being interrupted."

He laughed and paused. "I wondered if you'd give me another riding lesson up the valley? You promised you would, you know. These two kids have had enough, anyway … Mary's half asleep now, and I bet Dickie's so hungry he's nearly fainting." He turned to the twins: "You two get back with Tom. Peter and I want to talk."

"We'll stay and watch you fall off, David," said Mary sweetly.

"No, thank you, David," said Dickie. "I think we'll just go on as we are. I'm getting on quite nicely now, aren't I, Peter?"

"Captain's orders," Peter grinned. "Off you get. I'm the only one who isn't getting a ride today. Tom must have a turn soon."

"Not me!" said Tom emphatically, as he joined them. "I'd rather go on my own two feet – or on wheels, thank you all the same!"

Dickie and Mary looked carefully at David, and then the former said, "Acksherly I think – I think I'd rather walk now, after all. Maybe that's best. Old Sally is getting a bit bumpy round about here."

"Yes, David," added Mary. "P'raps you'd better have some practice. After all, it *is* your turn, I s'pose."

So David mounted and somehow he and Peter took the lead, and as the valley narrowed they were often out of sight of Tom and the twins toiling along behind. Although they would not have admitted it for untold gold, Richard and Mary were very tired. The sun was fierce and down here, at the bottom of the steep-sided valley, there were no welcome breezes to dispel the drowsy heat. The air was hazy, and from above the purple heather came the hum of millions of bees and insects. Although Tom had been quick enough to decline a ride on Sally he was, like so many Londoners, a poor walker and was just beginning to wonder why he had to suffer the discomfor of tired feet on a hot day like this, when Mary suddenly sat down.

"I'm weary and parched," she said. "I'm going to rest." Tom was glad enough of the excuse to stop, so all three stretched themselves on the heather at the side of the path.

"I don't like this valley," Dickie said abruptly. "It's he and it's ghosty. I hate it."

"So do I," Mary agreed. "There's no stream. Ever valley ought to have a stream in it."

Tom was lying on his back looking up at the sky through his laced fingers. He could see the top of the hill against the skyline on the opposite side of the valley.

"The stream is inside the pipes," he murmured sleepily. "Surely you know that? Peter showed you, didn't she?"

"Well," said Mary decisively, "I like the stream outside better. I want to put my feet in it."

"That's a good idea, twin," said Dickie. "It would be a good idea to swim in the reservoir. Nice and cool. Let's go on presently and catch up those two."

Tom sat up abruptly. "There's something moving on the top of the hill. There! Look! Can you see anything?"

The twins strained and stared along his outstretched finger, but had to confess they could see nothing. Tom was puzzled.

"P'raps not? But there's no wind, and I saw the bracken move as if someone was up there."

"Tiger, I expect," Dickie yawned. "Lots of 'em up here. Mary and me see'd them before."

"Or a pony," said Mary practically. "Peter says there are lots of them wild up on the hills."

For some unexplained reason Tom was uneasy. He jumped up and put out a hand to each of the twins. "No," he said, "it wasn't a pony. Come along! Let's catch up the others."

They went on for a little and soon reached the narrowest and steepest part of the valley. Always it seemed as if they would see Peter and David when they rounded the next bed, but still the others kept their lead. Mary was now quite unashamedly holding Tom's hand, while Dickie's steps were flagging. Tom watched the hill-tops, but saw nothing else to make him suspicious, but once he paused as if he heard something behind them. Macbeth, too, seemed uneasy, and anyway he hated the heat and the flies and the whole expedition, and finally sat down in the track with lolling tongue, and refused to move. Mary, as usual, picked him up and hugged him, and suddenly the silence was shattered by a great, dull, thudding explosion. The children looked up in alarm as the sound came rushing down the valley, reverberating from the steep hillsides towards them. When the echoes had died away like thunder in the distance there came another unrecognizable noise like a mighty rushing. At this Tom stopped gaping, grabbed a twin by each hand and started to climb off the path into the heather. Dickie began to protest, but found that Tom wasn't listening. Then, from ahead of them, where the twisting track was hidden by a high jutting rock, came a man's rough threatening shout. Tom paused, and then came Peter's clear and unmistakable call.

"Look out, Tom!" she called. "Mind the water."

Again, David's voice: "Climb, wherever you are! *The water's coming!*"

Then everything seemed to happen at once, and it was not until afterwards when they were able to talk it all over calmly that they got events in the right order. They all agreed that it was *after* Peter's warning, while they were standing still in the heather, that Sally came tearing round the rock with a strange man on her back. Her new rider was shouting and digging at her with his heels and doing all that he could to urge her into a still madder gallop. He seemed to be a very ordinary man, dressed in tweeds, and with a knapsack on his back. He was hatless and certainly was not an accomplished rider, for it seemed that at any moment he would be flung off.

They were all staring at this apparition in amazement when a man's voice behind them shouted, "Get off the path! Climb up into the heather! Hurry!" They turned to see a big man panting up the path they had just followed, and Dickie said, "Gosh! It's Bill Ward, our sailor!" And then Tom urged them forward up the side of the hill. And while they scrambled and climbed away from the path the hill-tops came alive with khaki-clad figures, and they heard Bill shout below them: "All right, boys! Leave him to me!" as the frightened Sally rushed down the narrow track towards him. And when the pony was only about thirty yards away Peter appeared on the top of the rock round which the pony had galloped.

For a moment she stood sharp against the background of the hillside, balancing herself on the uneven surface. The sun glinted on her fair hair, and her shirt was as blue as the sky above her. Then she raised a brown hand to her mouth and whistled loud and shrill – a weird, wailing whistle that the twins seemed to remember. Then Tom looked down at the flying pony. The whistle came again and Sally, with an odd little shake of her head, planted her four feet firmly in the track while her rider flew over her head into the heather almost at the feet of Bill Ward, who grabbed his prisoner by the coat collar with one hand, and Sally's bridle with the other, and began to climb up the hillside after the others.

David was now on the rock with Peter and shouting, "Higher, Tom! Higher! It's coming now!" There were confused shoutings also from the men on the hill-tops, and some with very grim faces were sliding down to meet them.

"Let the pony go, Ward," one called. "She'll look after herself."

Then strong arms hoisted the twins on to broad shoulders, and another gave a helping hand to Tom, and all climbed till they were as high as the rock on which Peter and David were standing, and the rushing noise became a mighty roar. They were all looking now at the spot where the steep valley was made narrower by the jutting rock.

"Jiminy!" breathed Tom. "Great Jiminy Cricket! The reservoir's gone!"

And even as he spoke the earth shook again, and the rock was hidden in a cloud of spray. They had a dim vision of Peter and David clinging together, and then a colossal wave of grey-brown water swung round the corner in a mad, whirling, tearing roar of fury. The first wave was crowned with bushes and trees and planks, and swept majestically down the valley. Actually they were standing well above its highest level, but if they hadn't climbed quickly they would all have been swept away in the flood.

"Gosh!" said Mary thoughtfully. "Just like the children of Israel."

"No," said Dickie. "I know what you mean, but it's old Pharaoh in the Red Sea."

The track had disappeared now under the swirling brown stream, but its force was lessening, and they could see Peter and David clearly again on the rock.

"It's going down now," David called. "Not much more to come. We'll be able to get round to you soon."

But Peter was pointing up towards the head of the valley, and then to one of the Home Guard on the opposite side of the hill. She put her hands to her mouth and called, but the twins could not hear what she said. Then the man on the hill waved reassuringly and gestured upwards with his thumb. Faintly they heard his answer: "All right, Peter! Your dad's all right. I can see him dancing about where the dam used to be."

The water was falling rapidly now as the main flood poured down the valley. Tom looked up suddenly. "What about those cottages down by the Onnybrook Road, Mr Ward! They're right in the way of it."

Bill grinned. "We warned them, son. The valley's clear. We thought maybe they might be too quick for us … but we ought to have saved Hatchholt, I reckon." He turned to the twins, who were looking up at him almost adoringly. "Well, you two! You're having a fine time, I must say. I told you you'd like this place, didn't I? I said it was a rare place for adventures. I hear you've been prisoners already and heroes all the time."

He laughed and showed his white teeth. "I'm going back to sea on Sunday. It'll be a peaceful change."

Then his smiled faded as he looked up the hill behind them. The white and shaken prisoner was being led – or rather dragged – up between two sturdy Home Guards.

"Aye," he said grimly, "but we've got one of 'em all right. I'd like to know what Ingles has found at Appledore."

Then Tom said, excitedly: "There's Uncle Alf. Look!

On the top behind you. He's waiting for them. Let's go up and see him."

But Bill called him back. "No," he said, "he's busy. Leave him alone now, and we'll see him later. He's got to take that beauty off, I expect … I suppose you twins would like to go home now, wouldn't you?" He winked broadly at Tom. "Guess you're too tired to go up to Hatchholt, aren't you?"

"We're jolly well not too tired," said Dickie indignantly.

"We're going just where you're going, Bill," was Mary's comment, and for once it looked as if she would have deserted Dickie for Bill.

Then came a shout from the rock. "Come down and meet us," Peter called. "You can get round the rock now. We're going up to see Daddy."

So Bill led the way down. Macbeth, who had participated in the mad scramble up the side of the hill with the same distaste and boredom as he had viewed the rush of waters, followed reluctantly; he would have preferred to lie in the shade by the stream at Witchend. He knew he had been a fool to follow them all today. He despised himself.

Sally, who had had a disturbing and exciting experience, submitted to Bill's caresses and picked her way delicately down over the sodden heather and bracken. The twins, a trifle awed by the adventures of the last twenty minutes, pranced along with Bill. Tom, glad after all that he hadn't missed anything, came last with his hands in his pockets and whistling cheerfully.

There wasn't much of the track left. The flood had torn away all loose soil by the pipe-line, and brought down many rocks and boulders in its mad rush. There was a dank, watery smell, and the hot sun was already drawing up a thin mist from the steaming refuse. At the very bottom of the valley – sometimes under the pipe-line, sometimes by its side, but already making its own course – ran a new stream.

"There you are!" Tom said as they stood watching it. "There'll be no water left for bathing at the top, I reckon, but you can paddle here now if you want to. You kids were complaining there was no stream in this valley. See what you've got."

Mary looked at the dirty water and wrinkled her delicate little nose in disgust. Macbeth approached languidly, sniffed disdainfully and then, doubtless because the water was muddy, walked into the stream and lapped. He always seemed to prefer a puddle or dirty water to clean water in a bowl.

Then the other two arrived. Peter's jodhpurs were wet to the knee, one hand was bleeding, and she had left blood on her face when sucking the cut, and her blue shirt was torn across the shoulder. She went straight to Sally and kissed the brown muzzle.

"Isn't she a clever darling? Didn't she throw him off beautifully? It took me months to teach her to stop short like that when I whistled. We used to have all sorts of games and tricks up on the mountains once, but she's never forgotten that one. I use a different whistle to make her come to me."

"I remember," David said. "You whistled like that to our father from the top of the hill the day we first met you."

"That's right," said Mary. "An' Sally stopped eating and – just stopped still. I remember too."

"Gosh!" was Dickie's comment.

"Nice work, Peter," said Bill, and slipped an arm round her slim shoulders and made her blush. "You kept your head, which was more than some would have done, and then you did exactly the right thing … And he fell right into my hands like a ripe plum…"

"You're right, Bill," David agreed. "She was grand. When the dam went up and I was wondering what to do, she had me off Sally before I knew what had happened. But before we could do anything that man jumped out of the heather just in front of us…"

"You saw who he was, didn't you, Bill?" Peter interrupted. "You saw he was Mr Evans – the man I found on the top last night, and who helped us look for the twins and then came back to sleep with us and bunked out before I was up?"

"Oh, yes," said Bill grimly. "I recognized the beauty And he knew that I knew, too, when he saw me standing in the path waiting for him … Go on, young man, give us the rest of the story."

"Well, Bill, I think he'd been hiding just there all the time, because when he jumped up I could see he'd a sort of black box arrangement between his feet, and I think he blew up the dam from there. I believe we surprised him anyway … You see, we were on the left of Sally, and the man was the other side of the path. As soon as he'd pressed that rod thing in the box – and it all happened so quickly we couldn't tell what happened first – and the explosion came, he made a great dash for Sally and was on her and away before we could do a thing…"

Peter took up the story. "And I was feeble then, because I s'pose I ought to have whistled Sally then and stopped her, though I don't think we could have done much with him on our own … You see, we didn't know then that the Home Guard were all out here looking for him. All I realized was that the water was coming down with a rush and that you others were behind."

"Yes," David interrupted, "but she wasn't feeble. She was just splendid. I was still goggling when the man shouted at Sally, and then Peter called out to you. Did you hear her, by the way?"

"Rather," said Tom, "and we started moving, too."

"Good," David went on. "Well, before I had time to wonder whether we ought to follow the pony back to you, Peter just grabbed me and hauled me up to the rock, and how we got there so quickly I just don't know. She was up first and did her circus trick while I was scrambling about and watching the water come round the bend at the top. It is all due to Peter that everyone's safe and that the man, whatever he calls himself, was caught so easily."

David was a little breathless when he had finished; Bill was grinning his praise, and Tom held out his hand to shake Peter's like they do on the cowboy films, and Mary squeezed her other hand.

Suddenly she felt so shy that she didn't know where to look. They were all *darlings* – every one of them! She felt her cheeks burning, so she jumped on to Sally and trotted her away from them, saying gruffly over her shoulder: "That man said that Daddy was all right. Will you all come up with me and see?"

The havoc was much worse on the other side of the rock. Here the flood had rushed down steeply with little to check its fury. Bill saw at a glance that Peter and David would have had no chance if they had not acted quickly. He saw, too, why the prisoner had grabbed Sally, for his own two feet would not have taken him quickly enough. At the foot of the rock, which had checked the full force of the torrent, was piled a great heap of stone, bricks and broken cement. From where they stood they could not actually see Hatchholt, as the reservoir was hidden by the last fold of the hills, but the little plank bridge over the pipeline had gone, and in one place the pipes themselves had been torn up and the broken ends were sticking up grotesquely from a welter of mud and debris.

Peter forced back a sob. Lovely Hatchholt! The valley in which she had known every stick and stone – every sheep track, every rabbit-hole, every nest – nothing now but a muddy, smelly waste.

The others seemed to understand, for they didn't say anything to her when they caught her up. Even Dickie and Mary were awed into silence. After a little David pointed to the other side of the stream: "Just about there the man was hiding. Shall we go and look?"

"There won't be anything to find now, David," Bill said. "Come on. Let's get out of this muck and see what Mr Sterling has got to tell us."

So they picked their way slowly uphill amongst the stones and rubbish. Dickie, who had always had weakness for water, stopped once or twice to assist the flow of the stream by clearing away obstructions, and sudden shout from him brought the others running back

"Look what I've found," he called. "Red and black wire!"

Bill picked up the two broken strands and examined them carefully.

"Just what we thought," he said. "If it's not broken again this will lead us to the dam. He didn't hide on the other side of the rock because his wire wasn't long enough to reach."

But the force of the water had snapped the wires a little higher up, and Dickie insisted upon coiling up the remnant he had discovered to keep as a souvenir.

When they came to the last corner Peter galloped ahead, and they heard her call excitedly, "Daddy! Daddy! Here we are. Are you all right?" Then she turned back. "I can see him. He's waving to me … Come on! Hurry!"

Nothing of the dam remained except the thick broken edges at each side. The little sluice-house was a ruin and where before there had been a lovely pool of clear cold water there was now nothing but a muddy-sided hollow and a trickle of water falling over the smashed stones where the explosion had made the breach in the wall. But the little house was still the same, and it looked as if Mr Sterling had remembered his potatoes, for a thin spiral of blue smoke drifted slowly upwards from the chimney.

Standing on the broken stones was Mr Sterling. He raised an arm slowly in salutation as the little cavalcade came into sight, but when he saw Bill Ward was with the children he put his hand to his mouth and called, "Did they get him?"

Everyone shouted the answer, and this seemed to be a great relief to him, for he pushed his old straw hat to the back of his head, lit his pipe, and started down to meet them.

Peter and the twins hurried on to meet him.

"Thank you very much for going out to look for us last night," Dickie began.

"Acksherly, Mr Sterling, we wished it was you that rescued us," Mary finished.

Mr Sterling took his pipe out of his mouth and regarded them gravely.

"Doesn't seem to me," he said solemnly but with a twinkle in his eye, "that you two can ever stay where you're put," but before they could answer Peter grabbed his arm.

"And you really are all right, Daddy?"

"I'm very well in my health and my body, Petronella, but I tell you that your father is an old fool ... Never forget what I say," and with this awful warning he turned away.

But Bill caught him up and slapped him on the back. "Nonsense, Mr Sterling. It wasn't your fault. You can't be blamed."

"That's where you're wrong, young man. I ought to have found his bomb, or mine, or whatever it was. Those Home Guard chaps and me searched everywhere early this morning after they knocked me up. We couldn't find the chap – and when I remember what hospitality we gave him and how he left his dirty boot-marks all over the floor, and me having to go out before my breakfast, and young Peter going off and leaving her dad..."

They soothed him down as best they could.

"Very well, very well," he said testily. "Don't pat me.

I'm not an old dog … I'm just an old fool."

Everyone felt rather embarrassed, and oddly enough it was Dickie who saved the situation.

"I suppose," he said clearly and distinctly, "I suppose, Mr Sterling, you wouldn't happen to have such a thing as a bit o' dry old crust in the house? I think we're feelin' a bit faint."

This remark was greeted with ribald laughter by everyone except Mary and the person addressed, but the tension was broken and they all turned towards the house. At the door Mr Sterling paused, and then those nearest to him saw a look of horror come into his eyes as he looked down at their boots. They were a dirty, bedraggled crew, and Mr Sterling had never in his long life seen anything like them. His own daughter, who had been licking her grubby handkerchief and trying to clean her face with it, was perhaps the worst. He shuddered.

"It's all right, Daddy," she said hastily. "I'll take my shoes off round the back … My shirt got just a teeny bit torn climbing up the rock, but I'll soon get it mended."

David was not much better. His corduroy shorts were torn and his leg badly scratched. He didn't appear to have any shoes on – just black mud spats. Tom, whistling cheerfully and trying a juggling act with two small dead trout he had picked up, was splashed from head to foot. Mary was the tidiest. Dickie was the dirtiest. Macbeth the most bedraggled. But Bill was the quickest to solve the problem of Mr Sterling's kitchen floor.

"Quick, chaps," he said. "Council of war out here in the sunshine. All in a circle. I'm the chief in the middle. Is that right, Dickie? Right! Now then; David tells me that

263

you Mortons promised to be back for dinner, so it's time for you to go. You mustn't worry your mother again. Tom can do what he likes – he can wait for me or go with you, but I've got a lot I want to talk to Mr Sterling about, and he doesn't want to be bothered with you now."

David got up. "Bill's right. What about you, Peter? Will you come back with us? Mother said you could come any time and you can sleep if you like. We could call at Ingles on the way and see what's happened at Appledore, and then I think we'll have to do some jobs about the house."

"Come on, Peter," Tom said, "I'm going back, too. I want to see Uncle Alf."

Peter shook her head, although the temptation was very strong. "No thanks. I'd love to be with you, but I'll stay with Daddy. I expect I can help him tidy up a bit."

David saw Mr Sterling's grateful glance at his daughter.

"Righto! Come as early as you can after breakfast tomorrow. We'll wait at Witchend for you till you come."

"Maybe I'll come up and see your mother before I go back," Bill called. "Maybe I'll come to Witchend tomorrow, too, and see what you've made of it. Good luck to you all. Don't go back along the top and don't go to Appledore. Go back the way you came. The Home Guard fellows will have told everyone what happened here."

The twins shared the favour of their "goodbyes" between Mr Sterling and Bill. Peter stood at the little gate watching them till they got to the turn. Then Tom and David both turned and waved.

Dickie and Mary walked side by side, with Macbeth drooping disgustedly along between them.

" 'Tisn't the trackless desert any more," remarked Dickie.

"No," said Mary firmly. "More like the Amazon or the great grey-green greasy Limpopo River in *Just So Stories*."

"Umm! That's good, twin. I didn't think of that first." He lowered his voice: "Smells a bit like that old bog, doesn't it?"

Chapter 11

Lone-Pine Party

David was dreaming. He was standing again on the "rocky plateau" in Dark Hollow, where they had found the waterfall and climbed up to the bog. In his dream he made up his mind that they must go there again to explore this valley, but even while he was considering it he was startled to see a large elephant coming down the track towards him. As it approached he saw that it was carrying a Home Guard wearing a sailor's hat. He felt that although the elephant was friendly its passenger was not, and as the former was now rushing towards him at a terrific speed it was only a matter of a few seconds before he recognized Mrs Thurston as the rider.

Nearer and nearer rushed the mighty apparition while his legs refused to carry him to safety. Then came a shrill whistle, and the elephant stopped short and their enemy began singing in a doleful voice. He struggled again to escape the hatred which showed on Mrs Thurston's white face – struggled fiercely, and woke to find himself clutching his pillow in a tumbled bed and the sun of a new day streaming in from the window. He grinned ruefully and sighed in relief to find himself awake and safe from rushing elephants. The singing continued, but with it now was mingled the clink of china as Agnes below in the kitchen prepared breakfast. From outside came his mother's soft whistle as she called Macbeth. He sat up and looked at his watch. Half-past eight. He was an hour late and nobody had called him. Dickie, in the other bed, looked as if he needed an hour or more yet, so he got up quickly and went to wash.

Mary wasn't down either, but there was a hungry smell of toast when he went through the kitchen. He found his mother sitting on the steps in the sun, tickling Macbeth behind the ears as the little dog lay on his back blissfully waving his bandy legs in the air. If he had been a cat he would have been purring!

"Hullo, David," she said as he kissed her. "Mary must bath him in the stream this morning. He's disgusting." Macbeth's tail lashed frantically to and fro as if this was a compliment, and Mrs Morton resumed her tickling.

"We'll have breakfast without the twins. Let them sleep on. They haven't had much rest since they came here, and I think it's about time you all quietened down after these adventures."

It was then that David had his stupendous idea and nearly blurted it out to his mother. He knew the others wouldn't really mind, but just in time he remembered that he ought to consult them first, so he contented himself by saying, "Can you and Agnes come out for a sort of picnic with us this afternoon about four o'clock? We're going to ask some other people as well, so perhaps we could have some potatoes and sandwiches and things? Could we?"

"Is that a proper invitation?" his mother smiled. "And how much food do you want?"

"Yes – I think it is. We want you, of course, Mummy, and I don't think we ought to leave Agnes behind … Do you mind if I talk to the others first, though, about how many there are to come? Peter will be here soon, anyway."

"Perhaps that would be best," she said. "It would be a great honour for me to have an adventure with my family. I don't seem to have seen much of them since we got here."

David looked at her in surprise. Then, as they went in to breakfast, he did wonder a trifle guiltily whether perhaps they had been inclined to overlook her. And he thought, too, that he certainly must write a long letter to his father tomorrow and tell him all that had happened.

The twins came down the stairs in step, looking slightly surly and sleepy just as Agnes was clearing away. One glance at them confirmed David's suspicions that this was to be one of "their days." There may, yesterday, have been a few brief moments when Mary's heart turned towards Bill Ward to the temporary exclusion of her twin, but this was not to be a day of such infidelities. Dickie glanced at the almost empty table, and their mouths opened in protest. Mrs Morton cut them short.

"Good morning, darlings. You've just come at the right time. It was such a help of you to sleep in this morning. Thank you very much … Agnes will bring in your eggs in a minute."

Slightly nonplussed, they kissed her and sat down.

Then Dickie said suddenly: "What have you been plannin', David?"

"We heard you saying something to Mummy," added Mary.

David almost blushed with surprise, but before he could defend himself there came the peewit's whistle from outside, and Peter rode through the gate. She tied up Sally and ran over to the open window.

"Good morning, everybody. Sorry if I'm early, but I couldn't wait. I've had my breakfast this morning, and when I passed Ingles, Tom was just off to work and said would we go down and see him presently, as he's too busy to come up here."

"You don't know any other news, then, Peter? Did Tom tell you what really happened at Appledore yesterday?" David asked.

She shook her head. "Mr Ingles was with him, and I thought he looked a bit grumpy, so I didn't like to ask any more."

"Pooh!" said Mary. "That's silly. He can't be grumpy with us. We'll go and ask him."

"Of course," said Dickie, "that's what we'll do. We'll get the milk and ask him."

"And you two can stay here if you like, and maybe we'll tell you when we get back."

"*If* we come straight back," added Dickie casually.

Peter looked at David. "They're like that today, are they?"

"I'm afraid so, Peter. It'll be a pity if they go off on their own today, because I've had a fine idea. I'll tell you about it when they've gone down to Ingles."

Two egg-spoons clattered on two plates as the twins glared at their brother with fury. Mrs Morton laughed.

"Tell me presently what you want, David. We shall need some wood and some water today, though. Don't forget."

Later, the four children strolled down the lane to Ingles. Tom was in the farmyard, whistling. "Can't stop for much this morning," he said, "but Uncle says I can have the afternoon off. Reckon there's lots to tell you, but I don't know it all yet. He won't say much."

"Quick, Tom," said David. "Just come behind the barn. I've got an idea, and I want to know what you think."

The meeting was broken up prematurely by a mighty roar from Mr Ingles. Tom ran off at once, but David followed him and was seen talking earnestly to the farmer, who after a while nodded dubious agreement and gestured towards the house. Peter went in to talk to Mrs Ingles, while the twins sat on the gate and swung their legs and smiled seductively at Mr Ingles whenever he crossed the yard. After a little Peter came out and called for David, and then they both appeared at the door, with Mrs Ingles hobbling between them, but smiling cheerfully.

When they got back to Witchend with the milk, David went off on his bicycle in a hurry, Peter cantered off on Sally, and the twins, after a successful interview with their mother and Agnes, staggered off with a heavy load up the valley in the direction of the Lone-Pine.

They all met again at dinner-time and looked very pleased with themselves. Even the twins forbore to complain that they were being left out, and if Mrs Morton had been a less understanding sort of mother she might have been very annoyed at the smug air of secret expectancy around the table. Agnes noticed little besides empty plates.

Tom arrived soon after and, with David, disappeared for about an hour. Both were carrying heavy baskets. Peter went off down the lane on Sally again, and the twins, twittering with suppressed excitement, sat restlessly on the gate.

Just as the two elder boys got back the first visitor appeared in the lane. Dickie recognized him only because Peter was with him. Mr Sterling was wearing a yellow, battered panama straw hat, and a very tidy-looking blue suit with a magnificent yellow and blue tie. The twins jumped down to open the gate and he shook hands solemnly with them before removing his hat with a charming bow to their mother, who came across the turf to meet him. David found some more deck-chairs and Mr Sterling stood and fanned himself with his hat as he was thanked for the trouble he had taken to search for the twins, and for his hospitality to them all.

Then Mr and Mrs Ingles arrived, with the latter riding on Sally. Both were looking very smart, and Mr Ingles had changed into his uniform for the occasion. He lifted his wife down while Peter held the pony and joined the group by the porch. David was now feeling very nervous and wondering whether the others really would come, but his attention was mercifully distracted by the appearance of Agnes, dressed most unsuitably in black with a black hat upon the rim of which waggled four enormous scarlet cherries. Just as the twins ran over to her a car came up the lane and the party was complete. A jolly-looking man in officer's uniform was driving and by his side was Bill Ward, who jumped out and proudly introduced his father. Captain Ward saluted the ladies, gave Peter a hug with one arm, and clapped Tom on the back with the other. Then he shook hands with David.

"Well, my lad? Very much honoured by your invitation, but you didn't tell us much. What are we to do?"

David cleared his throat and began his speech. He had been planning what to say all day, but now that all these grown-ups were here round him he forgot the words he had rehearsed and began rather incoherently:

"Thank you all very much for coming, and we're all very glad to see you … It's like this … We – Peter and Tom and the twins and me – have formed a secret club with a secret meeting-place near here with a camp fire … We want you all to come as our guests to the camp this afternoon – we've got some rations for you, thanks to Mother – and then we thought we could all tell each other what we found out on the hill and Appledore and Hatchholt…"

Before any of the grown-ups could answer, Dickie broke in:

"An' there's something else jolly important and serious, too. You've all got to be blindfolded."

At this startling pronouncement Captain Ward and Mr Sterling looked mildly astonished, Agnes showed signs of alarm, while Mr Ingles roared with laughter and slapped his knee.

"Well, did you ever hear the like of that?" he boomed. "Blindfolded, eh? Me – that's lived hereabouts for forty years! And what is it you're going to do with us when you've covered our eyes and got us helpless?"

Then Peter spoke up. "We're going to lead you to our secret camp, Mr Ingles. Of course we regret the inconvenience very much" – she was rather proud of this grand phrase – "but we know you'll understand."

Mary sidled up to Bill, whose appearance always unsettled her allegiance to Dickie.

"If you *like*," she said, "I'll lead you myself. Then you'll be quite safe. Would you like me to look after you?"

"Thank you, Mary. I would. I only wish I could take you to sea with me!"

"If we've got to go through with it, I suppose we'd better start," his father said briskly. "Come along! I'll be the first victim," and he took off his cap and produced a khaki handkerchief.

Tom, Peter and David supervised the bandaging while the twins danced round exultantly. Mrs Ingles was the only exception to the blindfold rule. Her ankle was still too weak for her to walk far, and she was already reconciled to travelling on Sally. Peter helped her on with the aid of a kitchen chair and said solemnly: "I'm afraid we shall have to ask you for your parole, Mrs Ingles."

"God bless the child," answered the panting and uncomfortable rider, "and what's that, might I ask?"

David came up and explained. "You're the only stranger who will see the route to the camp, Mrs Ingles. We knew you wouldn't feel comfortable riding on Sally if you couldn't see…"

"You're right there, lad," she broke in. "I'm not even comfortable when I *can* see on this pony."

Her husband laughed again and David gulped and went

on … "So we must ask you please to give your solemn promise not to tell *anyone* the way to the camp."

"And that's a parole," added Mary brightly.

"It's really a solemn swear," said Dickie.

"Well, if Peter will lead me safe and sound and not let me fall off I'll never tell anyone, I promise."

" 'Specially Mr Ingles?" said Dickie.

" 'Specially Mr Ingles," she confirmed.

At last the cavalcade was ready. Only Agnes seemed particularly perturbed and indeed she had already made several half-hearted attempts to retire to her kitchen. Her hat with the dangling cherries was now cocked rakishly over one ear and she would undoubtedly have cheated with her bandage if Mary had not been watching her. Then Tom proudly produced a length of rope and the strange procession started – each member of the party holding the rope for guidance – with David in the lead. His mother came next, then Captain Ward, followed by Mary holding Bill's free hand; then Agnes with one hand groping grotesquely in the air before her; then Mr Sterling, who had been very silent throughout all the proceedings and who now wore the expression of a martyr being led to the torture; next Mr Ingles, laughing stumbling and shouting; and finally Peter leading Sally with Mrs Ingles aloft. Dickie took no useful part in the procession but danced first on one side of the line and then the other, and generally made himself rather a nuisance.

"Lucky you can't see where you're going now," he said once to the pilgrims. "Jolly lucky it is for you all. Wild beasts all round you. Tigers lurkin' everywhere."

Then again: "Wild and desolate country we're in now. Just comin' to the crocodile swamp."

Once the line wavered and broke in the centre when he called urgently, "Mind your head, Agnes. We're in the jungle and there's whackin' big blood-suckin' spiders all hanging from the bushes."

Soon they came to the stream, crossed it, and began to climb. Here it was that Mrs Ingles wished that she had stayed at home. The pony was sure enough on her feet but the track was narrow and very steep, and not being an accomplished horsewoman she found the angle at which she was forced to proceed particularly trying. But David gave them no rest and led them quickly up the hill.

"Mount Everest now," Dickie said.

"Just coming to the glaciers," Mary explained to Bill.

At last they came to the Lone-Pine. The fire, lit earlier in the afternoon by Tom and David, was burning brightly and the kettle was steaming. The sides of the clearing were strewn with bracken as a welcome resting-place for the weary guests, and on one side of the fire was a spread cloth covered with plates of sandwiches and mugs.

"You can take off your bandages now," said David. "Peter! Will you please take charge of the cooking and the food? We brought some potatoes for roasting presently, and it looks as if the kettle is nearly boiling." Then he turned to Mrs Morton, "What do you think of it, Mummy? Isn't it a grand place? We've never had a better camp, and you do understand why we had to keep it secret, don't you?"

"It's splendid, David. You must keep it nice and show to your father when he comes home on leave. He'd love
"

The other grown-ups were looking round with varying expressions. Bill was laughing as usual, while his father offered a cigarette to Mrs Morton. Mrs Ingles, very red in the face, was being helped to the bracken couch by Peter while her husband roared, "Well I'll be jiggered! I never knew this place before, although I suppose I've seen the tree often enough."

Mr Sterling looked fixedly at the crockery and the table cloth, but as everything was spotless turned his attention elsewhere. Agnes, now looking battered and weary, leaned against the trunk of the pine, mopped her face with her handkerchief as she wondered whether the children had really brought enough food for this big party.

Dickie climbed the tree to act as look-out, but soon came down when he saw Peter making tea. Then all except Peter and David – cook and host respectively – sat down in a big circle and when every cup was full David looked over to Captain Ward and said, "We do hope you're going to tell us all about Appledore, sir, and what' really happened there. If you like we'll all give our separate stories, but I expect there's nothing new we can tell you."

Captain Ward put his tea-cup down and looked round the circle of eager faces. The twins were struggling hard to keep back their questions until he had spoken. Bill, his only son, was tickling the back of Mary's neck with piece of bracken and laughing as she shook him off. Peter flushed and excited, was handing round sandwiches while the two elder boys watched him from the foot of the tree. Mr Sterling, with a clean handkerchief spread across his knees, was looking at him a trifle anxiously; Mr

Morton nodded imperceptibly as he caught her eye, and Mr Ingles winked encouragement. Agnes was concentrating upon a few curious flies who wished to sample the dangling cherries in her hat.

"Very well," he said at last, "the grown-ups shall tell their stories first. You all deserve to hear just exactly what has happened, for if it hadn't been for you young people we might never have caught these devils ... By the way, young man," he said, turning to David, "didn't you say before we started on this trip that we were all to be made honorary members of this secret Society?"

"Yes, sir," said David. "We'll be very proud if you all will. Presently you must all sign the book. We're the Lone Pine Club."

Captain Ward smiled. "Fine," he went on. "Now we know where we are. Speaking for the other grown-ups I think I can say we're all very honoured by the invitation .. Well, fellow members, if you have no objection I will start the story and then perhaps friend Ingles here, and Bill, and Mr Sterling may have something to add to it. Afterwards you can fire questions at us as hard as you like. Is that agreed? Right!"

And here he settled himself back on his bracken couch and began to fill his pipe as he talked.

"It so happens that you original members of the Lone Pine Club discovered – or helped to discover – a very dangerous plot by our German enemies. By now you will all have guessed, I expect, that Mrs Thurston was a German spy. We have not yet had time to find out all about her, but there is little doubt that she has lived for some years in this country and I expect she was in the pay of the enemy for many years before the war. It is true that when she first came to Appledore we did not make many enquiries about her. Why should we? We are friendly, neighbourly people up in these hills, and strangers are welcome if they do not interfere with us, and behave themselves. Mrs Thurston was pleasant enough although I hear now that occasionally her man-servant was not so obliging or friendly, and it is rather strange that she should have used someone so noticeable as this man Jacob. Actually I believe we shall prove that he was a very able engineer and scientist, and for this reason alone I suppose they thought the risk worth while. I was told by the Chief Constable this morning that our countryside is almost certainly harbouring many such unpleasant and dangerous people, and it is everyone's duty to do what you children have done and report anything unusual or suspicious.

"Anyway, it is important for you all to realize that in war like this, the enemy will do anything to any of you civilian or soldier – if he thinks it will help him to win. Up here – and indeed for many miles around – is stored much of the water for the Midland cities. The Germans have tried to break our spirit by bombing and have failed, and this latest idea was particularly unpleasant as its purpose was to smash up the reservoirs and deprive of water those who work in the cities and towns and make munition. There are several reservoirs in these hills, and the only way of destroying them is to blow them up. The only way to blow them up efficiently is to put the explosive in the right place and to have it placed there by an expert. Bombing from the air couldn't possibly do this, so it mus be done by what we call *saboteurs* – men or women whose particular job is to smash up or slow down the war effort. Thank God there are not many Englishmen who would stoop to such dirty work against their own country, and so such jobs as this must be organized by the spy who is definitely settled down and accepted in this country and then carried out by men and women who are dropped in the dusk or at night from German aeroplanes. I expect you all realize that the Long Mynd is ideal for the landing of enemy troops. You youngsters, except Peter, have only seen a small part of the mountain, but it is wild and lonely for miles, and consequently very safe for landings by parachute. It won't be so lonely in future, I might add, as we shall be watching it very carefully!

"Now what we think happened is this. Clever and unscrupulous spies were stationed in various parts of the country to organize plans for the destruction of water supplies. Mrs Thurston was, of course, the agent in this district. She made herself at home amongst us and even if it took years to get herself known, liked and trusted, it would be worth while in the end. It was her job to send to Germany regular reports so that at a fixed time the Nazis could begin to send her carefully disguised assistants. Mr Sterling will tell us, I've no doubt – and Peter, too, for that matter – that he has often seen her on the hills with field-glasses and camera, and that she has always been there for some purpose which seemed reasonable and unsuspicious."

Here Mr Sterling looked at his plate in some embarrassment, and was heard to murmur something about bird-watching.

"Anyway," Mr Ward continued, "we think that she must have personally examined and explored the reservoirs in this district to be destroyed, made maps, and then somehow got the messages to the Germans."

"Please," said Dickie abruptly. "I would like to know how she could do that."

"Well, Richard," he went on, "there are some good opportunities for doing that, and you can take it that messages do go in all sorts of ways and often by sailors through a neutral port like Lisbon ... However, I think her plan was to photograph the various reservoirs first or send maps and particulars over, and then, as I said just now, the most suitable men were chosen and disguised accordingly and dropped round about here at dusk or at night. It would seem that Appledore was the *rendezvous*, and that they all had to find their way there before they could do anything definite. Most of them seem to have brought some equipment and explosive with them, and I can't think why as we found a laboratory and powerful wireless set in the cellar at Appledore."

David interrupted this time – "Of course," he said, "and they all used the signal of the owl's cry. I heard one on our very first night at Witchend! I remember now that I woke up and heard an aeroplane and then an owl."

"Yes," broke in Dickie with shining eyes, "and we heard old beast Jacob hooting, and the man with the parachute, *he* hooted too!"

"Wish I could," said Mary. "I tried and tried, but I can't."

"Tell them what happened at Appledore," said Tom with a wink.

"No. I shan't do that," said Captain Ward. "I'll leave that to your uncle presently … I think you would like to know that all the other attempts were unsuccessful and that we caught the other three men and Jacob. Fortunately Hatchholt is not so very important compared with the other reservoirs. I dare say Mr Sterling will tell you how he thinks they were able to blow up the dam. Certainly the man who called himself Evans was clever and enterprising … wasn't he, Peter?"

Peter flushed and laughed. "Oh, I know I said he was nice. He certainly fooled Daddy and me."

"That's all very well," David broke in hotly, "but if it hadn't been for Peter and the way she whistled to Sally and stopped her, we might not have caught him at all."

"There's not much else to tell," Captain Ward continued. "As soon as you passed on your suspicions – and I'm told that David was the one who most deserves thanks and praise for this, although Tom here found Mrs Thurston's map – we not only warned the county, but the police and military all over the country were notified of our suspicions. It's too early yet for us to have news, but I dare say that special efforts are being made now to check up on suspicious persons, and to search at wild and lonely places for *saboteurs* … Now, would any of you like to ask any questions before Mr Ingles and Mr Sterling tell you their part of the story?"

"There's one thing I've never been sure about," Peter said. "I still can't work out how many men there were. The place seems to have been full of strangers, and I could never keep count."

"Well," said Captain Ward. "You caught the man who

called himself Evans up at Hatchholt just after he'd done his job. That's one."

"There's the stranger in the raincoat we tracked the first day on the Mynd," David went on. "We never saw where he went, but I suppose he slipped down through the woods to Appledore. I remember Peter saying that he was a stranger, and now I think of it he was looking at a scrap of paper which I suppose was a map. That's two."

"Gosh, Dickie!" Mary said with a sigh. "An' John Davies too, I s'pose. But I can't really and truly believe he was as bad as the others, can you?"

" 'Course he wasn't," said Dickie. "He was decent to us. He was all right…" Then suddenly he turned to the Captain. "But he *can't* have been a spy. He knew all about Spitfires and Hurricanes, and he was in AIR FORCE UNIFORM."

"I'm sorry, Dickie, but he was one of the worst. I think we shall find that he'd been in England for a long time before the war – probably a schoolmaster – and it's quite easy for them to get a British uniform. They could either get one from a prisoner of war or make them. Lots of spies come in uniform. That's three, isn't it?"

"Well, anyhow," Dickie muttered, "I think he was one of the best. He was a decent sort of spy. Jacob was the worst."

"Then the fourth must have been the one we found in the wood in the fog," said Mary. "He said he was a British officer testing parachutes and things for going over Germany."

"I say," Dickie broke in, "spies are awful liars, aren't they?"

When the echoes of Mr Ingles' hearty laugh had died away over the Long Mynd, Dickie went on: "But he really had hurt his ankle, and the fog was awful when he came out of the aeroplane. We remember how low the 'plane came, don't we, Mary? The pilot was lost, I s'pect, and kept coming back."

"We all heard the 'plane that night," Peter said. "I thought he was coming to knock my head off as I went back up Hatchholt ... And, of course, they all *knew* about Appledore and Mrs Thurston, didn't they?"

Captain Ward nodded. "Yes. They wouldn't hide that. I think they all came separately so that if they were seen in such a lonely place they wouldn't attract so much attention as a party of strangers. Mrs Thurston would never be quite sure when each one would arrive, but they all used the owl's cry as a sign, we know, and I think it was David who told me how she tried to keep you all off the top of the mountain the first day that you met her. Maybe the man in the raincoat hadn't arrived at Appledore by then, and yet she had heard the 'plane and thought he might be wandering about in the woods and that you might meet him. You can understand why she didn't want any of you at large round Appledore, and how furious she must have been when the twins turned up again that night in the fog with two spies or perhaps more already in the house, and another on her doorstep with a twisted ankle."

David nodded as the twins nudged each other with pride. "Could we hear Mr Ingles' adventure with the Home Guard at Appledore now, please?" he asked.

Mr Ingles lit a cigarette and was prevented by his wife from lounging back on the bracken as he began his story.

Peter in the meantime had given everyone a fresh cup of tea and was now pushing potatoes into the glowing embers of the fire.

"I must say," he said heartily, "that I wished you two lads could have come along with us, but we didn't know that there might not be a bit of shooting, and I didn't think Mrs Morton would have said 'Thank you' if I'd got you into that. Anyhow, after I'd got my instructions through the Captain here, twelve of us started off in a lorry. We did what we'd done the night afore and stopped her down the lane and came up quiet. There's not really a lot to tell, because it was so easy. Some of the boys went quiet to the back, and I saw Jim Rogers putting bracken in his tin hat like we'd been taught. Some went round the side, and I took four with me and went to the front door. Nobody seemed to have noticed us, and old Jacob answered the knock like he always does about two inches. I puts my foot in and gives a real push for once, and over falls the old man in a heap. Very touchy he was, but I never liked him, and as he began to use bad language in English as well as German I passed him outside and then someone else tapped him on the chin and down he went quiet as a lamb. Three of the boys ran upstairs, and I went in to find Mrs Thurston. She was annoyed, and so was I about her locking up these kids and sticking me out she'd send Jacob to look for them because she'd never seen them! Then there was a fair bit of noise upstairs as the chaps found the fellow with the bad ankle and after a bit of argument they had to put him to sleep too … While I was talking to her I heard someone outside and there, in the hall, was another fellow creeping past. He was much

284

more enterprising and threw a grenade at me. Down I dropped on my knees and right through the window went the grenade and that was lucky because it exploded at once and has messed up the lawn. Mrs Thurston made a run for it while I was discussing the situation with the bomb-thrower but she met some of the boys who soon looked after her. When we'd got the three beauties under control we searched the house. I can't tell you all we found, but it was enough to convict a thousand people. Maps there were in plenty, and down in the cellar a wireless receiving and sending set, miles of wire, some detonators and explosives in all manner of forms, revolvers, and grenades too … And that's about all there is to tell, I reckon … We all went back together in the lorry just like a Sunday School treat, except that Mrs Thurston did a lot of spitting and snarling in German and I heard the others 'Heil Hitler' a few times … Funny lot of blokes they were … After we'd delivered the goods we came across to you at Hatchholt soon as we could because we found out that the reservoir was to go up today, and we knew that we hadn't bagged all the beauties …

"And now you know everything I reckon…"

And here Mr Ingles produced a large red handkerchief and mopped his face. Everyone started to talk at once and even Agnes was heard to say to Mrs Morton, "Never been such goings on round here in my time, Missus. Who would have thought those Nayzees would have the imperence to come traipsing all over our hills … and the children being all mixed up in it and all … it fair makes my blood run cold."

Then the hot potatoes were handed round and Captain Ward sauntered over to Tom and David who were standing with their back to the pine congratulating themselves on the success of the party. Peter was trying to persuade Dickie to go down and fetch more water for washing up when she heard the Captain say, "How d'you think Evans managed to fix his charge to blow up Hatchholt? Some of my men are supposed to have searched the place early."

She looked up at this. "That's what I was going to ask. I was pushed out of the way before breakfast and so I don't know what happened till Evans jumped out of the heather at us and bagged Sally. Did you tell them to get rid of me, Mr Ward?"

"Yes, I did. There might have been trouble and we knew something was afoot. I heard about the search party by then and told them to find out whether Evans had actually spent the rest of the night at Hatchholt as we were anxious to ask him a few questions ... But your Father hasn't told us anything yet, Peter. Let's ask him."

Mr Sterling was sitting uncomfortably and stiffly upright, looking with distaste at the charred potato between his fingers. When he heard his name called he dropped it thankfully and started guiltily.

"How do you think he laid the charge, Mr Sterling?" Captain Ward called. "He must have been smart to have got past your examination."

Mr Sterling looked embarrassed. "He *was* smart and I was slow," he said. "Reckon I've been a foolish old man all along over this business. I've always tried not to believe the worst, but I was all wrong this time. I trusted the fellow and now I've failed in my trust," he finished almost in a whisper.

Peter dropped what she was doing and went over to him. "Nonsense, Daddy. He made a fool of us both. They made fools of us all. I told you how nice and helpful and friendly he was on the hill ... Don't you worry, darling."

Her father beamed at her. "Well," he continued a little more cheerfully, "I reckon I've worked out how he did the job. Reckon he stripped and dived in deep and fixed the charge under water. What he did with the wires I don't know, because we searched all the front of the dam when the Home Guard lads told me what they thought was like to happen. He may have found a loose stone in the wall under the water, or fixed the charge in one of the outlet-pipes. He may have meant to have come back to the cottage after he'd hidden the wires and his gadget for exploding the charge, but as the Home Guard chaps came up so early he must have laid up somewhere in the heather, and we missed him. Peter told me where he was hiding when he blew the place up – reckon he didn't bring enough wire, and that was as far as he could get ... Suppose we can soon build her up again, but maybe they'll fix a telephone now – not that I can abide the things..."

Mr Sterling looked round and pushed his spectacles farther up his nose ... "Reckon I'd like to say I'm much obliged to all who have helped and been so neighbourly to me and my lass."

There was a short embarrassed silence until Bill broke in quickly: "There's something Mr Sterling's forgotten to mention. He didn't tell us that he insisted upon coming out on the hill in the middle of the night to search for the twins. It was only because young Peter here couldn't keep awake that we persuaded him to go home. I think we should all be very grateful to him."

There was a murmur of polite appreciation before the sailor went on: "And isn't anyone interested in what happened to me? Only my girl friend Mary, I suppose? I shall be glad to get back on board for a real rest. Haven't done so much walking for years."

"Why, Bill," laughed Peter, "you were wonderful when you collared Evans when he shot off Sally."

Captain Ward took the centre of the ring again.

"Any more questions now," he asked, "because time's getting on and we must get back."

"I've got one," said Dickie. "It's about John Davies. If he came down from an aeroplane what would he do with his parachute?"

"He hadn't got it with him when we found him here," added Mary, "and he told us he'd come by train and lost his way."

Bill smiled and tickled her neck again. "That just shows all you know about it, baby! There isn't an early train in war-time, and I expect he was dropped the night before. He'd hidden his 'chute for sure, and if you searched the wood or the hillsides for long enough I expect you'd find it. That'll be a job for you when I've gone back to sea."

Then Captain Ward said: "I don't want to hurry away, but I ought to go. I hope that now we've all been made honorary Lone-Piners you won't blindfold us on the way down. I suppose we all have a right to come here again if a meeting is called, and we ought to know the way?"

David looked at Tom and Peter. "Yes, of course, sir. We shall have some more meetings, and hope you'll all come. We must have one for certain when Bill comes home again. You won't be blindfolded again, but we haven't really sworn you all in yet. Will you please wait and sign the book ... You don't mind swearing secrecy, do you?"

While Peter and the twins began to wash and clear up, David unearthed the sardine tin and the secret document which they had all signed on the day when the Club had been instituted. The paper was oily and smelly, and the signatures in blood looked rather odd, but the wording was still quite readable.

"I don't think you need sign in blood – pencil will do for honorary members – but will you please listen to the Rules, and then promise to keep Rule 3 which says you must keep it secret."

"An' we've got a noath," said Dickie.

"You must say that too," added Mary.

So one by one, led by Captain Ward, the grown-ups repeated the promise "to be true to each other, whatever happens," and signed their names in pencil on the back of the oily paper. Agnes seemed uncertain and unhappy about adding her name, but Mrs Morton encouraged her, and Mrs Ingles rattled off the oath cheerfully enough as an example.

Then they cleaned up the potato-skins, collected the waste paper to take home, and buried the tin again under the tree. The fire was carefully put out and everything, as Bill said, "made snug and shipshape." Mrs Ingles was hoisted on to Sally's back again, and as Peter led the way out of the clearing Bill said: "Thanks for the party, Lone-Piners. I'm proud to be a member. You'd better send me reports of your adventures and meetings while I'm away. Does anybody want to ask any more questions?"

"I can't think of any now, Bill," Peter said over her shoulder as she held the swaying Mrs Ingles more firmly to Sally. "I shall think of lots tonight in bed, of course. I always do."

"I want to know something," Tom said suddenly. "It's about your little dog. You told me he seemed to hate Mrs Thurston as soon as he saw her. Why did he do that?"

"Difficult question to answer, Tom," said Captain Ward. "I don't know this little chap properly, but it is a fact that sometimes animals show an uncanny instinct about people. I had a wire-haired terrier once that showed a fierce dislike of a gardener of mine. The gardener turned out to be a thief, although I'd always thought him pleasant enough. If Mac here showed his hatred of Mrs Thurston, his taste was sound, wasn't it?"

They were crossing the stream now, and Peter waited for the others to come up.

"That reminds me of something I've wanted to know ever since we met. It sounds a bit silly, but I really do want to know why you call him Macbeth. I did *Macbeth* last Christmas term, and it's such a funny name for a dog, even though he is a Scottie."

Mrs Morton laughed. "If you know *Macbeth*, Peter, it should give you an idea. I'll tell you why, though. We've had him three years. We didn't know what to give the twins on their sixth birthday, and on the day before in London Mr Morton saw Macbeth in a shop-window. He couldn't resist him, and I remember that on the way home he bought him a scarlet lead. The twins loved him at sight, but argued for days about a name for him. I know that most of the names suggested were silly, and we just couldn't agree. Macbeth was a very destructive puppy, so after one awful night when he was left by mistake in the drawing-room and had a fight with a feather cushion, he was put in the kitchen and everything 'chewable' was put out of reach. He resented this very much, and showed his annoyance by waiting till we had gone to bed, and then barking. For a week he was so noisy that we thought he might have to go, and then one night my husband quite suddenly sat up in bed and named him. Do you know why?"

"Something about sleep," Peter answered. "I can't quite remember, but wasn't it after Macbeth had murdered Duncan?"

"That's it, my dear. Well done … Do you remember?"

" 'Methought I heard a voice cry "Sleep no more!
    Macbeth does murder sleep" – the innocent
        sleep,
    Sleep that knits up the ravell'd sleave of care …' "

She laughed. "I remember Daddy saying 'The little devil murders sleep. We'll call him Macbeth.' "

By now they were home again. Agnes slipped in to make up the fire, and Captain Ward and Bill started their "Goodbyes." Everyone hated saying it to Bill – specially Peter and Mary. He promised to come back again on his next leave, promised to write, promised never to forget today's adventure. When at last the car disappeared round the bend of the lane Mary remained a lonely little figure by the gate with one hand raised in salutation. Dickie went over to her after a time, and while the others lingered chatting by the porch, the twins took their usual position on the top rung of the gate.

Mr and Mrs Ingles were the next to go, and Peter noticed the farmer nudge his wife so violently that she nearly fell over. Then he cleared his throat and went up to her father.

"Any time you want a bit o' company and a different bed, Mr Sterling," he bellowed in what he believed to be a confidential manner, "there's both waiting for you down the lane. Tonight maybe you won't want to go trailing up to Hatchholt again. You're welcome to a bite and bed at Ingles, and it'll do you good to get away from that mess up there."

Mrs Ingles added her welcome, but before Mr Sterling could reply Mrs Morton chimed in.

"It's strange you should say that, Mr Ingles –" and Peter wasn't positive but she thought she detected a slight wink as she spoke – "but I've just insisted that Peter stay with us tonight. We'll squeeze her in somehow, and perhaps you'd allow Tom to stay to supper too, would you?"

Peter murmured something about "no night things" and "better stay with Daddy," but to her intense surprise her father thanked the Ingles and agreed that a change would do him good!

So that was settled, and as the sun went down in glory behind the gaunt ridge of the Long Mynd the Ingles and

Mr Sterling shook hands with Mrs Morton and started off down the lane. Mrs Ingles refused point blank to subject herself to Sally again, and, taking an arm of each, hobbled slowly off between the two men.

The twins stayed on the gate till supper-time, and afterwards were driven protestingly upstairs to bed. The boys and Peter helped Agnes wash up, and then went out to the porch. It was nearly dark and as the moon came up softly they could smell the wood, the stream, and the heather on the hill.

Peter slipped between the two boys as they strolled over to the gate. She was very happy. It had been a wonderful day and the end of a perfect adventure. None of the girls at school could ever imagine an adventure like it. She felt warm and comfortable when she thought of Mrs Morton's kindness, and she was with friends she loved best and still able to sleep in the shadow of her beloved mountain.

"You'll get the dam mended, I expect," David was saying, "and the valley will soon be clean and decent again … Mummy said to me just now that you can stay with us all the hols if your father will let you. With Tom so near that would be grand … I want to explore Dark Hollow properly one day soon. Shall we, Tom?"

Tom, who always preferred whistling to words, nodded. "I'll let you know when I'll be off work," he said. "Won't be often, I reckon, but I'd like to go there with you. It's where the waterfall comes in but doesn't go out, isn't it?"

"That's right," David said. "Come when you can, Tom, and we'll try and arrange meetings whenever you're available. It's funny," he went on, as they sat on the top rung of the gate, "but the day we came and met Bill in the train the twins told everybody that we were going on a great adventure. Just think how right they were! Look what's happened to us in a few days … I remember a chap at home telling me that the country was dull and that we wouldn't know what to do … There won't be anything left for us to do by the end of the hols if we go on like this."

In the still air his voice must have carried far because, before the others could answer, the twins were heard from an open bedroom window behind them.

"Beasts you are," came Dickie's unmistakable treble. "Utter beasts plannin' new adventures without us … But we don't care. Mary and me have thought of a new one…"

"Yes, and we've a jolly good mind not to tell you."

"Don't tell them, Mary."

"All right then, I will. We're going to those old Stiperstones to find that old Devil we saw sitting in his Chair…"

As Mrs Morton removed them from the window, Peter, with a hand on the shoulder of her two friends, said: "Perhaps we could go. I've got an Uncle over there on a big farm. He'd have us, I believe. Specially if we helped a bit. It's different country from this – wilder and more rugged. Perhaps we could go in the Christmas or Easter hols…"

Before they could answer there came loud and clear from close by the cry of an owl, and they all looked up half expecting to see the shape of a parachute against the sky.

But as they watched they were in time to see the old fellow himself – the owl of Witchend – come swaying silently like a dusky shadow out of the wood on his way to find his supper.

THE END

Cwm Head, Church Stretton
Westend Farm, Wheathampstead, 1942

THE MALCOLM SAVILLE
SOCIETY

The Malcolm Saville Society was formed in 1994 to bring together fans of Malcolm Saville's work. Through newsletters and meetings, the society allows enthusiasts to exchange news, information and speculation about the books and the real locations which inspired them.

For further details please send an SAE to:

The Malcolm Saville Society
10 Bilford Road
Worcester
WR3 8QA